An Evans Novel of Romance

THE ENCHANTER

CHRISTINA HAMLETT

M. EVANS & COMPANY, INC. NEW YORK

Library of Congress Cataloging-in-Publication Data

Hamlett, Christina

The enchanter / Christina Hamlett
p.   cm.—(An Evans novel of romance)
ISBN 0-87131-610-2 : $15.95
I. Title.   II. Series.
PS3558.A4446E53   1990   90-0000
813'.54—dc20   90-37364
CIP

M. Evans and Company, Inc.
216 East 49 Street
New York, New York 10017

Manufactured in the United States of America

2 4 6 8 9 7 5 3 1

To Lizanne Barker, for teaching me the craft
of storytelling and continuing to be my most
encouraging mentor

To Ardie, Julie, Kathy, and Melanie, for telling
me to write faster so they could see how it all comes out

To Pat Teal, for believing in enchantment
as much as I do

And to the real Kyle Falconer,
without whose magic there would be no story

Prologue

IT WAS THE LADY'S VOICE that stirred the old man from the refuge he had sought in daydream. "It is time," she spoke from the depths of the turquoise lake, its surface as smooth as the finest glass.

Wearily the old man raised his head and rubbed the sleep from his eyes with fingers too crippled to hold fast even the lightest chalice. His chest-length beard and mane of hair—once the most glorious shade of chestnut—were now difficult to distinguish from the ashen cobwebs clinging to the folds of his dirty cloak.

"Haven't you anyone else?" He sighed, the words passing barely above a whisper through his thin, cracked lips.

A defiant ripple broke the lake's tranquillity, sending a splash of water neither warm nor cold across the old man's sandaled feet. "We've spoken of this a hundred times before," she said with a perceptible edge of sharpness. Her waters darkened in the blink of an eye to crystalline amethyst.

"And a hundred times more, I suspect," he muttered, impatient for his audience with her to end, that he might return to the solitude of his cave and to the memory that was Bryn Myrrdin, the place of his youth.

"You have seen her face," the Lady sternly reminded him. "The time has come to take your leave and find her."

Futile as it was to challenge her authority, it was a habit born of long association. "I'm too old for this," he protested, his rheumy eyes too weak to make out much more than the lake's transition to a churning crimson.

"Your destiny has already been chosen!" she hotly commanded. "As Protector, you have no choice but to recover that which never should have been taken from us."

"And if I should fail?" he queried, bitterly cognizant that he had failed once already in his lifetime.

It was a question that fell on deaf ears. "I will show you her face one more time," she announced with the irritation of an exhausted parent reprimanding a recalcitrant child. "Now pay close attention. . . ."

As gracefully as clouds that part to reveal the stark beauty of a midday sun, her waters magically shimmered and turned clear. "Gaze deep within and remember what you see," she instructed.

A mosaic of wrinkles creased the old man's face as he squinted painfully at the vision of young womanhood shown to him.

"Find her," echoed the Lady's voice on the fragrant winds. "Find her. . . ."

Chapter One

"HAVE YOU EVER caught his act?" her boss asked.

Even the mere mention of Kyle Falconer's name still had the capacity to send a shiver of excitement through Catherine. Three and a half years hadn't dimmed the memory or intensity of the magical night she had first seen him. Three and a half years later she was still trying to reconcile the conflicting sensations of attraction and fear.

"Only once . . . back in California," she absently replied to his question. "He's quite a showman." The understatement of the century.

"Just *once?*" Johnson echoed with a snort of incredulity. "I'd have thought you'd be hitting Tahoe every weekend, living that close and all."

A tolerant smile curved Catherine's mouth in response to his unalterable views of the freewheeling California life-style. A BMW in every garage . . . breakfast in Tijuana . . . lunch at Disneyland . . . dinner and nightcaps at the South Shore casinos.

"I guess I just didn't have the time," Catherine glibly lied to deflect any further inquiry. In truth, of course, the opportunities to see Kyle Falconer perform had been plentiful, opportunities she had consciously chosen to avoid. Whether she was fearful of the mystical power he exerted over her or wistfully apprehensive that she might not experience it again, she had never been able to determine.

And now her editor was making her attendance at the Washington D.C. show an assignment. That, and an interview.

3

"I hear he's going to make the Washington Monument disappear," Johnson continued, adding with a wry smile, "Too bad he can't do the same for the deficit."

'Tall order," Catherine observed, nonetheless secretly convinced that there were no limits to the man's talent.

Like the rest of his television specials, the magician's Washington performance had garnered a lion's share of national publicity, tickets selling out almost immediately.

"Oh, by the way," Johnson added, handing her an envelope, "did I mention that he doesn't give interviews?"

"But you just said—"

"Consider it a challenge." He shrugged, stretching his bulk across a pile of papers and strawberry Danish to grab the insistent phone. "Johnson here," he barked, "whatcha got?" Their meeting abruptly drawn to an unceremonious close, Catherine let herself out, slipping the ticket envelope into her pocket.

It wasn't until the late-morning break that she discovered the envelope Johnson had given her contained not one but two passes to the nine P.M. performance. Her first reaction was that the office grapevine obviously didn't extend beyond the frosted glass panel that read EDITOR-IN-CHIEF. Ev Johnson surely had to be the only one on the planet who didn't know that she and sportswriter Nat McClure had broken up right after Christmas. Then again, maybe he *did* know. Maybe, like everyone else, he just assumed that anyone who friends said resembled a young Katharine Hepburn wouldn't stay unattached for long. Or at least until Thursday at nine.

The thought of Nat brought with it the customary stab of pain. He had been one of the first friends she met when she settled into her new responsibilities in the Arts and Entertainment section at the *Trib*, a friendship that quickly ripened into romance. He was also the last person she believed at the time would fall prey to jealousy and betray her trust. Hard work—the traditional salve of all that ails the human heart—had not only pulled her through the emotional loss but continued to propel her toward a list of credits astonishingly impressive for someone under thirty. It was her very track record of accuracy and dedication that enabled Catherine to frequently land some of the *Trib's* most plum assignments. To beg off taking this particular one, of course, would inevitably raise questions she just wasn't prepared to answer. Not yet, anyway.

As she closed her office door to dull the incessant clatter of typewriters and the cacophony of phones, her thoughts were already sliding back to a disquieting replay of what her conscience kept stubbornly refusing to let her forget.

Magic had always held a special fascination for her. Card tricks, rabbits pulled out of hats, people vanishing from one trunk and reappearing in another. From the first time her mother had hired Marco the Magnificent to entertain at her sixth birthday party, the power of this mystifying art had enthralled her. Naturally, as she got older, she knew it was all an illusion and that there were perfectly plausible explanations for every kind of trick.

Yet as she sat in hushed silence with the crowd of two thousand that had packed the community center that evening over three years ago, the levelheaded intellect that governed her life was overwhelmingly assailed by sights that defied all laws of logic, gravity, and common sense.

Transfixed, her green eyes never once left the face of the dark-haired magician from the first moment he came onstage. Initially it was a reaction she tried to dismiss as perfectly normal. Who *wouldn't* stare at a man as handsome as Kyle Falconer, she asked herself, amused by the thought that he could probably stand on stage doing absolutely nothing and still make women swoon in the aisles.

His flashing brown eyes had teased the audience, dared inanimate objects to move, winked, and caused a Jaguar and its occupants, four giggling audience volunteers, to vanish momentarily and then reappear on the other side of the stage, and sparkled in appreciation of well-deserved applause. His thick black hair encouraged fantasies of lazy Sunday mornings in bed. His tall body, surprisingly lithe, moved with the grace of a dancer, each step and gesture a measured perfection.

It was more than looks, though, that held her attention. In retrospect she felt as if she had been hypnotized, his magnetism and energy effortlessly reaching across twenty-nine rows to take her prisoner.

Her rational mind had resisted his pull as being audience manipulation, but the part of her that had always been enamored of the world of magic—*his* world—was completely in the man's grasp.

"Let's see if we can get his autograph," Catherine's companions had urged her when the show was over. To their surprise she declined, falling back on the weak excuse of a headache to disengage herself from eagerly mounting frenzy of fans who waited in the lobby to meet their hero in person.

Maybe I *should* have, she chided herself in the months that followed. Maybe it would have succinctly dispelled then and there the unfounded obsession she had carried ever since: that there was some sort of bond between them. Why else, she wondered, would she have imagined so distinctly the sound of his voice whispering her name as she exited the theater parking lot?

"Kyle Falconer?" Larry whistled when Catherine called him after lunch. "Awesome! When?"

Larry Mitchum was one of those priceless souls who could always be called upon to pick up dry cleaning, water plants, type copy, or even baby-sit cats on short notice. The salt of the earth and a number-one buddy who never minded dressing up to play escort or replenishing the Kleenex when tears hit the flood stage. Freckle-faced and halfway through college, Larry had been unofficially adopted by the entire female staff as their favorite kid brother.

"Tomorrow?" he repeated. "Damn! Tucker's being neutered."

"But the show's not till nine," Catherine explained. "At night."

"Yeah, but I'm having him done tomorrow morning." Tucker was Larry's distinguished sidekick, a gray schnauzer that he never let out of the house in winter unless he was wearing a hand-crocheted doggy sweater. Tucker, Catherine would have bet, probably had a bigger sweater wardrobe than most of the staff. "Maybe next time," Larry begged off, genuinely sorry to be saying no, a virtually nonexistent word in his vocabulary.

Back to my Rolodex, she thought with a sigh. Since the demise of her relationship with Nat, Catherine's A list of companions for these working evenings had narrowed precipitously to include only Larry, who enhanced her enjoyment of many an otherwise mediocre event with his youthful enthusiasm. Her B list—a long line of appreciative coworkers, neighbors, and acquaintances from the local press clubs and arts groups she belonged to—were constantly vying for tickets to the numerous pre-Broadway tryouts, visits from European opera companies, showings of rare Picasso prints, and even poetry readings by aging soap operas stars—that filled her work calendar.

But this particular Thursday evening found each one of them with an unbreakable previous engagement and numerous expressions of regret that they would have to miss this extravaganza, a standout in a city known for its exceptional access to world-class entertainment. Catherine began to wonder—a little unreasonably, perhaps—if fate was conspiring against her to force her to brave the web of Kyle Falconer's enchantment alone, when she would have felt so much safer sharing it with a familiar—and very mortal—face.

Still trying up until Thursday afternoon quitting time, Catherine finally resigned herself to the fact that she'd be dateless for what was being billed as one of the major events of the year. Well, she'd hold on to the tickets anyway. Surely there'd be someone deserving in the standby line to whom she could give an impromptu gift. Her good deed for the week.

In spite of the hour, 14th Street and Constitution Avenue were still congested, primarily with tourists looking for places to park their rental cars. Catherine had to smile to herself as she emerged from the Smithsonian station. Much as she enjoyed driving, her own car had unquestionably spent more time at home in the underground garage than on Washington streets, owing to the convenience and economy of the Metro. With long, purposeful strides she crossed Fifteenth Street and proceeded across the grass.

A temporary amphitheater had been built on the grounds of the Monument, its high wall partially obscuring the view from the crowd of people outside—in some places now six deep—still hoping to purchase tickets. Catherine remembered the extra one in the envelope, wondering at the same time how best to get rid of it. An old person? A young person? A person who'd have to eat toast and beans for a month to pay for it?

But it seemed that fate, in answer to her quandary, had already provided the solution. The second ticket was missing.

In annoyance her mind raced back to the last time she had definitely seen it. Think back, she told herself. The envelope Johnson had given her. Putting it in her pocket. Coffee break at her desk. In her hand when she called Larry. She scowled. Had she taken it home Wednesday night? No, she had tried four more coworkers in the office on Thursday morning. What had she done with it then?

Up ahead, the ushers were starting to admit the people with passes, the television crew having finished their setup with forty-five minutes to spare. Silently chiding herself for being so careless, Catherine stepped into the line that was slowly pushing forward, its members chattering in anticipation of what they were about to see.

Given that her entire day had been plagued with frustration, Catherine wasn't surprised she had misplaced the ticket. None of her calls to the Hyatt Regency had been returned, and she was no closer to getting an interview with Kyle Falconer. As a last resort she had even gone there in person right after work, only to be told crisply at the desk, "Mr. Falconer does not accept calls or guests." Her persistence had not worn them down.

Nor had they been swayed by her credentials. If anything, her connection with the *Tribune* had only intensified their commitment to protect their prestigious celebrity's privacy. All that she had gleaned—and only then by an accidental slip of the tongue—was that he would be there until Sunday.

As the memory of her first impression of him had come crashing back, where the passionate ferocity of his presence was as frightening as it was exalting, she rationalized that maybe it was better she wasn't going to get the interview. One lingering glance, one touch of his skin in their handshake, and she would likely have been reduced to Jell-O. On the other hand, it might have been *good* for her to come face-to-face with the fact that her secret hero was just flesh and blood. Over and over in her budding career she had witnessed dazzling performances of world-class actors, opera stars, even other magicians—and then been amazed and perhaps a little disappointed upon interviewing them to discover how commonplace and mundane they usually were once the footlights, glitter, and adulation of thousands of amassed fans had been stripped away. Why should Kyle Falconer be any different?

She contented herself with studying the black-and-white glossy program, its text offering only meager supplement to what little she had found in Archives. He was thirty-two. He came from a small town in New Hampshire, the name of the town itself curiously omitted. He had appeared ("magically," one article quipped) on the Las Vegas entertainment circuit ten years ago and seemingly achieved overnight acclaim as the world's greatest magician. No relatives. No romantic links. Apparently no other life than the one he chose to project onstage. A true twentieth-century enigma.

His specialization, the program continued, was making the impossible a reality. Two years ago he had astounded an audience in Cairo by walking in one side of the Great Pyramid of Giza and out the other. Two years before that he had escaped from a sealed vault in the heart of Fort Knox, bringing with him as evidence a single gold bar. And now, on a moonless night in April, he was going to make one of Washington's most famous landmarks vanish from its base.

The crowd was growing restless. Members of the camera crew had given up pacing the aisles. The frenetic, pulsating beat of music from the speakers positioned at the base of the massive obelisk stirred the senses rather than calmed them. Suddenly the air was charged with the electricity of his arrival.

"Where did *he* come from?" the crowd murmured in surprised delight. Indeed, no one could remember the precise moment, caught up in the spell of the music and the lights, anticipating the sheer spectacle their own eyes would behold in the hour to come.

Yet there he was in front of them all, a charismatic hero in black slacks, white silk shirt, and black leather aviator's jacket, the collar roguishly turned up to meet his wavy, black hair. "Just thought I'd drop in," he announced with a wink, the microphones sending his sensuous voice into the farthest reaches of his sea of admirers. In reply the crowd went to their feet, their hands sending thunderous applause into the Washington sky.

Boyish dimples creased his lean face as he jokingly urged them to stop. "Really," he insisted, "I haven't even *done* anything yet."

Pledging to justify the high compliment they had just paid him ("Not to mention the ticket price," he added in good humor), he immediately proceeded to nimbly pluck objects as if from an invisible sack, levitate a blushing volunteer, subject his assistants to complex rites of disembodiment by sword and saw, each illusion more breathtaking than the one before.

9

As the hour of ten approached, Catherine could sense the audience's hearts furiously pounding, their curiosity begging him to fulfill his climactic promise, its spellbinding magnificence to be retold again and again.

"Well, what would you like to see now?" he teased, then indicated with a toss of his head the tower of marble and granite that loomed over five hundred feet tall behind him. "Maybe a little disappearing act?" Their hysterical applause was answer enough.

Catherine felt her own pulse quicken as she watched him prepare for the final enchantment, her body uncomfortably aware of his all-consuming effect on her. A tingling shiver through her arms caused her to reach for the linen jacket that lay on the empty seat next to her and, leaning forward, her eyes once again made Kyle Falconer the total focus of her concentration. Whatever spell he had cast on her, she found herself helpless to resist, reluctant to fight.

Transference, she attempted to label it. Clearly her aching loneliness and her memories of Nat were transferring what she had felt for him into an erotic fantasy about a total stranger she had seen only once before in her life. Yet even as she thought it, an undeniable truth floated through her consciousness. Not even with Nat had she felt the surging, feverish bond she was experiencing now with the figure in black and white, the feeling that they had been one . . . and would be again.

"The Washington Monument," he began in a voice that would melt butter, "was conceived in 1847, a pseudo-Greek temple to honor the country's first president." Slowly building in volume, the orchestral overture from *Back to the Future* provided a suspenseful backdrop to his narrative. "One fourth of the way up in 1848," he continued, "all work ceased . . . not to be resumed until twelve years later." An upward wave of his hand pointed out the definitive coloration that marked the marble's origins from two different areas of the Maryland quarry. "Tonight you shall see where the work originally came to a halt."

Had the wisps of blue and lavender smoke already started at the beginning of his story? Or, summoned by a magical cue, had they only just then begun their menacing spiral upward from the four corners of the Monument's base? Like flickering tongues, they swirled higher, becoming a thick cloud that soon enveloped its prey until it was no longer visible to the spectators below.

Suddenly—and without warning—every light between the Lincoln Memorial and the Capitol itself went out. Even the streetlights and the television Portapaks fell victim to the blackness. The grounds plunged into impenetrable depths of blindness for six seconds, long enough for the final phase of Falconer's wizardry to take place. Then, one by one, four floodlights at the corners of the Monument's base came on to cast their brilliance upward. The veil of blue and lavender smoke was gracefully descending like a goddess shedding her silken robes. A gasp rose from the audience. The top three quarters of the landmark had indeed vanished. So, too, had the magician, though Catherine apparently was the only one to notice.

"My God! What's that?" a woman in one of the lower rows of the amphitheater screamed, then laughed at herself or what she had momentarily glimpsed in the remaining wisps of lavender smoke. A reddish-brown bird, confused by the bright lights and the noise, had strayed into the space where the Monument had stood in full glory but a minute before. Darting off into the night sky, it missed the spontaneous applause that its unrehearsed appearance had generated. Still aware of the magician's absence, the crowd was simultaneously clapping and speculating out loud how he possibly could have pulled off such an incredible stunt.

It might have been a leaf or a breeze, as gently as it had grazed her cheek. Without thinking, Catherine automatically touched her face, recoiling as her fingers made contact with what felt like a feathered wing. Her short gasp was drowned out by the applause still bursting out around her.

And then, before she realized what was even happening, a bright beam of light was shining directly at her. Or, rather, on the seat right next to her. For standing on the chair, his arms raised triumphantly above his head, was Kyle Falconer.

"Hey, how did he get up there?" The spectators mumbled in awe, laughing that once again they had been fooled. So distracted were they now by his sparkling presence in their midst that not a single one thought to turn any attention to the Monument, its full height slowly rebuilding from out of thin air.

"I'm sorry," he said gallantly to Catherine. "Was this seat taken?"

Chapter Two

HE WAS ALREADY gone by the time Catherine reached the lower level, the security guards obviously having followed to the letter their instructions to smuggle him to the waiting limousine on 15th. "I don't know," one of his assistants replied blankly to Catherine's inquiry of whether he was returning to the hotel.

Off to the side, two of the cameramen were engaged in a heated debate about Falconer's use of giant mirrors or mass hypnosis to pull off the trick that film had captured for posterity. "What about the bird?" one of them contested, grinding out the butt of his cigarette with the heel of his boot. "It flew right through the Monument, remember?"

"Yeah, but it probably wasn't a *real* bird," the other one pointed out. "I'll bet it was one of those Disney critters he worked by remote."

As she left the confines of the noisy amphitheater Catherine realized she was trembling almost imperceptibly, her heart still racing from having been so close to him at the show's finale. When he had looked down and spoken to her, his eyes—a deep, fathomless brown—had locked with hers as if to communicate a silent message. "It's you, isn't it?" they seemed to say. Or had she only imagined the subliminal text? For in the next instant he was already proceeding down the steps to take a much-deserved standing ovation.

Not once after that did he seek her out in the rows of faces that shouted praise, nor did he wait for her outside. It was as if he had completely forgotten about her, as if she had been only a random spectator and his flirtatious remark only a well-rehearsed element of the total theatrical package. If telepathy were part of his repertoire, it had failed to alert him of her ardent desire that they meet.

Annoyed at circumstances that had thrown them together for one brief, breathless moment but was otherwise keeping them firmly apart—and her from fulfilling her obligations as a reporter— Catherine felt suddenly drained by the intensity of her experience. Still, despite everything, she determined not to let the otherworldliness of the past few hours distract her from the task ahead. *Come on, Cath,* she told herself finally as she hailed a cab, *you're not going to let some latter-day Houdini get the best of you, are you?*

"Sorry, miss," the hotel operator apologized. "He doesn't answer." Even Catherine's ruse of pretending to be a long-distance caller hadn't worked. "Would you care to leave a message?" the woman asked. Catherine declined, dejectedly returning the receiver to its cradle and sinking back into her bed pillows.

Determination to meet Johnson's challenge and secure an interview for the *Trib* had long since faded as her prime motivation to make contact. "You really *are* getting obsessed," she reprimanded herself. But why? What had possessed her into taking a cab to the hotel, waiting in the lobby until midnight and then pretending just now to be a foreign caller in the hope that she could trick the night clerk into putting her though?

Common sense told her that she should be writing her review instead of daydreaming. In seven hours Johnson would be expecting something brilliant on his desk. The lack of an interview he could forgive; he had as much as said on Wednesday that he wasn't really counting on one. But a cohesive, solid review was something he *did* expect. Demand, in fact, particularly from a writer as talented as Catherine.

I'll get up in few minutes, she decided, pulling the afghan over her shoulders. *I'll get up and put on a robe and type my little heart out.*

Exhausted from a long day and disturbed by the feelings that Falconer had evoked, she was an easy target for slumber. Its blanket of comforting darkness softly descended on her, enveloping her in a velvet cocoon.

Outside the railing of her bedroom balcony, unseen, the reddish-brown bird kept vigilant watch until morning.

A kaleidoscope of bright green and yellow and the pungent smell of sweet flowers assailed her senses, so real that for a moment she had to stop and remind herself that it was only a dream.

She was deep in the heart of a forest, the sun barely casting its warm light through the lacy umbrella of trees above. Soft, moist earth caressed her bare feet, and as she walked, the fabric of the coarse black gown she wore made a rough whisper over the leaves and twigs in her path. Without thinking, she pushed up her sleeves past the elbows, aware now of how pale her arms were against the black cloth. Aware, too, of her clipped, unpolished fingernails and lips that felt dry beneath her tongue.

Like ageless, towering sentinels, the trees around her offered no clue as to her whereabouts, yet she hardly felt frightened or lost. This could have been any forest. Maybe a forest from her childhood in Oregon. Or later on, in California. And yet it was different somehow—mystical yet comfortingly familiar—each branch and each leaf teeming with fresh color and vitality.

Onward she walked, down a little-used path, drawn to the sound of moving water up ahead, even more aware now of her thirst and the dryness of her skin.

There in the clearing it stood: a lake that shimmered with iridescent beauty. Its surface was so still, it might have been made of glass.

The melodic voice had not been audible from a distance, but here at the edge of the forest it was clear and precise, the soothing tones of an unseen woman. "You have always had the power to go," the voice said. "You have no choice but to use it."

Cautiously Catherine crept forward, for even though it was her own dream, she felt as though she were trespassing, playing witness to something forbidden. "You must return with it," the voice continued, "or all shall be lost forever."

So intent was Catherine on listening that until he spoke, she didn't notice the cloaked figure in brown and gray patiently sitting on the bank of the lake.

"And if I fail?" he said. His voice was one of someone who had seen years of sorrow and wisdom. Each word was carefully measured. The hood of his cloak obscured his face; the tentative movements of his limbs beneath the ragged material suggested frail health or advanced age or perhaps both. She wanted to move closer to get a better look but dared not.

"You *must* not fail!" the woman's voice replied, a defiant ripple breaking the tranquil surface of water. Only then did Catherine sense—and by reasons unknown to her—that it was not a breathing human companion with whom the cloaked figure was conversing but the crystal lake itself.

Half in anticipation, half in fear, Catherine crouched down into the bushes, wary of being discovered and thrown at the mercy of something not quite natural. The barrier imposed by her hiding place behind the thicket now forced her to strain to hear the conversation as it continued.

"But how will I know her?" the old man asked, a hint of urgency in his manner. "The passage of time is long and its corridors many."

"Trust the vision," the lady of the lake murmured back. "She is the only one who can lead you to what you must find." Her voice was fading, as if it were on a ship being carried farther from shore.

"I must see her face one more time," the old man implored, raising a gnarled hand so bluish and pale as to be nearly translucent. "To remember," he whispered, "to be sure when I have found her . . ."

Catherine then found herself standing alone at the lake's edge and looking in, a circle of water before her turning purple-black and swirling like a miniature whirlpool. "She is the one you must find," the woman's voice—nearly gone now—echoed up through the liquid depths.

The blackness of the whirlpool slowly dissolved, and in its place materialized Catherine's image. As it appeared, Catherine felt herself gasp. And then the cave faded into darkness. . . .

Larry was quick to express his concern when Catherine called in sick the next morning. "So you need me to pick up anything or take you to the hospital?" he offered. Good old Larry, always at the ready to drop what he was doing and come to the rescue.

"Just a run-of-the-mill bug," Catherine protested.

"You sure?"

"I'll be fine by Monday," she insisted, feeling guilty for lying to someone whose own honesty was practically his personal trademark.

"There is *one* thing you could do, though," she added.

"Name it, kiddo."

"It's about my review."

"Oh, yeah—how was the show?"

"You'll be the first to read about it," she promised. "I was wondering if you could pick up the copy and run it in for me."

"No prob. See you in a few minutes."

"Actually—"

"Hmm?"

"Could you get it at lunch instead?" Out of the corner of her eye, two skimpy paragraphs in longhand taunted her from the kitchen table. "I haven't typed it yet."

"*I* can do that for you," Larry volunteered, but Catherine quickly declined.

"You're saving my neck as it is," she informed him, firm in her resolve to stall for the time it would take to write something worth handing in. "How about twelve-thirty?"

"Whatever is best for you," he said. "No sweat, anyway— Johnson's out with a root canal." He paused a second. "Or was it a brain canal?" he joked.

"See you later," Catherine said, laughing.

"Hey, wait a second," Larry interjected just before she hung up. "How *was* the show? Was he everything you thought he'd be?"

"Everything," Catherine agreed, the tingling sensation returning. "And more."

Running a hand through sleep-tangled hair, she sluggishly strolled to the bathroom, still angry at herself for having fallen asleep in her clothes and not getting up until twenty minutes before she was supposed to be out the front door.

She had awakened with a start, disoriented by the sun streaming through her window. What day was it? With a short-lived spurt of adrenalin she entertained the idea of trying to beat the clock, abandoning it when she remembered the review she still had to write.

Still dressed, she had pulled out one of the kitchen chairs and sat down to collect her thoughts. She dismissed the ridiculous thought that she could write about the effect Kyle Falconer's performance had *really* had on her. After that the first sentences came easily but quickly degenerated into mindless drivel as she exhausted her supply of synonyms for *spectacular*. Shortly before she called Larry, exasperation drove her to snap her pencil in half. Finally she gave up the hope of writing the review at that moment and, hoping a hot shower would clear her thoughts, headed for the bathroom.

It wasn't until she had shed her clothes and stood under the welcome blast of hot water from the shower that the details of the dream returned, as rich in clarity as when she had been asleep. Disturbed by the content, she tried to dismiss it as the result of something spicy she had eaten before bed, remembering that she hadn't even taken time for dinner the night before. Aware now of how hungry she was, she turned her thoughts to the luxury of a leisurely breakfast, a treat usually reserved for rainy Sundays and infrequent vacations.

Like a stealthy intruder, Falconer invaded her consciousness as she slid the warm bar of soap down supple limbs and worked it into a frothy lather. She felt her stomach muscles tense. Felt the bar of soap slip out of her fingers. Fumbling to collect it, she reminded herself firmly that Kyle Falconer was only a man. She even said it out loud, as if to emphasize the point. Her heart, however, was not convinced.

She could still feel herself melt under his penetrating gaze, still feel the heat his body had generated from an hour of nonstop entertainment. Under the pulsating rush of water she closed her eyes and imagined the scene all over again, carrying it a step further. In her mind they shared a smoldering kiss, the crowd around them vanishing as easily as the Monument, leaving the two of them alone and locked in each other's arms beneath a moonless sky. "You've been reading too many romance novels," her subconscious interjected sarcastically. "Better switch the tap to cold or you'll be in here all day."

Later, her hair wrapped in a turban-style towel and a cup of lukewarm coffee in her hand, Catherine sat staring at the same eighty-seven words she had written an hour and a half earlier. Deciding that she needed the fresh air a short walk would afford, she dumped the remains of coffee into the sink and let the silky kimono slip from her shoulders as she crossed the hall to her bedroom.

At any time of year the nation's capital was a breathtaking city to explore. The stately elegance of Federalist architecture was just within blocks of contemporary steel and glass. Whether winter snows draped Embassy Row in a blanket of white, or summer sun heightened the frenzy of protesters on the fifty-four acre Ellipse, Washington, D.C., was a setting that crackled with energy and encouraged further discovery.

Springtime remained Catherine's favorite season. The abundance of color made it a natural for would-be artists with sketch pads and chalk. Mrs. Taft's legacy of three thousand trees donated by the mayor of Tokyo still burst forth in bright pink profusion, just as they had done for over sixty years, punctuating the landscape with strawberry-colored blossoms.

Catherine had walked all the way to the Vietnam Memorial before she realized how far she had gone from her apartment. Solemnly, still lost in thought, she walked past the grim, black wall of servicemen's names. Here and there, visiting mourners had paid their respects with single, beribboned flowers. A mother lifted her child to touch one of the engraved lines. A trio of men in their forties openly wept and clung to each other for support.

As she neared the end of the wall her upward glance fell on the towering obelisk visible through the trees. Without thinking, she thrust her hands into the pockets of her jeans and started walking toward it, inextricably drawn to the site where Falconer had worked his magic the night before.

In the hours since the Falconer performance the city had performed its own vanishing act, crews skillfully dismantling the huge amphitheater until nothing remained save for the trampled impressions in the grass where the makeshift structure had stood.

Now it was business as usual at the Monument, a crowd of tourists circling the base as they stood in line for the elevator ride to the top. Shielding her eyes from the sun, Catherine looked up to the column's full height, still astounded that something so huge could be rendered invisible in a matter of seconds.

"The elevator was the hardest part," an amused voice said behind her. Startled, Catherine turned, already recognizing the man to whom the voice belonged.

Chapter Three

HIS DISARMING SMILE and casual approach caught her off-guard. So, too, did his treatment of their meeting as premeditated on his part rather than accidental. "I had a hunch this is where I'd find you," he remarked, apologizing for what she might have earlier misconstrued as deliberate evasion.

"How did you know that I—" Catherine abruptly stopped short of the complete question, conscious of the warm blush that was spreading over her face.

His lips parted in a dazzling display of straight teeth. "That you've been trying to reach me?" he filled in for her. "I just had a feeling, Catherine."

It wasn't until later that his use of her first name prior to their formal introduction struck her as frightening. After all, she had left her card and countless messages at the hotel. Someone could have described her to him. He, himself, could have remembered her from the previous evening. Maybe he had made a lucky guess at what the gold initial pin on her scarf stood for.

Before she had a chance to consider any of the options, he had changed the subject and started walking toward Pennsylvania Avenue. Catherine quickly fell in step beside him.

Minus the trappings of fame and his trademark ensemble, Kyle Falconer could easily have been anyone. His appearance in broad daylight failed to attract any attention—a condition that obviously pleased him. Dressed in jeans, open-necked shirt, and tennis shoes, his only common link to the same magician who had performed to a capacity crowd the night before was the tear-shaped crystal that hung from a slender gold chain around his neck. Catherine found herself staring at it as they waited for the light to change.

"Would that be okay with you?" he repeated, amused by her distraction, touched by her childlike wonder.

"I'm sorry," she started to apologize, the disquieting embarrassment returning to intimidate her usually reserved manner. Seeking to put her at ease, he was already restating his invitation.

"Late breakfast? Early lunch?" he offered. "It's the least I can do for keeping you waiting."

For the first time she noticed the subtle age lines about his mouth and eyes, which muted his youth with quiet strength. Wisps of dark hair curled against the vee of his open shirt. She felt the power that lay coiled within him, even at rest.

"I know a great café on Capitol Hill," he continued as, urging yet protective, he touched her elbow as they crossed the street.

"I haven't said yes yet," Catherine pointed out as they reached the other side, a defiant show of bravado to counterattack the complete lack of defense she felt in his presence.

Her hesitation was reflected in a flash of disappointment behind his sensual brown eyes. "If another time would be better . . ." he began, but even then she was letting forth a smile that betrayed her real feelings.

"No. That is—I mean, I guess there's no time like the present." She shrugged, trying to sound noncommittal.

His response was accompanied by an enigmatic smile. "That's a matter of perspective."

Still puzzled by the remark as they waited for their order at the Candidate's Choice, Catherine asked him what he had meant.

"You mean about time being relative?" he paraphrased. "When you're young, it can't go fast enough. When you're old, you want to grab hold with both hands and make it stand still."

"You're a long way from having to worry about *that*," she observed, recalling his age cited in the program.

A scant furrow crossed his brow. "What about you?" he asked, offering her the basket of biscuits.

"What about me?" Puzzled, her senses told her that he had intended to say something else just then but changed his mind.

20

His dark eyes appraised her thoughtfully. "What do you do with *your* time?"

"I thought *I* was the one doing the interview," she reminded him, nonetheless flattered by his curiosity.

"Is that what we're doing? An interview?" Long, tapered fingers wielded the butter knife in smooth swirls over the fresh bread. An easy grin played at the corners of his mouth. "You're not writing anything down."

Embarrassed to admit it was because she didn't have any paper, Catherine met his challenge with composure. "I have a good memory," she replied.

"A useful trait," he nodded appreciatively. "As you were saying . . .?"

Later, halfway through their meal, Catherine realized he had successfully turned every question back into one of his own about her. "Naturally inquisitive." He smiled in response. "What exactly did you want to know?"

The problem, of course, was that there were too *many* things she wanted to know. Her thoughts harkened back to her first journalism class in college and the instructor's repeated admonition against predictable questions. Ask the unexpected, he had stressed time and time again to his students. Ask your subjects things they've never been asked before. In the absence of any prior interviews with the media, of course, Kyle Falconer would be considered open territory. She could ask any question she wanted—unexpected or otherwise. Overwhelmed by the possibilities, her mind had gone blank.

"So how long have you been practicing it?" she asked at last, annoyed with herself for the total lack of creativity but too uncomfortable to let the uneasy silence continue.

"'It' being . . .?"

"Magic."

"Illusion," he said, gently correcting her.

"Aren't they the same thing?"

"Magic is the alteration of reality," he explained. "Illusion is a perception of the mind."

"I don't think I understand," she confessed. "Wasn't it magic that made the Monument disappear last night?"

"Did it really?" he teased. "Or did it disappear because you *expected* it to?"

"I don't know *what* I expected," she said, her words tumbling out. Most of all, she hadn't expected to feel possessed the way she did just now, intoxicated by the look in his eyes and the masculine scent of sandalwood across the short distance that separated them. "Are you going to tell me how you did it?" she probed, already certain of his response.

"An artist never divulges his secrets," he replied with a wink.

"What about your family, then?" she went on, determined to pursue new ground. "What are *they* like?"

For an instant an undeniable look of pain stole into his expression, prompting Catherine to ask quickly if she had said something wrong.

His mouth curved with tenderness at her compassion and sensitivity. "They've been gone a long time," he said. "It's still difficult."

Catherine nodded sympathetically. Although her own father had died when she was just a little girl, the tears still came on each anniversary of his death. Probably they always would. "Tell me more about illusion," she insisted, hoping to relieve the somber lull that had entered their conversation.

She watched him settle his slender frame back into a relaxed position in the booth they shared, the sun through the window glistening off his black hair. Sad in the certainty that the opportunity to be this close to him would never come again, Catherine found herself memorizing every detail of his face and voice so as not to forget. Like a discreet ghost, the waitress silently reached across them to refill their coffee cups as he talked. Catherine was oblivious to everything but the man with whom she felt an inescapable bond. Prismatic colors danced across the surface of the table as the crystal, catching the light, moved in concert with him as he spoke.

"An illusion is like . . . a dream," he was explaining. An involuntary jerk of Catherine's hand caused a splash of coffee to spill from her cup and saturate a large spot on the tablecloth.

"Clumsy," she muttered as she accepted the napkin he chivalrously held out to her. Random as his allegory had been, the mere mention of dreaming had triggered disconcerting recollections of her sleep that were still subconsciously bothering her. Determined to dismiss them, she urged him to continue with what he had been saying.

"The logical side of the brain," he obliged, "tells us that we're not really there, intense as the dream might seem to be at the time. The fantasy side, though, wants to fight the inevitability of waking up." He fingered his cup reflectively. "Much as everyone likes to speculate how a person can walk through pyramids or survive impalement on a sword, a secret part of them *wants* to believe the illusion, believe that it all actually happened the way their eyes saw it."

"Even skeptics?"

"Maybe skeptics the most." He smiled. "If there wasn't a tiny part of them that still believed in miracles, they wouldn't keep getting up in the morning." His glance fell on her arms, folded in front of her on the table as she had leaned forward to listen.

"Cold?" he asked in concern.

She lowered her eyes in confusion as his hand made gentle contact with the bare skin of her forearm. Beneath his fingers lay a perceptible trail of goose bumps. Catherine felt her cheeks color under the heat of his gaze and the electricity of his touch. As her mind raced to think of something to say, she was distracted by the face of her watch, quickly comparing the time it read against the grandfather clock across the room. A mild expletive escaped from her lips after confirming what she hoped was a mistake. It was almost two.

"I'm keeping you from something," he observed.

"No, really," she protested. "I just didn't realize it was getting so late."

"If you have to be somewhere . . ."

Catherine was quick to deny it, suddenly fearful that their time together might end. "It's nothing important," she insisted. Larry would understand. She'd call him as soon as she got home. With an ache, she realized that going home was the last thing she wanted right now. Unsuccessfully she tried to ignore her quickening pulse and the knot that had formed in her stomach.

Falconer made no attempt to hide the fact that he was watching her closely. Nor did he retrieve the hand that had slid to rest softly on top of hers. "Are you all right, Catherine?" he asked.

Spontaneously and without thinking, she pulled back and

shrugged, breaking the slender thread of contact that had united them. She immediately regretted the action. Her mind reeling with confusion, she said the first thing that she could think of. "I guess I'm just"—she searched for the right word—"overwhelmed."

He offered her a forgiving smile, tilting his head in puzzlement. "Not by me, I hope?"

"It's not every day I get to sit for hours talking to a magician."

"Illusionist."

"Call it what you like," she replied, looking at him and conscious once more of his sensual magnetism. "It all looked like the real thing to me."

Thoughtfully he sipped the remains of his coffee. "It's as real as you *choose* for it to be. That simple."

"I wish that *writing* about it were simple." She sighed, pangs of guilt returning as she thought about the two pathetic paragraphs she had composed that morning in a disheveled stupor. "My muse must be on vacation."

"But it always comes back to you," he commented matter-of-factly. "Like it will *this* time."

A cloud of suspicion registered on her face. "How do you know?"

"Hasn't it?"

"Yes, but—"

"Assumption," he explained before she could go on. "You're persistent in what you want. If you didn't believe in what you were doing and what you're good at, you wouldn't be so dedicated to your job."

Smiling at the irony of his comment, Catherine replayed the events of the past twenty-four hours. Selfishness had clearly overridden whatever dedication she liked to think she had toward her chosen career. Ceaseless, inward questions nagged at her, prominent among them the worry that she was losing her most valuable asset as a writer and reporter: objectivity.

His voice cut into her private reverie. "You seem lost in thought."

She blinked, feeling light-headed and self-conscious. "I've been lost before," she replied.

There was a faint glimmer of humor in his eyes. "I'm not being much help to your article, am I?" In retrospect, she realized, he had said little more than what was in the black-and-white brochure she had received at the performance.

"My boss wasn't really expecting me to come through," she admitted. "He said you didn't give interviews."

"He was right. I covet my privacy like a miser covets gold."

She hesitated. "But you came *looking* for me," she reminded him a little sharply. "Even though you knew I worked for the paper."

He was already nodding. "Yes, I did." His casual glance around the restaurant prompted his suggestion that they leave and go for a walk. "I think we're overstaying our welcome."

"Wait," she objected, uncomfortable with his ability to avoid direct answers. "Can't you at least tell me why?"

Once more his face displayed an uncanny awareness of her inner turmoil. "What I think you want to know, Catherine, doesn't have anything to do with the interview, convenient as it was to pretend that it did."

"Pretend?"

"On *my* part," he added, his voice softening as his fingers reached across to close over hers. Awkwardly she cleared her throat, unable to take her eyes off his hand, its touch insistent and possessive.

"I'm not sure what's going on here," she murmured. Impatiently she waited for him to explain, dreading that he had seen through her schoolgirl crush and now tactfully sought to dissuade her from it.

"I don't expect you to understand what I'm going to say," he said preparing her for his response. "Only to listen."

Cautiously she nodded, hoping to hold her emotions in check. The silence lengthened between them as he seemed to weigh how best to explain his actions.

"I should have known there wouldn't be an easy place to begin," he said, more to himself than to Catherine.

"Most people," she ventured, "try the beginning."

He laughed. "I was thinking of something a little more recent," he said.

"Like what?"

For a long moment he explored her face, settling at last on her eyes, which regarded him with a curious mixture of passion and fear. Nothing on earth could have prepared her for his reply, simple in its delivery but chilling in its significance.

"The dream you had this morning."

Chapter Four

PANIC, STARK AND vivid in intensity, flashed in her eyes, her senses reeling from the privacy he had shattered. Driven by an inward crescendo of terror that his revelation was the harbinger of something dark and threatening, her first impulse was to bolt from the table. How could he have possibly known a secret as intimate as a dream?

Paralyzed by his words, Catherine glanced down to see the knuckles of her captive hand turning white. Not from *his* grasp, however, but from her own fingers engaging his in a feverish grip, as if she were afraid to break their electrifying contact. Her pulse skittered in alarm, her instincts split between the emotional urge to escape and the physical gravitation not to let go, to move even closer.

A suffocating sensation tightened her throat as she tried to bring forth the one-word question that was thundering inside her head. Across the table, his handsome face was a study of composed tenderness and concern.

"Catherine?"

His voice seemed to come from far away, and she found herself straining to hear, distracted by her own whirlwind of conflicting emotions.

Sharp and assessing, the eyes that met hers read the fear his statement had generated, imploring her to accept an unspoken apology for what had been a premature transgression. Respectfully he started to let go of her hand, reconsidering it in the brief moment it took to feel her fingers tighten. His hand remained where it was.

"How?" she asked her voice stiff and unnatural. With quiet but desperate firmness and a barely noticeable quiver in her chin, Catherine found the nerve to challenge him. "Tell me how."

For an instant a wistfulness crept over his face that Catherine found bewildering. "If you believe only one thing that I tell you, Catherine," he began, his eyes melting the distance between them, "trust that I haven't come this far to harm you." The crystal shimmered like a capsule of radiant stars as his free hand reached out to caress her wrist. "That's something I'd prevent at all costs."

With a start Catherine realized that his lips hadn't moved, that the voice she had heard just now had come to her precisely as the telepathic affirmation she had fancifully imagined in the stands at the Washington Monument.

The warmth of his smile echoed in the thoughts he sent. "Yes, Catherine. I had to know it was you."

Dupont Circle—a pulsating confluence of privileged and poor, of activists and indifferent bystanders—was a favored Washington spot for people-watching. That afternoon, though, Catherine was not among those dedicated to the unobtrusive observance of Washington's masses. Sleek limousines that ordinarily would have kindled mild curiosity passed her by unnoticed. Elderly chess players and impromptu evangelists in the shadow of the magnificent fountain sculpture might have otherwise evoked her interest or amusement. So, too, would the sprinkling of lovers walking hand in hand, revelling in the balmy spring day. Instead Catherine's preoccupation had rendered all of them invisible, her attention centered on the man she had chosen, against her better judgment, to accompany from the restaurant.

He had not abducted her by force, nor lured her by the false pretenses of promised enlightenment. Indeed, if something *should* happen to her now, Catherine could not help but play out in her imagination that witnesses would recall the hours they had attentively spent in each other's company and the earnest way they had clasped hands across the table. They'd describe, too, how the young man had been the first to get up, how the young woman had quickly moved to join him the second he turned from her and toward the door. Whatever she had walked into, she had gone willingly.

Her actions at that moment defied all logical thinking, for even then he had given her a choice. "I'll give you what time you need, Catherine," he told her as he started to take his leave. Yet Catherine could not ignore the strange sensation that what he was offering her from his heart was also the one thing he could little afford to waste. Her own heart pounding in her chest and her defenses scattered, Catherine saw no other way to learn the truth than to pursue and confront it. With steadfast determination she clung to reality. Kyle Falconer, whatever his intentions, had dangled a key that inexplicably linked them; she had to find out why. Stranger that he was to her, she was as transparent as glass to him, a realization that alternately intrigued and disturbed her.

To her surprise he had not initiated any physical contact with her once they left the restaurant, seemingly conscious of the anxiety that his previous touch had caused. By tacit consent they had started to walk together, Catherine matching his pace with her own as he strode with the confidence of someone who had lived in D.C. all his life.

If she had been expecting his answers to be direct and immediate, clearly she had already forgotten the pattern of their earlier conversation. His continued talk of illusion only served to annoy her further, its mention yet another smoke screen to avoid responding to her demand for an explanation.

Twice more he had attempted to speak to her without talking. Both times she had forced her mind to block out his voice. Until he could offer an explanation, she found it an unwelcome violation as offensive as a physical assault.

Only once before in her life had she felt as vulnerable and unprotected as she was feeling in his presence. Shortly after her father's death Catherine and her mother had come home from a movie to find that a burglar had ransacked their house. She could still close her eyes and see all the dresses from her closet strewn on the floor, drawers perfunctorily emptied out on the bed, her ceramic penguin bank lying broken on the floor in jagged pieces. The nauseating feeling of crude exposure had remained with her for months after it happened, the memory recurring in the company of a stranger who had the power to reach deep into her thoughts and dominate them.

But now her stomach also churned with the conflict that simmered inside her. His actions alarmed and repelled her—and yet his very being seemed to draw her inexorably closer.

She could not deny the smoldering sexuality he exuded, nor its stimulating effect upon her. His proximity was a passionate challenge, hard to resist. The vibrant chord of desire he had struck in her secretly dared her to imagine the physical perfection that lay beneath the broadcloth shirt and form-fitting jeans.

In truth, though, it wasn't just the virile exterior that captivated her. His innate sensitivity and warmth were rare and unexpected in a society that seemed to pride itself on apathetic relationships. Indeed, if one considered the search for a soul mate as a perilous journey of the heart, it would not be difficult for Catherine to fantasize that her own search had finally ended, so strong was her sensation of already belonging.

The subtle dimple of a suppressed smile appeared in his cheek as Catherine turned to look at him. Momentarily abashed, she stiffened, recalling his ability to read her mind. If he had read it just them . . .

For her own peace and sanity she had to shake the possibility from her mind. Instead she watched with curiosity, wondering what it was about the fountain's inscription that now held his attention.

"Have you ever navigated by the stars?" he casually asked. The glittering luminosity of the crystal in pure sunlight abruptly distracted her from his inquiry, prompting the blunt accusation that had been dancing like a specter in her consciousness for the past hour.

"You hypnotized me."

He glanced sideways in a cool surprise, reflecting on her statement a moment before he replied. A wry but indulgent glint appeared in his eyes, catching Catherine off-guard. "You sound so sure, Catherine."

"Didn't you?" she countered, determined to stand her ground. To her way of thinking, it remained the only plausible excuse. Somehow, against her will and without her knowledge, he had tricked her into revealing the dream herself, then claimed responsibility for it. Even the voice she heard in her head must have been some kind of illusion. But for what purpose?

With quiet emphasis he assured her that her fears were misplaced.

As she opened her mouth to protest, he was already explaining why. "You're an intelligent woman, Catherine. From what you've probably heard about hypnosis, you already know that it can't make a person do something that's against their basic nature."

"Then how did you know about my dream?"

"You give me more credit than I deserve." He smiled. "I didn't send it to you if that's what you meant."

"But you *knew* about it," she countered.

"I knew that you'd *have* the dream, yes."

"How?" In annoyance, the thought flashed before her that her repetitive insistence was not unlike a child who had been told no.

With his hand gently touching the small of her back, he was leading them both toward an empty bench.

"Do you know what a dream is?" he asked as they both sat down.

Flustered by his continued maneuvers to keep her off-balance, she tried in vain to bring him back to her original question.

"A dream is the soul's way of travel," he went on. "It goes forward. It goes back. It enables you to rehearse a problem before the problem gets here—the feeling you call déjà vu."

"What does that have to do—"

"All it takes to trigger a dream" he continued, "is something familiar that gets you thinking as you fall asleep." With a tilt of his head he indicated the marble figures representing the Arts of Ocean Navigation. "The spirit can find its way across the stars and back again by morning. All it takes is a reminder to get it started."

Catherine's gaze was riveted to him, dissatisfaction evident on her face. "I thought you were going to give me answers," she reminded him crisply.

"I'm trying to."

With dramatic impatience Catherine turned her left wrist inward to look at her watch. In one swift movement he caught her hand, his eyes deep and imploring. "I'm telling you in the best way I can, Catherine."

"And what way is that?"

"The only one that you'll believe."

Her expression clouded in anger. "You haven't answered *anything*! On top of that, you've made me miss whatever chance I might have had to turn in a halfway decent story!" Her green eyes narrowed in suspicion. "Was that it? You didn't *want* me to write about you so you—"

His hands shot up to take hold of her shoulders firmly, urging her to calm down. "That was never my intention at all."

"What *was* then?"

Surprise drained the blood from her face when he replied. "To tell you who I really am."

Lazy and seductive, the slow-moving Washington Channel had an almost hypnotic effect on anyone who watched it. It was not until they had reached this setting—graced by the winding boulevard of Yoshino and Akebono cherry trees—that Kyle Falconer began his story, acutely aware that their continued relationship hinged entirely on her acceptance of the truth.

"About ten years ago," he began, "a Latvian freighter got caught in a late-summer storm in the North Sea. On that ship and headed for home was a sailor with a dangerous obsession."

Puzzled as to where the story was leading, Catherine nodded vaguely. She was faintly conscious of the water that lapped against the barrier below them in soothing accompaniment to his narrative.

"The chance, if it came at all," the magician continued, "would last only a split second."

"The chance for what?"

When he lifted his eyes, a flicker of sorrow lingered in them. "Where he came from," he said at last, "life was oppressive and without hope. At least if he took a risk on the open sea . . ." His voice trailed off as he hesitated, studying Catherine's face.

Uneasy beneath his unbroken gaze, Catherine parried with another question. "Who was he?"

"I don't really think the name makes that much difference," he replied with a shrug. "He wasn't someone who would be missed in his own country. For all intents and purposes, his peers on the ship and his family at home would think that his body had been claimed by the sea that night in the storm."

Catherine felt a shiver course through her spine. "He jumped overboard?" The pressures that would have motivated so suicidal an action were beyond her comprehension.

"He saw the storm as a godsend," he explained. "In the confusion of securing the ship and fighting the elements, no one would notice him slip away from his post on the bridge."

Catherine drew her knees up to her chin, huddling on the bench in rapt attention as his words painted the chilling scenario, bringing it to life in her imagination.

In her mind's eye she could almost hear the crash of thunder and see the scurrying silhouettes of frantic seamen on a rain-drenched deck, shouting at each other above the wind in a guttural language that was foreign to her. She could see, too, the dark-clothed figure with black hair who cautiously moved apart from the rest, his eyes never leaving the leeward side that had been left unattended momentarily.

With the agility of a cat the sailor darted among the shadows. Even through his coarse sweater and heavy coat, the winds of the North Sea cut through to his bones, his flight to freedom now less than twenty feet away.

For luck, he reached up once more to pat the left hand side of his life vest, its bulky padding concealing the oilskin pouch he had securely strapped to his chest. Lack of time and fear of discovery had prevented him from being able to add a flare gun to his limited supplies for survival. The whistle, signal mirror, and waterproof flashlight would be his only salvation once he hit the waves. Gritting his teeth in grim determination, he waited until just the right moment to vault over the side and into the icy depths. His last coherent thought was that no one on board had witnessed his escape.

"But if they weren't anywhere near shore . . ." Catherine anxiously protested.

"His gamble," the magician said, "was to be picked up by another ship bound in the opposite direction."

"Even so," Catherine challenged, "wouldn't it be hard to get rescued in a storm?"

"Hard, but not impossible," he replied. "Men that desperate for freedom often have a corresponding balance of faith. If he were meant to be saved, he trusted that he would. If he died in trying, at least he'd die free."

It was a long time before he continued, or so it seemed. To Catherine's astonishment a pink-and-gold dusk was descending on the park, bringing with it a cool evening breeze.

"A freighter of British registry found him almost two hours later," he said quietly.

A gasp escaped from Catherine's lips. "What h-happened?" she said, stammering. "Wouldn't they have had to send him right back?" Stories like that made the press on a regular basis.

"Not with the papers he was carrying."

"Papers?" she repeated. He hadn't mentioned any papers before.

"Identifying him as an American citizen." His eyes held a burning, faraway look. "An American from New Hampshire named Kyle Falconer."

Stunned, Catherine had the same feeling she sometimes experienced as she was going to sleep at night—the sensation of jerking awake after falling helplessly and almost endlessly in a dream. In dizzying frustration she sought to form a rational conclusion. "The sailor," she finally murmured, "it was you?"

In the dying light of day she saw him shake his head negatively. "I was the one who rescued him."

Catherine faltered, her voice slow and unsteady. "I don't understand. You mean, you were on the second ship?"

Semidarkness masked the brief smile that touched the corner of his mouth. He turned his face to reflect on the broad expanse of water gliding before them. The amber light cast by the nearby rotunda of the Jefferson Memorial made his profile stand out in sharp contrast.

"I told you," he said, "that no one had seen the sailor go over the side. . . ."

Catherine held her breath, anticipating the next piece of the puzzle. "Except you?" she ventured, at a loss to understand what he meant.

His words once again transported her to the night of the storm and the black sky crackling with sound and fury as, far below, a swimmer was losing the battle of his life. A bolt of lightning illuminated the heavens—enough for the hawk that dipped through the steel-gray clouds to catch a glimpse of something human that was being thrown about in the tumultuous waves.

Slowly the creature circled in descent, aware that the young man's strong will to live was no match for the sea's strong desire to claim him. The hawk dropped lower, the feathers of its chest and wings harshly slicked back by the force of the wind and rain. One last scream died in the young man's throat. And yet in his last moments of life the sailor's heart found a peace he had never known, for above the roar of the storm he heard an unfamiliar voice. "You are free," it said as a shadow passed before his eyes and a warmth penetrated his skin in spite of the ocean's bitter cold.

For only a second both souls—one leaving, one arriving—hovered in communion above the crashing waves. Protectively, as the waters closed over the lifeless body, the hawk spread its wings and dived straight down, disappearing as a vertical jag of lightning ripped apart the blackened summer sky.

Catherine choked back a cry of alarm, for so powerful had been his description of the moment that the feathered image of red and brown stabbed through her head as clearly as if she had seen it herself. In astonishment she recoiled. She found herself shaking as she realized that indeed she *had* seen the winged creature, last night at the Washington Monument.

"Yes, Catherine," he said slowly. "It was one and the same." She felt the muscles of his forearm tense beneath the sleeve she had absently clutched during his story.

As if from a distance, her tumbled thoughts heard him ask if she knew what kind of hawk it was. Whether he had already sent her the answer or, buried within her subconscious, she remembered a word long forgotten, the name that escaped from her pale lips was barely above a whisper. "A merlin."

"Yes," he replied. "Merlin. As in Camelot."

Chapter Five

IN HER BREATHLESS scramble to unlock the front door Catherine nearly overlooked the bouquet of daisies and envelope propped against it, scooping them up at the last second as she hurled herself inside . . . to safety.

Her face and hair were moist with perspiration, owing to the fact that she had run almost all the way from the park. She was still shuddering at the thought that at any moment she'd hear him shout her name the way he had done when she escaped from him. Fingers trembling, she hastily turned the key in the dead bolt and affixed the safety chain. Even as she did so, a ludicrous notion crossed her mind—that locks and keys would hardly be a challenge to a man who practiced sorcery. Thank goodness he didn't know where she lived, she thought. Or did he? Had she told him without knowing it?

Her thoughts veered back and forth between visions of a man who had somehow managed to escape his rightful place—in a padded cell—by charming his captors with glorified card tricks and disappearing rabbits, and the more frightening alternative—that she had made herself the prey of someone who could see inside her mind, plant thoughts there without her knowing—and for an unknown and perhaps sinister purpose.

Her nerves were raw with trepidation and flickered apprehensively at the idea that perhaps he was already there ahead of her, waiting. Over her pounding heartbeat Catherine listened for clues of an intruder in the stillness, her eyes scanning the living room for subtle evidence that she was not alone.

Not until she had checked inside every closet and behind every curtain did her erratic pulse begin to slow down. For now, at least, she was safe.

Safe from *what*, though? was the question that rioted in her consciousness. Common sense kept her from flying to the phone and dialing the police. He hadn't hurt her, she reminded herself. He hadn't threatened her. He hadn't done anything that a person would normally call the police to report. Yet, deep inside, the same common sense that kept her from reaching for the phone was sending a warning signal that his presence represented a danger she was ill-equipped to fight; specifically his control over what she was thinking.

Although he had repeatedly denied it, she reasoned that hypnosis had to be the only answer. Somehow he had tricked her into forgetting the things she told him, playing on her shock and surprise. Yes, that *had* to be it. Even the story he had told her about the sailor—so vivid and strong that she had imagined it all as if she had personally witnessed it—that, too, had been some sort of a mind trick to scare her. But why? Just remembering it now silently shattered her with a feeling of total vulnerability. She found her breath was coming in shallow, quick gasps, the tension in her limbs serving as a reminder of her aloneness . . . and her jeopardy.

Get hold of yourself, she thought. *You're building this whole thing into something dark and melodramatic. So he hypnotized you—so what? Now that you know what he's doing, you just have to see that he never gets the chance to do it again. Let him play his mind games on the people who pay to watch him perform. You have a nice, normal life to live, remember? A life that doesn't have room for men who tell farfetched stories.*

With a jolt she was suddenly aware that she had been sitting and staring at the white-and-yellow bundle on the floor without really seeing it. Moving as if in a trance, she got up from her chair and bent down to examine the fallen bouquet, the carelessly splayed fragile stems. Gingerly she reached for the envelope, breathing a sigh of relief when she recognized Larry's scrawl beneath her name: "I was here. Where were you?" Inside, a sunny get-well card featured an elephant in traction.

Her smile was quickly replaced by a scowl as she recalled the professional and personal deadline she had missed at the magician's bidding. In nearly the same breath she was taking part of the blame herself. If only she had kept better track of the time . . . if she had insisted he keep to the interview . . . if . . .

Catherine could feel the two bright spots of hot pink already forming on her high cheekbones. In quiet admonishment her heart completed the sentence. If she hadn't felt so determined to pursue him until he took notice of her, she never would have been subjected to the feelings of confusion and anxiety she was experiencing now. Clearly infatuation had blinded her.

Upon reasoned reflection she could have accepted his identity as a foreign sailor and empathized with the critical despair that had led him to risk his life for a narrow chance at freedom. And understanding that motivation to start over in a new country, she would have respected his privacy and his painful secrets. Whatever he chose to share, she would have kept in confidence. *Why* he had chosen to share it with *her*, of course, was another question. How did he know she wouldn't turn around and make it a feature story? Why break the very mystique he had worked so carefully to preserve? Unless he trusted her. . . .

She hadn't forgotten the look in his eyes at the restaurant when the subject of his past first came up, nor had she stopped questioning herself about what that look could have meant. If his loyalties to loved ones ran as deeply as her own, who was she to attack his reasons and demand more truth than he was prepared to give?

She even could have accepted that his near-death trial in the turbulent clutches of an angry sea had somehow endowed him with psychic abilities beyond the ordinary realm of explanation. Only a year before the *Trib* had published a front-page story about a construction worker who had survived a four-hundred-foot slip from a scaffolding, awakening in the hospital with a fluent French vocabulary and a long-winded diatribe against Louis XIV. Catherine still found herself wondering from time to time how the man had gleaned so precise a knowledge of an earlier century . . . unless it really was, as he claimed, his own recollection.

Kyle Falconer, however, was well outside the parameters of such open-minded acceptance. If he truly believed that his spirit had entered a drowning man's body at the precise moment of death, then his was a dangerous personality—bordering on insane—and she had been wise to get away from him as quickly as possible.

As for the other possibility . . . Catherine shook her head. There *were* no other possibilities. Devil incarnate or intense lunatic, Kyle Falconer was permanently out of her life. Or so she hoped.

Determined to dismiss him from her mind, Catherine strode to the bedroom to retrieve her address book, thinking out loud about the apology she owed Larry.

The answering machine came on after three rings, the message prefaced by an energetic piano concerto that continued throughout the tape. "Tucker and I are practicing for Carnegie Hall." She recognized Larry's voice. "But if you leave your name and number, one of us will get back to you."

Catherine hung up at the sound of the beep without leaving a message. What could she say into a machine that would make her predicament seem reasonable? Under these circumstances, she needed the reassuring response of a real, live person. With a shudder she realized once again how alone she was feeling.

With a pang she flipped through her address book, aware that most of the people she could call up and talk to were probably out celebrating that it was finally Friday night, the end of the work week.

Owing to her returning feelings of anxiety and isolation, the apartment—usually spacious and airy—suddenly seemed constricting. For a moment she considered packing a bag and going to a hotel. She would welcome a change of scenery and the opportunity to be pampered. Even as she rejected the whim her heart faced an undeniable truth: she was afraid to leave the apartment because her instincts told her that he was out there, looking for her. She'd be safer where she was right now. Catching her image suddenly in the hall mirror, she quipped grimly, "Snap out of it, kid—you're going to wind up in the padded cell right next to his."

Her annoyance with her blatant cowardice was overshadowed by a lingering, but very real memory, a remembrance of the distress he had evoked in their conversation. Although his dark eyes had contained nothing of sinister malice or raving madness, her skin had prickled with the sense of nearby danger.

"So much for putting him out of my mind," she chided herself out loud, disturbed to see that her bedside clock now read a quarter to ten, the address book still open on her lap. Wherever her thoughts had gone, she couldn't remember.

As she wandered out to the kitchen her glance again fell on the bouquet of flowers lying next to her dictionary on the table. It was probably too late to call Larry; she'd try first thing in the morning. About the only thing she could do now was put the daisies in a vase and go to bed.

Her glance fell, too, on the handwritten paragraphs she had started what now seemed like a very long time ago. The words didn't even seem familiar to her now, in spite of her having written them just that morning. Well, she decided flatly, there was no point in finishing it now. Timeliness was everything in the newspaper business, even for "fluff" articles like arts and entertainment. With a smirk she remembered that was the label that Nat had once given her work, subtly discounting the talent that others had openly praised. Stupid remark, she thought at the time, especially coming from someone who covered sporting events.

Disappointment ran through her as Catherine read the last sentence before wadding the sheet of paper into a ball. "Mercurial," she read, recalling that she had pulled out the dictionary to make sure the definition had fit what she wanted to say. The book was still open to that page, right where she had left it before her walk.

As she reached over to close it her hand nearly froze in midair. For there, on the same page with *mercurial* was another word that now jumped out at her, a word accompanied by a postage-stamp-sized picture of a bird. A mixture of astonishment and curiosity compelled her to pull the book toward her. "A variety of bold, small hawk of the genus Falco," she read, her eyes darting to study the simplistic sketch. A sudden, thin chill hung on the edge of the words she had just spoken.

"You must have picked it up subconsciously," she said to herself, speculating. For as long as she could remember she had possessed a photographic memory, a definite plus when it had come to taking tests at school. It hadn't failed her in her career, either, enabling her to recall details of text she had skimmed only briefly. Obviously it had also been at work that morning, although there still existed the freakish coincidence that he had asked her about the hawk at all.

Angrily Catherine snapped the heavy volume shut before her eyes could drop down to the definition, the one that began with a capital M.

Steady plops of dripping water echoed through the darkness, falling into unseen pools. Catherine squinted, trying to find her way through the rose-colored mist that was slowly lifting around her, leaving upon the moist ground a thin cover of powder-soft glitter. As her eyes grew accustomed to the shadows, spiral objects of lavender and gold began to materialize around her like a thick forest, their enormous height well beyond her vision.

Catherine gasped as she accidentally brushed against one of them, its damp surface hard as coral. The encounter left an ugly scrape on her bare arm. She touched it tenderly with her left hand, conscious now of the shimmering light filtering down through the mist from cracks above to dimly illuminate her surroundings.

The forest, in which she imagined herself at first, was not a forest at all but a cavernous chamber of stalagmites, rising like pointed cones from the earth, their length sparkling with crystalline deposits. Directly overhead, their counterparts dipped down like monstrous icicles.

Far off in the distance, there came a sound her ears had previously missed—the distant strains of a harp. Confused, Catherine looked around, unsure of the source. The hollow walls of the cave turned each noise into a distorted reverberation. Peering past the farthest cluster of rocky columns, she could barely discern a low opening previously shrouded by the mist. Still touching her bruise to shield it from further injury, Catherine cautiously moved forward.

Her intuition did not go unrewarded, for the stringed tones were louder now, a melody emerging that somehow Catherine recognized as oddly familiar. Mesmerized, she listened, certain that it was coming from the other side of the wall, its lilting aria soothing her like a forgotten lullaby.

An exclamation of disappointment escaped from her lips as she bent down to examine the opening, for it was smaller than she had estimated. An easy enough feat for a child but a very tight squeeze for an adult.

Suddenly she laughed at herself, remembering that she was, after all, only dreaming. People could do things in dreams they couldn't do in real life—things like flying and becoming invisible. Why not become smaller, Catherine rationalized, recalling the adventures of *Alice in Wonderland*. Firm in her resolve to discover the source of the song, Catherine flattened out on the damp ground and proceeded to wriggle forward, her fingers groping to push aside the pebbles and earth that cluttered the hole's dark entrance.

The walls of the smaller chamber in which she emerged danced with lavender shadows of flickering light as if from a nearby fire, and yet no flames were visible. Like the outer cave, this one, too, smelled damp but not unpleasing.

It was the music though, that captured her full concentration as it came floating toward her through the dusky tunnel. Decisively she inched her way closer, able to stand now to her full height. As she put out her hand to grope her way along the edge of the wall, she was surprised to find its surface polished and smooth as a mirror. Surprised, too, to discover that the light she had imagined as reflected from a fire actually shone from within the wall itself in a dazzling display of minuscule crystals.

The music continued, louder now. Yet neither the instrument nor the musicians were in sight. Catherine reasoned that they must have been cloaked by the darkness of the cave.

Suddenly the music stopped, prompting Catherine to stand very still, barely daring to breathe. Had her presence disturbed the occupant of this place? In a rush of panic she realized that she had never paused to consider who or what she might find, drawn single-mindedly to the source of the melody. She took a hasty look over her shoulder, disturbed to see that the low opening through which she had just crawled had vanished.

Be reasonable, she told herself. After all, she hadn't come that far. If she simply retraced her way, keeping close to the wall, then surely—

A metallic thud just a few feet away made her jump in alarm, suppressing a scream with her hand. In the long silence that followed, she waited, fearful that the slightest noise would betray her presence. Her eyes could barely make out the fallen object. She leaned forward for a closer look.

It was deep red and gold, its elongated shape unfamiliar to her.

Catherine crouched down and stretched toward it, her muscles tensed and ready to react if she had to.

Pain squeezed her heart when she saw what it was. She reached out with tentative fingers to touch it. A harp of indeterminate age lay broken where it had tumbled from the darkness, its neck cruelly twisted by the impact and its strings ripped from their place.

From deep within the cave's dark corners came a low, tortured sob, and Catherine quickly withdrew her hand from the harp, torn between consoling the owner and running away lest she be blamed for the instrument's fate. Her pulse furiously racing, Catherine held her breath.

"The risk is too great" came an unsteady voice, its tone forced and thin. It may have been a whisper of the wind, so quickly did it travel to where she lay crouched against the wall. Again the same words were repeated, the asthmatic voice weary and choked, and Catherine—in spite of her fear—strained to determine where the voice was coming from, for no one was visible.

"The risk is greater if you stay," a woman's voice replied, clear and strong, its power emanating as if from the crystal walls themselves. Catherine laid her head back against the cave's sheer wall and closed her eyes, trying to recall where she had heard the voice before.

When she opened them again, she had to blink from the brightness and intensity of light shining at her. Not from the crystals of the darkened cavern but from the midday sun directly overhead. Disoriented, she looked around, astounded to find herself on the edge of a lush green forest—the forest that bordered the same lake from her dream the night before. She sat up quickly, her eyes scanning the lake's edge, already anticipating what she would find. There, just as he had been before, sat a frail figure in tattered robes, his head hung low in despair. "What if I should die?" he asked. "What then?"

An impetuous ripple skittered across the surface of the lake as the woman laughed. "Have the years taken your courage as well?" she inquired.

"Sometimes," he said with a sigh, "I'm afraid they have."

Before Catherine's eyes, the waters seemed to change from sparkling turquoise to an angry, velvety purple. "You are the protector," the lady of the lake reminded him sternly. "Whosoever possesses our treasure is invincible."

"Yes, yes. . . ." The old man nodded in resignation, reaching for the gnarled oak stick that lay at his side.

"Then you know what must be done," she stated emphatically. With difficulty the old man was struggling to his feet.

"But what if the secret should fail me?" he began to protest once more. Already the lake was voicing her reply.

"Nonsense," she teased, her surface returning to its earlier shade. "You always said you could do it in your sleep."

Catherine watched as the man's frail shoulders heaved an exasperated sigh. With one last pause of reluctance he cast aside the weathered stick, now standing shakily on his own at the water's edge. He was mumbling something that Catherine couldn't hear. Slowly his arms raised, the folds of ragged fabric hanging like brown, opaque cobwebs from his thin wrists.

As he lowered them, almost gracefully in their descent, Catherine stifled a cry of surprise, for the fringed edges of cloth had turned into feathers the color of sun-burnished sienna. And as she stared, the cloaked figure seemed to be getting smaller and lifting higher from the ground. She blinked her eyes for only an instant, long enough for the final metamorphosis to take place. Swooping directly toward the spot where she sat hidden, a hawk was vigorously stirring the wind with his magnificent wings. Catherine let out a scream as it passed by her face, blinded by the fiery brilliance of the jewel embedded in its chest.

A violent spasm jerked her out of sleep, as if she had been struck by a thunderbolt. Instinctively she reached for the bedside lamp, noticing only then that she had thrown both pillows off her bed and that her nightgown was soaked with perspiration.

It was only a nightmare, she reminded herself. Not even a nightmare, really, if she stopped to think about its individual elements. Cave dreams weren't all that unusual, were they? Neither were dreams about music or trespassing. Catherine shuddered, recalling the dream's surrealistic end.

Angrily her heart was already pronouncing an accusation; hypnosis or not, she was certain that Kyle Falconer had prompted the twilight drama in a further attempt to manipulate her. In the next moment she was scoffing at her theory's total lack of logic. No one could be made to do something against their will . . . not even dream. Then whatever happened that night and the night before had to have been her own fabrication, its roots a bizarre mystery and its interpretation no doubt a waste of time.

"This is insane," she muttered, stripping off the wet gown and throwing it over the back of the chair. Some strong herb tea was what she needed to calm her nerves, she decided, removing her kimono from its hook inside the closet door. Hot tea and a strong dose of reality to return her life to normal.

Beneath her breath, Catherine cursed the very assignment that had plunged her emotions into such turmoil. If Kyle Falconer had remained at the comfortable distance of fantasy, she might be sleeping peacefully now instead of pacing her kitchen at five minutes past midnight, obsessed with involuntary visions, suspicious that he was their source.

As she waited for the water in the kettle to boil, Catherine wandered back to the bedroom, unlocking the French doors to the balcony and feeling the cool breezes caress her face and neck. "Put him out of your mind," she told herself again. "It will all look better in the morning."

The city had not yet retired for the evening, its lights glittering like earthbound stars. Her elbows resting lightly on the railing, Catherine pensively leaned forward, drinking in the fresh air. Slowly her serenity began to return.

It was only a subtle wisp of fragrance carried on the night wind, but it was enough to make Catherine stiffen. Even as her memory identified the unmistakable scent of sandalwood, a rustle from the potted fig tree behind her made her wheel around in fright. As if he had been waiting, Kyle Falconer stepped from the shadows.

Chapter Six

THE NIGHT AIR that had felt so cool and refreshing but a second before now chilled her in its icy grasp. Her eyes wide with the terror of a trapped animal, Catherine realized that escape would be futile. His lean body conveniently blocked the door. Without thinking, she attempted to back up, immediately feeling the pressure of the waist-high steel railing through the silky fabric of her robe.

Spontaneous concern for her safety flashed across his face, and he remained where he was, speaking her name gently.

"Please don't be afraid," he sought to reassure her, extending his hand palm upward.

From the kitchen Catherine could hear the kettle begin to whistle. The sideward inclination of his head indicated that he had heard it, too.

"Tea?" he inquired as naturally as if he were the polite host and she the unexpected guest. Catherine remained motionless, too stunned to acknowledge his words, aware only of her increasing anxiety beneath his enduring gaze. Against the light of the room beyond, his stance emphasized the force of his thighs and the slimness of his hips; his athletic physique would easily put her at a disadvantage if she chose to run.

To her surprise he turned and stepped inside the bedroom without a backward glance, leaving her alone to weigh her options, limited as they appeared to be.

Within seconds the high-pitched whistle of the teakettle slowly died to a thin whimper. Tentatively Catherine stepped inside, conscious now of the sound of cupboard doors being opened and shut.

Her mind raced for some means of escape. Atop the nightstand nearest the balcony, the telephone represented her most likely hope of rescue. Grabbing the touch-tone receiver off its cradle, Catherine crouched down as low as she could behind the bed, alert to the noises still coming from the kitchen. With lightning speed she punched in the three-digit access code for emergencies and pushed the receiver up to her ear. Nothing. Nervously she depressed the switch hook and tried again. And again. The line was dead.

Catherine let the receiver clatter back into its cradle, caught up in the hopelessness of her situation. She was oblivious to the tall figure with lustrous black hair that now watched her from the darkened doorway. The sash of her kimono had loosened, allowing the front to fall open as she knelt on the floor. Angrily Catherine pulled it closed, a cascade of her brown hair carelessly tumbling across her face as she looked down to retie the material. As she tossed her head back she caught his reflection in the narrow panes of glass.

Realizing that to let him sense her fear would make her all the more vulnerable, she turned to confront him with as much courage as she plausibly could manage. "Just what do you want?" she demanded.

To her surprise his reply was neither threatening nor patronizing. In truth, if she were to label it at all, the description that came to mind would have been that of earnest sincerity, a dramatic contrast to the duplicity she perceived lay beneath the surface of his masculine veneer. "You haven't heard all of the story," he replied, his eyes discreetly fixed on her face, seemingly respectful of her semidressed state. His voice was smooth but insistent. "You'll need to hear it to make your decision."

Catherine opened her mouth to ask the obvious, her question abruptly preempted by his thoughtful suggestion that she might want to change before they continued their conversation. His half smile, in response to her puzzled expression, was almost apologetic. "For someone who can pull off minor miracles," he observed, "you'd think I'd do better with things like this."

"Things like what?" Catherine asked, still wary that his smile and attempt to put her at ease might disguise a ploy to break through her resistance.

He hadn't moved from the doorway. "Having your trust," he said after a long silence "is more important to me than I could ever explain." Beneath long lashes, the liquid brown eyes regarded her with quiet respect. "If your heart tells you that I'm asking for something impossible, Catherine, just ask me to leave and I will."

"Just like that?" she murmured, suspicious of the offer's simplicity.

"Even magicians," he replied with an affectionate wink, "can recognize when they've met their match."

Two china cups of steaming raspberry tea had been carefully set out on the table when Catherine emerged from the bedroom dressed in a beige camp shirt and jeans, her hair swept back in a ponytail.

"I wouldn't blame you if you hadn't come out," he remarked from where he stood in the living room, studying the photographs in the brass étagère.

"You asked me to trust you," she reminded him, still not sure why she had agreed to his request and hardly convinced herself that she was doing the right thing by continuing the conversation. Catherine had to admit, though, that even if Kyle Falconer was a lunatic, he clearly wasn't going to hurt her.

At her words he gave a subtle nod of gratitude, returning his attention back to the collection of pictures. "Your parents?" he asked, touching one of the larger frames with a reverence she found strangely comforting . The telltale fashions and hairstyles betrayed the decade of origin.

Catherine nodded, sensitive to the fact that that, and the smaller one next to it, were the only reminders she had left of what her father had looked like. "He died when I was a little girl," she volunteered, somehow certain that he was about to ask her more about them. "My mother's been gone for three years."

His glance dropped down to the circular collage that chronicled Catherine's growth from birth to fifth grade. Amused, he compared the precocious youngster to the striking adult who now watched him, arms folded, from across the room. "You haven't changed," he complimented her, indicating the ten-year-old's implacable air of determination.

As quickly as the feeling had come over her, Catherine dismissed the idea that his remark referred to anything more than the physical traits that become refined with maturity yet still hint of youth.

"I see you've poured the tea," she commented, remembering her earlier initiation to his methods of sidestepping personal disclosures by twisting the focus back on her. Girding herself with resolve,

Catherine firmly recalled the reason he had given for his nocturnal visit. She'd simply refuse to answer any more of *his* questions until she had obtained some vital information of her own.

A moment later, pleasantly acquiescing to her request, Kyle Falconer sat across from her at the table, the bright lights of the kitchen adding emphasis to the feathered age lines at the corners of his mouth and eyes. "I suppose it goes without saying," he said, sighing, "that I'm not just your average guy from New Hampshire."

"Where then?" she asked. Fingers laced around the delicate cup, she regarded him over the rim with a mixture of curiosity and doubt.

"Britain," he answered. "In a village that's not on the map."

"Why didn't you say so in the first place?" Catherine said reproachfully. "All that talk before about the sailor and the ship and—"

Imploring her patience with a wave of his hand, he embarked on an explanation that was as comfortable to him as it was mystical to her. If nothing else, he promised her, it was the truth.

"In less than the space of a day," he began, "you've met someone who knows your dreams, seems to read your mind, and claims to be renting someone else's body."

Catherine wrestled with the smile trying to tug at her mouth, annoyed at herself for how difficult it was to ignore his gift of humor, much less his arresting looks.

"Where *I* come from, though," he continued, "surprises like that are more commonplace than not."

Behind her cup, Catherine raised a quizzical eyebrow, not yet ready to eliminate the possibility of mental imbalance.

"Your world is very different from mine, Catherine," he announced, disappointment apparent in his tone. "The people of your time are too slow to trust and too quick to condemn."

"My time?" she repeated. "My world? What are you talking about?"

"Centuries," he replied as he sipped the hot liquid contentedly. "Twelve, to be exact."

Their previous exchange at dusk in the park had already confirmed to him the challenge that existed in winning her friendship, if not her tolerance. He stretched back in the chair, prepared for the explosive response that predictably would follow his statement, the accusation that he hadn't stopped playing games with her. His patrician features deceptively composed, he allowed her heated censure to run its course before he spoke again, continuing as calmly as if nothing had happened.

"What I'm going to tell you, Catherine," he said, "isn't anything that you haven't already suspected from the first time we were together in the same room."

The annoyance in her voice was barely concealed. "You mean, this morning in the restaurant?"

"What I meant," he clarified softly, "was about six months before you mother passed away." Compassion made him want to touch the slender fingers that automatically tightened on the handle of the cup; instinct told him his touch right now would be unwanted. "You were in the audience of a show I did in California."

Like a flashback in a movie, Catherine's memory swiftly called to the surface every detail of that night—the clothes she and her girlfriend Diane had worn, the sequence of illusions Falconer had performed, the voice she had heard in the parking lot. Dominant among those recollections was the intensity of her attraction back then to the man onstage, rekindled now in her imagination, as sizzling as a white-hot flame.

"From that night on," he continued, "I knew without a doubt that the vision of the lake hadn't lied."

His intentional reference once more to the dream snapped her out of her reverie, and she firmly demanded that he account for his knowledge of it.

He chose, instead, to point out an observation about their strained alliance. "You've never called me by my name," he remarked, as if the omission amused him.

Even as she opened her mouth to protest that it had nothing to do with what they were discussing, an uneasy realization pervaded her thoughts. She *hadn't* yet called him by name, in spite of the accelerated company they had kept since they'd met. To call him Mr. Falconer would have seemed too formal; to revert to Kyle would have implied an intimacy not yet nurtured with time. Yet a third possibility lingered on the edges of her consciousness, fostered by an intuitive sense that neither name was really his. Quickly her suspicion was replaced with a disturbing reality that she had forgotten in the course of the day's developments.

"How did you know who *I* was in the park?" she countered. His casual mention of names had triggered the fleeting astonishment she had felt the first time he spoke to her. "You never *did* tell me that."

A faint light twinkled in the depths of his dark eyes. "I knew who you were," he replied, "because I've been looking for you . . . for a very long time."

"Centuries?" she asked, wondering if her theatrical sarcasm would conceal the sudden surge of indefinable excitement that had just raced down her spine. *He* was looking for *her?*

Irrevocably his response quelled her blossoming fantasy. "Not for the reason you might think," he said, "but a reason just as important."

Catherine sat back, momentarily rebuffed by the cool neutrality of his voice, sour disappointment supplanting the impulsive rush of passion. Conscious of his scrutiny, she proceeded with the obvious question: "Why?"

"To locate something," he answered matter-of-factly. Hands folded, he hunched forward, his expression stilled and serious. "Something that never should have been brought here."

"Here?" Catherine echoed. Like a shadowy veil, a sensation of dèjá vu passed in front of her, a feeling of recognition that she had heard only recently, a similar phrase. Puzzled, she couldn't place its source.

Oblivious to her distraction, Kyle Falconer was still talking.

"Whether or not you choose to believe who I am or how I got here," he said, his velvety voice urging her attention, "you're all that I have to help me recover what I've come this far to find."

Catherine's mind was spinning with bewilderment, her previous anger evaporating into total confusion. "Assuming any of your story is true," she speculated, "why would you need a—"

He was already helpfully supplying the missing word. "Mortal?" he offered. With a fluid motion he picked up the two empty cups and was taking them over to the kitchen counter. "Ordinarily it's a quest I could handle on my own."

Catherine blinked at the archaic term, a word she normally associated with knights and crusades. "Quest?"

With meticulous care he was rinsing the china cups and gently laying them aside. "Under the circumstances," he continued, "I was lucky to hit the right century, much less find the right country to start searching."

"*What* circumstances?" Catherine cut in. "This whole thing is beginning to sound pretty cloak-and-dagger."

"What do you mean?"

"*Proof,*" Catherine said flatly. "You ask me to believe you, and yet you haven't given me anything or told me anything I can verify."

He was leaning against the counter now, his legs casually crossed and his arms folded. "You're absolutely right, Catherine, I haven't." The face that looked up at him held the same measure of defiance as the youngster's photograph in the next room, the eyes abandoning all pretense of acceptance. "There's nothing I can do or say that you couldn't explain away as illusion or psychic trickery." His steady gaze bored into her in silent expectation, mentally caressing the qualities he had known from the beginning that she would possess. "All you really have to go on," he advised, "is the truth in your own dream."

"You still haven't told me what it means," she protested. "Or how you knew."

"I think your time has an expression for it," he recalled, "the tingling feeling a person gets when he thinks others are talking about him." He smiled. "It's not exactly the same where I come from, but it's close enough for comparison. I knew about your dream because I was in it."

Catherine scowled, remembering only the silvered tones of the unseen lady and the ragged figure of . . . "That's impossible," she argued, unwilling to accept his bizarre proposition.

"The spirit itself is ageless. Unfortunately the physical body isn't as resilient to the tortures of time."

He was moving toward her. Catherine raised her eyes to look at him, her glance halting on the dazzling sparkle of crystal at his chest as it reflected the overhead light. The combination of the jewel's bright gleam and her point of perspective replicated the encounter that had flung her awake earlier. Stunned, her memory superimposed a shadowy image over his, the view of a hawk in flight as it soared toward her through a clearing of emerald trees, its screech piercing the silence. As mystically as it had appeared, the image vanished, leaving only the man who stood above her.

"Come with me a moment," he quietly invited. As she sat clutching the seat of the chair, shaken by the unearthly vision, he offered both palms out to her.

Reluctantly she placed her hands in his and allowed him to help her up, her legs curiously weak and unstable.

Against the backdrop of stars Kyle Falconer leaned forward on the balcony railing as he spoke, the muscles of his forearms taut and firm as his hands rested on the narrow ledge. Somewhere in the night the church bells chimed three times, tolling the hour.

"Deep in the Summer Country beyond Camelot," he said, his voice a sensuous whisper, "there are hills that hide a cave of crystal, its underground entrance long ago sealed by enchantment. I intended to spend the rest of my days in that cave, waiting until I was needed." As subtly as the evening breeze, sorrow crept into his narrative, and he turned his head to look at her. "It's not for us to choose our destiny, though, Catherine. Not any more than I could have refused an order of the Goddess."

His haunting statement sparked a new rush of questions in her mind, and anxious that they'd be answered in his words to come without her having to ask, she bit her lip to keep from blurting them out.

Mindful of the dark apprehensions that still reigned in her assessment of him, the magician extended his hand and delicately touched her cheek, his fingers trailing downward to trace the outline of her jaw. "Every act of man and beast—no matter how small it seems—is dictated by a pre-vision beyond understanding." His eyes clung to hers, analyzing her reaction as he brought the same hand back into view. Sandwiched between his thumb and forefinger lay the missing ticket she had searched for on the night of the performance.

Startled, she watched him flick it off the ends of his fingertips into the night sky, gasping as she saw it burst into a gold-and-scarlet display, its circular shape reminiscent of a giant dandelion. For a moment it hung motionless in the cool air, and then, beginning its descent, the sparkling sphere broke apart, as if violently shattered from within.

Her eyes and mouth wide with surprise at the spectacle, Catherine watched the particles fall like crimson snowflakes to the city street below.

"How did—" she began to say. But he was gone.

Chapter Seven

IN THE HOURS remaining until daylight, Catherine slept fitfully, as enslaved by the remembrance of his silky touch as she was unnerved by the brusque manner of his departure. Not a word had been spoken of when she would see him again, nor a clue as to the role she might play in his mysterious "quest."

Catherine's first thought in the dove-colored morning dawn was of the double image she had witnessed that night at the kitchen table. The sensation she had felt at that moment was like no other she could recall, for in spite of her panic as the creature's curved ivory talons and sharp beak drew threateningly close to her body, her intuition sensed that it meant her no harm. Moreover, his visit had proven that Kyle Falconer meant her no harm, either.

As he led the way to the balcony Falconer had given no indication that he was aware of her hallucinatory experience. Although she would be hard-pressed to substantiate the point, there *was* one fact of which Catherine was oddly beginning to feel certain: that he wasn't the cause of it. A catalyst, perhaps, of something deep in her subconscious with which she had yet to come to terms. But a purveyor of nightmares? Catherine rubbed her eyes, unable to erase the features of the man who had gazed at her beneath last night's starlight and tenderly stroked the side of her face. Undeniably her heart wanted only to believe him, even faced with a story that predominantly favored the supernatural. The promise he made that he would never hurt her still lingered, deep and sincere.

Again and again Catherine turned over the elements in her mind, seeking unity and cohesion. Exasperated, she flipped on the bedside lamp and reached for the telephone message pad, scribbling the random items as they occurred to her, attempting to establish a sequence or a correlation that might explain the seemingly impossible.

How, for instance, had he come into possession of her second ticket from the Thursday night show? Maybe, she thought, playing devil's advocate it wasn't her ticket at all. Like any performer—amateur or professional—he'd probably have a ready supply of comps for friends and associates. The pass he produced by sleight of hand on the balcony could have been *any* ticket. She had only *assumed* it was hers.

Her creative juices bubbling, Catherine jotted down a related theory: that the ticket had been nothing more than a theatrical prop designed to ignite like a book of matches with one flick of the wrist. That, she decided, would explain the mini-fireworks display.

It would also explain his disappearance. The spontaneity of a spectacular distraction would have been enough for . . .

Annoyed, she scratched out the idea. Certainly she wasn't so simple-minded and one-dimensional that a minor diversion would keep her from seeing him move out of the corner of her eye or hear him close the door of her apartment. Especially not after the sum total of energy she had invested in their conversation and the all-consuming focus she had maintained on his every movement.

Once again her mind toyed with the notion of hypnosis, recalling how his eyes had locked with hers, prolonging the magical moment that appeared destined to end in a single kiss . . . and yet did not. He easily could have transmitted a suggestion that she remain in a trance until such time as he could conveniently exit from the building. What seemed to have been a few seconds could have, in fact, been a few minutes, maybe longer. Maybe an hour.

Fine. Catherine smirked. Her analytical mind had come up with a plausible basis for every perceived illusion. What it *still* couldn't answer was *why*. Why would Falconer deliberately lie? Why would a man go to so much trouble to make her think that he was a lunatic? Or that maybe *she* was?

With a scowl she read over the notes she had just dashed off, dismayed that the entire writing exercise had been one of futility. Futile because all paths led to the one conclusion her logical side refused to accept: that maybe the greatest magician of the twentieth century wasn't from the twentieth century. That maybe the incredible illusions his audiences applauded were, in fact, not illusions at all.

Catherine snapped off the light and rolled back into the cozy warmth of the covers, determined, for the moment at least, to block out the sound of his name in her head, obliterate the memory of his face and the breathless grip he had on her emotions. Whether he's for real or not, she reminded herself, he's already made it clear that he's not interested. Hadn't he said as much last night? Although he may not have intended the remark as hurtful, its truth had jolted her with a harsh impact. Even now she was annoyed with herself for succumbing momentarily to the romantic notion of a handsome figure traveling across centuries to find his one true love—her.

Still, she knew she wasn't just making up the unspoken interchange that had passed between them or the energy of their brief physical contact. Her instinctive response to him had been more powerful than she had ever imagined possible, fueled by the flame she had perceived in his own eyes each time he spoke to her. And yet all trace of passion had vanished from his voice when he answered her question of why he had been searching. It was clearly something else—not Catherine—that had brought him here. To *her* time.

"I'm beginning to talk like I believe it," she said out loud. "Make up your mind, Cath. Is this guy telling the truth or not?" Too preoccupied to tackle further efforts at sleep or speculation, she swung her legs over the side of the bed and headed for the bathroom.

Catherine's usual weekend beauty regimen involved little more than some moisturizer for her face, a few quick strokes of mascara, and a dab of lip gloss. In the absence of a more complicated routine she found it easy to entertain a host of possibilities about the object of Kyle Falconer's search, firmly as she had reproached herself for such senseless woolgathering.

What on earth, she mused, would bring a so-called sorcerer across centuries and into the heart of the nation's capital? Images from her dream spilled over into her thoughts. What had the lake called him? The protector? Protector of what? Gold? Jewels? A book of his own spells? In her attempt to suppress a chuckle Catherine fumbled the mascara wand and sent it rolling into the sink. A wizard who had to rely on a book instead of his own memory wouldn't be of much use where he came from . . . wherever *that* was. No, it had to be something more serious. Something worth risking one's life for. Wizard or not, his fear of mortality had permeated her dream, a fear that she had subconsciously sensed in the restaurant and last night in her apartment.

She was still thinking about it half an hour later as she nibbled on a Spartan breakfast of toast and grapefruit juice, her stomach too agitated to handle anything more substantial.

Absently she slid her index finger under the green rubber band that loosely bound the Saturday edition of the *Tribune*. Predictably the paper's arrival had jogged her memory on the apology she still owed Larry, not to mention the excuse she'd have to come up with for her boss. At least the latter scenario had a respite until Monday. Maybe, if she was lucky, Johnson would take an extra sick day. Even better, maybe he'd forget whether she had turned in anything or not. Sure, she thought, and chickens will grow lips. Well, at least the track record she had maintained up until yesterday would weigh in her favor when she confessed. Her conscience temporarily placated, Catherine poured another glass of juice and removed the Metro section from the unrolled stack in front of her.

Washington, D.C. was well known as one of the country's most photographed cities. Its grand architecture and inspirational monuments were often being captured for posterity by free-lance shutterbugs and *Tribune* staff. On any given day, usually no less than three candids graced the pages devoted to local news, their indomitable spirit and timeless beauty accompanied by references to the weather or urbane remarks about the power of the people.

Given the frequency of the historical landscape's exposure, it wasn't so unusual, then, for a dramatic evening shot of the Washington Monument to dominate the prime slot beneath the Arts and Entertainment masthead. Catherine's attention, though, was now riveted to what lay beneath the photograph in bold typeface: FAL-CONER SHOW IS PURE MAGIC.

In confusion, her eyes dropped to the end of what amounted to a quarter-page review, blinking in astonishment as she read the byline that credited her as having written the article. "What's going on here?" she muttered under her breath. Johnson never would have sent two people to cover the same event. Nor would he have let a mistake slide by like putting her name on someone else's work.

Hooked on curiosity, she began to read, a disturbing awareness slowly beginning to take form within the first few sentences. She read a paragraph more, uneasy with what she was discovering. For as her eyes flew over the words it became obvious to her that someone had taken great pains to create a structure and tempo imitative of her own journalistic style. Only those who knew that style intimately might have discerned that the Saturday review was a well-constructed mimicry and not Catherine's text at all.

"Imagination," the piece stated, "is the intelligent mind's way of proving that it has a sense of humor. Before a capacity crowd at one of Washington's most recognizable trademarks, Kyle Falconer demonstrated that magic—like an amusing story well told—has the universal capacity to spread smiles. This writer, however, can not begin to translate into works the mystical power of suggestion and the technical precision of wizardry that kept Thursday night's spectators gasping in awe. Even the televised version of Falconer's performance—scheduled by CBS to air throughout the country during Thanksgiving week—will no doubt be a pale copy of the vibrant original."

Halfway through the article Catherine was stunned once more by a pervasive sense of dèjá vu. Somewhere—and recently—she had read something that followed a curiously similar line of argument. From a teaser opening, the text fluidly slid into a recap of Falconer's prior accomplishments, devoting nearly three paragraphs to his triumph in Egypt. Not until she had completely finished did Catherine realize that the author—whoever it really was—had cleverly skirted any direct references to exactly what had transpired two nights ago, reiterating that the illusions themselves defied description and analysis. It was almost as if the writer had not attended the show at all but had paraphrased from previously published critiques and documentation.

Then it occurred to her why the basic outline had struck a chord.

She padded across the kitchen to her junk drawer. There, right where she had thrown it yesterday morning, was the glossy brochure she had been handed outside the amphitheater. Tentatively she opened it and read the first paragraph, relieved to see the subtle duplication of format but even more perplexed as to how it had come to be incorporated with her own name in an unrelated publication. Further, how could such an article have gotten into the *Trib* to begin with when the Friday press deadline would already have come and gone? If there was one thing on which Johnson was a tough taskmaster, it was deadlines with a Capital *D*. She and Larry would have cut it close enough as it was if she *had* diligently stayed home, written the article, and delivered it into his hands the way they'd planned.

Unexpectedly a smile lit Catherine's face as the mysterious became clear. Obviously Larry—probably more familiar with Catherine's style than anyone else—had taken it upon himself to do her a favor when it became apparent to him that she needed one. Accounting for the lack of specifics and the playful "You had to be there to believe it" closing statement, she reasoned that he'd somehow managed to obtain an extra copy of the program.

Warmth spread over her as she basked in the appreciation of having such a good friend. Her still unrehearsed apology would be accompanied now by a thank-you, as well as a suitable payback for his efforts, accompanied by a stern warning never to try it again unless he wanted to ruin his chances of ever being a full-fledged reporter.

Catherine glanced at the kitchen clock, noting that it was still too early to call him on their morning off. Inspiration was quick to follow. She'd go for a bicycle ride, telephone Larry from the midway point between her apartment and his, and offer to take him to a full breakfast at her expense. He consistently joked at the office that he and Tucker subsisted on quarter pounders and fries. Breakfast at someplace like the Atrium or Copernicus would be a genuine treat. From a selfish standpoint it would also give her someone levelheaded and rational to talk to, and the chance to assure herself of her own sanity.

The warmth of the new day's sun coaxed Catherine out of her reflective gloom as she cycled down the tree-lined streets, putting the grandeur of government and the humble testimonies of its weakness behind her.

The idea of having breakfast with Larry was definitely a good one. Fresh air, leisurely exercise, and the knowledge that she was saved from having to provide excuses on Monday not only eased her earlier anxiety but also brought on an appetite as she pedaled her way south of the city. The diversion had also minimized her preoccupation with Kyle Falconer, though her heart already sensed it was not going to be a permanent condition. Too many questions still lay unanswered.

Larry—sounding as if he were out of breath—pounced on the phone at the third ring. "Feeling any better?" Tucker was barking his head off in the background.

"I'm really sorry about yesterday," Catherine apologized as soon as she could.

"No big deal. Stuff happens. So what's up?"

"Well, first of all," she proposed, "I thought I could pay you back with breakfast."

Larry insisted he hadn't done anything to merit the treat. "I'm just sorry we got our wires crossed," he said. "I must have barely missed you."

"Long story. That's why I thought—"

"So did they help?" he interrupted.

"Did what help?"

"How quickly she forgets!" He sighed dramatically. "The flowers. They were okay, weren't they?"

In her enthusiasm to lead into her thanks for the review, she had completely forgotten the bouquet. Awkwardly she stammered that they were fine and that it had been a thoughtful gesture.

"Long as the get-wells get you back on track," he said. "Listen, Cath, I hate to be a flake on your breakfast invite, but Tucker's sort of jazzed to get to the park."

"About the review—" she started to say.

"Makes me want to catch it on TV in November," he remarked. "You sure didn't give away any state secrets on *that* one, though. I guess I was hoping maybe you would."

His comment didn't register at first. "What do you mean?"

"Always the woman of mystery." Larry laughed. "Well, I thought it was pretty good, anyway. I just wish I could have saved you a trip to the office."

With that Larry blithely signed off to attend to an impatient Tucker before Catherine even had a chance to ask him straight out what she had assumed, only an hour ago, to be a reasonable deduction. His cryptic phrase implied something quite different.

Far above her, camouflaged by dark lacy branches, the merlin's sharp eyes missed nothing as the young woman stepped out of the phone booth and discontentedly turned her bicycle back in the direction from whence she had come.

Chapter Eight

"YOU'VE GOT TO start thinking and acting like who you are—a reporter, remember?" Catherine chastised herself out loud in front of her bathroom mirror. "If you don't, you're going to drive yourself completely nuts!"

The easy explanation she had been expecting to hear from Larry hadn't come. Obviously, by his inference, he thought Catherine herself had written the review. How could *that* be, though, she thought with a scowl, when she had so clearly lacked the wits and the time ever to create a passable opening paragraph? Had she experienced temporary amnesia and forgotten it? Scratch that one. She smirked. That only happens in soap operas.

Blinking with bafflement at the article that still lay faceup where she had left it, Catherine mentally replayed her actions of the past twenty-four hours in search of an answer. In the tumble of confused feelings that assailed her, her mind consistently returned to the dizzying effect the magician kept having on her well-ordered sense of logic and balance. Had he distracted her so much that she no longer knew whether she was coming or going? For that matter, was she writing reviews in her sleep?

Suppose *he* had written the review and submitted it under her name? she speculated. But why would he have done it in the first place? Besides, someone surely would have noticed him dropping it off at the *Trib*. A visit like that wouldn't go unnoticed, she determined. Finally, Catherine mused, there was the bottom line of simple logistics. He had been with her. Where would he have found the *opportunity* to write his own review, much less deliver it in time to make the deadline for the morning edition?

He's a magician, her conscience cut in. He can do whatever he wants. Yes, but not just *any* magician, she countered. This one isn't from present-day New Hampshire; he's from England—and the Middle Ages. An idea came to her.

If he was going to persist in this fixation about being from another century, he'd have to keep tossing off facts to keep up the facade. Obviously he would have to have read them somewhere and committed them to memory for her benefit. What if *she* were to use the same approach?

With a chuckle of satisfaction Catherine realized she had been attacking the problem from entirely the wrong perspective. Sooner or later, she rationalized, he was going to trip over his own story. All she had to do was lay the right bait to make that happen. While it still wouldn't explain *how* he had pulled off some of his more baffling escapades, at least she'd finally be able to rest with the knowledge that he wasn't any more supernatural than *she* was.

Where to start, of course, was the next question. Her eyes scanned the two living-room bookcases in search of a suitable resource with which to start her homework. When at last she found what she was looking for and withdrew it from the shelf, Catherine suddenly felt ill at ease with her own plan. What if her research *did* expose him as a hoax? Was that actually what she wanted? Or did part of her want proof that magic and Kyle Falconer really *weren't* just fantasies? Not sure of her expectations, Catherine proceeded to open the thick green volume in her hands.

"*Selby's Encyclopaeida of British Myth and Legend,*" the foreword advised, "*has made every reasonable effort to ensure the historical accuracy of its content. In the absence of formal records during the Empire's early centuries, editors have attempted to identify regions of origin and significant corresponding events to enable readers to establish a general time frame. Where applicable, related writings are cited, as well as speculative analysis of how some of these colorful mainstays of the British Heritage may have evolved.*"

"So, in other words," Catherine mumbled to herself, "Take it all with a grain of salt." Armed with a piece of paper and a pencil, she turned to the table of contents, conscious of the one reality she didn't want to lose sight of during her research: that anything *she* read just as easily could have been read and utilized by Kyle Falconer. What she had to do was find something that wouldn't be common knowledge.

There are still those places in the British Isles where time has woven an unbroken spell of enchantment.

Deep in the forests, moist with English rain, modern visitors can close their eyes and almost hear the ghostly murmurings of the ancient sects as they gathered to worship in their secret ways.

Along the Welsh streams that once projected their fresh bubbles upward into shimmering mists of Wedgwood blue, it's also easy to imagine—if only in the blink of an eye—a hoofed creature of pure white and a single golden horn lowering its head to drink long and deep before moving on, ever wary of sounds of approaching danger.

Impressions trampled deep on forgotten roads to the north were believed to have been made by dragons, the soil of deep carmine ruthlessly stained by the blood of unlucky knights who had failed to slay them. To this day no flowers dare grow where the lizardlike giants had tread.

Impregnable fortresses of stone could still be found as well, although their present purpose was a shallow testament to their original intent. Gone completely were those castles of which the most popular legends were made, their stately towers long ago destroyed by invading warriors, their walls and drawbridges having likewise fallen to an even more merciless adversary—nature itself. Gone was the pageantry once praised in song. In its place is only the haunting spirit of its past and the mournful wail of the wind through empty meadows.

"This," Catherine muttered in disappointment, "is getting me absolutely nowhere." Idealistic and pretty as the text might be, its blatant lack of substance forced her to set it aside before she had even reached the midway point of the first chapter.

What I really *want*, she told herself, *is an undisputed authority on this stuff, an expert who knows Arthurian legend like the back of his or her hand.* Almost immediately Catherine brightened. She *did* know someone, someone who would be more than delighted to share his knowledge.

To everyone but Professor Wilfred Zalunardo, the operative word in the Visiting Lecturers Program was *visiting.* Nine years before, Georgetown University had invited the professor to spend half a semester sharing his expertise on political expression in fifth-century Europe. Nine years later he still had demonstrated no signs of leaving, having appropriated a basement office, a desk, a phone, and full clerical services from the dean's private secretary.

The fact that no one in Administration ever challenged his self-appointed status as a permanent fixture on campus, of course, was primarily traceable to the hefty endowments the university had come to appreciate every Christmas. Certainly in the face of five-figure checks drawn on his personal account, a little eccentricity could be tolerated, if not completely ignored.

Popular rumor had it that Professor Zalunardo had come into an inheritance, shrugged off all traditional shackles of responsibility, and by and large had lived his life for the past quarter century as a free spirit. History was his passion, a love he was able to generously indulge in the convenient absence of a spouse or an employer.

Though nearly two years had gone by since their brief introduction in the lobby of the Kennedy Center, Catherine could still picture his angular features, lanky frame, and disheveled white hair, suggestively inspired by Einstein. A personality perpetually in a state of hyperspeed, he was also one for whom it could be accurately said that interrupting him in a conversation was like trying to thread a sewing machine while it was running.

"I really appreciate you seeing me on a Saturday," Catherine thanked him when she arrived at the university, still amazed at her good fortune in catching him by phone on her first try.

"By all means, come in, come in," he urged her, throwing the door wide open to an office that would have caused even the most stalwart of housekeepers to faint in her tracks. "You say we've met before?"

"The Coventry Concert at the Kennedy Center?" Catherine jogged his memory. "It was back in—"

Professor Zalunardo dramatically smacked his forehead with the palm of his hand. "God, yes! Of course! That's it!" Beneath electrified white brows his eyes sharply narrowed like an intense bald eagle. He was already pulling out a chair and pouncing toward a hot plate to offer her a cup of tea. "So you're writing a book?" he inquired. "Dungeons, dragons, damsels in distress, search for the Holy Grail . . .?"

In truth Catherine had volunteered nothing of the sort. Was he mistaking her for someone else? No matter. It was actually a pretty good excuse. "Camelot," she said matter-of-factly.

"Big mistake." He clucked his tongue. "Overdone, overrated. Plays, musicals—you name it. Just joking of course. But seriously, it's all overkill unless you go for a new angle."

"Yes, as a matter of fact, I—"

With a flourish Professor Zalunardo swept up a messy sheaf of papers from the top of his desk. "Now *this* is the stuff I'm talking about! Sex, scandal, trade-offs, inhumanity . . ." Proudly he fanned the pages under her nose. "It's got it all right here!"

"About Camelot?"

"Camelot!" He snorted. "Good God, no! It's about Washington, D.C. A lot of similarity if you get down to brass tacks, right?"

"I hadn't really thought about it," Catherine confessed.

Professor Zalunardo's eyes blazed with zeal for his theory. "*Think* about it, then!" he insisted. "War, peace, lords in the castle, and peasants on the grass, hypocrisy running rampant, corruption from within. Of course we don't have dragons or unicorns, but that's beside the point. Did you know that unicorns were sexless? Makes you wonder how they reproduced if they didn't have a gender."

"If we could get back to Camelot?" Catherine politely recommended.

"Back to Camelot . . ." Professor Zalunardo echoed with a sigh. "God, what a concept *that* would be! Of course, you'd have to have a plan, make a list of who you'd see, what you'd do . . ."

Catherine stole a glance at her watch.

"But enough about *my* work," Professor Zalunardo responded to her subtle hint of impatience. "This book you're writing is about what?"

"Well, what I'm really looking for is that new angle you mentioned, something no one has used before."

"Hmm." The professor's brows drew downward in a frown as he paced the room. "That would depend on where you're going to *start* it. The beginning maybe? With Uther?"

"You mean Arthur?"

"I mean Uther. Uther Pendragon, Arthur's father."

"Actually—"

"Quite a character, that Uther. He was High King, you know. Bedded the Duke of Cornwall's wife right in her own castle, had her husband killed, and then married her so she wouldn't be out on the streets. Figuratively, of course. They didn't *have* streets then. How's your tea?"

"It's very—"

"Sort of negligent, though when it came to acknowledging his own son. Not that you could blame him, times being what they were. Kill off a High King's son and you've pretty much eighty-sixed the dynasty, right? So he sent him away with Merlin."

In the fortuitous break of Professor Zalunardo taking a sip, Catherine urged him to tell her more about the High King's wizard.

"All supposition, of course," the professor said, prefacing his reply. "Nobody knows where he came from. Just sort of arrived full-blown on the scene when the Pendragons came to the throne. Couldn't even account for his parentage, not that anyone ever hassled him about it unless they wanted to be turned into potato bugs. Anyway, the legend was that his mother was a princess who was raped by the devil, and that's where he got is power."

"He seems like an odd choice to look after the king's son," Catherine pointed out.

"Odd, but fate," Professor Zalunardo replied. "You see, it was his destiny, and everybody knew it. Just like it was his destiny to get seduced by that little harlot in the woods."

"Harlot?" Catherine felt her pulse suddenly quicken.

"But I'm getting ahead of myself," he apologized. "Merlin kept Arthur out of sight until Uther's death fifteen years later. Now when Uther died, all of Britain went crazy, not knowing who would take over. That's when Merlin proposed that they have a contest. You remember the sword in the stone story, don't you? Well, that was

Excalibur, a little bit of wizardry conjured by the Lady of the Lake, also known as the Goddess. The rules in this contest were that whoever pulled the sword out was meant to be the next king. Merlin and Arthur show up, Arthur pulls it out, and ta-da! The rest is history."

"What about Merlin?" Catherine probed. "You had mentioned—"

"Oh, he stayed at Camelot for a while after that," he went on. "I mean, how many fifteen-year-old boys do *you* know who could run a kingdom without help? Anyway, he got Arthur married off to Guinevere, and that's about the time everything started going to hell. And then, after he disappeared—"

"Disappeared?"

Professor Zalunardo shrugged. "Some say he got fed up with Arthur's stupidity and just walked off one day. Others say he was defeated by powers greater than his own."

"Such as?"

"Who knows? Another wizard maybe . . . or the Goddess herself. Personally I always thought it was a big mistake for him to teach his bag of tricks to that lady friend of his." With a gasp Professor Zalunardo took note of his watch. "God! Look at that! I'm late for my meditation. You can only do it at certain times, you know. Listen," he said, proceeding to grab books off of his shelves until he had acquired an armful, "why don't you take these and we can get together again next week? No," he said, suddenly scowling, "next week's bad—I'm having my office repainted. New curtains, too. Did you notice I've got curtains and no windows behind them? Illusion!" he laughed. "God, I love it!"

As he ushered Catherine out the door there was only time for one more question. "When Merlin disappeared, where do *you* think he went?" she asked.

"It's not where he *went*," the professor replied matter-of-factly. "It's where he ended *up*."

"Which is?"

"Locked in a cave of crystal in the Summer Country." Professor Zalunardo gave a wistful sigh. "Not even Merlin himself could get out of *that* one and live to tell about it."

• • •

When Catherine finally looked up at the clock in her apartment, she was stunned to discover that it was past three and that she had been reading steadily ever since she got home. Admittedly she had read over many of the passages three or four times, especially those that pertained to the magician. When she had finally reached the end, she felt the same crushing disappointment as reaching the end of a compelling novel or exciting movie. She didn't *want* to get to the end, not when the beginning and middle had sparked so many questions. All that she knew for certain was that she had to see Kyle Falconer again.

Catherine stretched across the bed for the phone book.

"I'm sorry, ma'am," the Hyatt Regency operator informed her, "but Mr. Falconer checked out last night."

Catherine's protestations did little more than annoy the woman, who firmly insisted that there had not been a mistake. Kyle Falconer and his entourage had had a change in plans, and accordingly, departed earlier than scheduled.

"If any of them should call . . ." Catherine began. The words died in her throat as she glanced up to meet the eyes of the hawk that gazed at her from the corner railing outside her French doors.

"Ma'am?" the operator said.

The receiver dropped from Catherine's hands to the quilted bedspread. She rose and moved toward the glass.

Chapter Nine

FOR A LONG TIME the two of them regarded each other through the transparent barrier, neither moving except to blink in the brightness of the midday sun. Finally Catherine put a tentative hand on the doorknob. The hawk stiffened in alert apprehension. Cautiously she stepped outside.

As if carefully assessing her, the hawk's satanic eyes narrowed, gleaming like glassy volcanic rock. Compelling and magnetic, they seemed to pierce straight through to her soul, dropping down only once to her ankles, then immediately back up to her face. Locked in a stalemate, both barely dared breathe, each waiting for the other to break the spell of silence. Mesmerized, Catherine used the time to study its powerful body and physical beauty, the tips of its feathers gold-lit by the sun, as if dipped in glitter, its bearing proud and confident.

That it was the same bird from the dream and the sea and the moonless sky over the Washington Monument, of this she was inexplicably certain. Though what it wanted from her was as much a mystery as the man who seemed to be associated with its presence.

The remembrance of Kyle Falconer brought with it the quick and disturbing thought she had experienced on the phone just a moment before: that his premature departure from the hotel now left her with no way to contact him, no way to pursue the question his story had sparked.

Momentarily distracted, she looked back up to see that the hawk had moved a few inches closer, its head slightly tilted in a way that suggested either skepticism or amusement. Almost sensuously it flexed the talons of one foot, then the other, the exercise emphasizing their length and sharpness. Barely perceptible beneath the thick feathers of its chest, a sparkle of light danced as the bird resettled on its narrow perch.

Catherine felt a strange thrill of frightened anticipation, for she realized that if the bird were indeed linked with Kyle in ways she couldn't fathom, it also represented a way to reach him beyond the conventional. She took an unsteady step toward it.

The hawk was instantly on guard, its early informality replaced by a dark warning behind icy black eyes. Catherine froze, conscious of the ugly beak that menacingly dropped open as the bird straightened to its full height. "It's okay," Catherine whispered soothingly to reassure the creature that she meant it no harm. "Take it easy, it's all right." Urgency quivered in her voice, although Catherine herself was unable to tell whether it was from fear that the hawk would fly away or attack. "I didn't mean to scare you," she said, faintly reminded that *she* had been the one initially frightened.

The hawk once more tilted its head to the side, its body neither advancing nor retreating. "It's okay," Catherine repeated, wondering what her neighbors would think if they could see her engaged in a one-sided conversation with a falcon.

Gone—as quickly as it had come—was the steel glint of evil that had previously flashed in the bird's eyes, the veiled threat supplanted by guarded curiosity.

Catherine's lips parted, hesitating on the question that imagination urged her to ask but that logic insisted would be foolish. "How do I know you'd even understand me?" she said out loud, seeking a sign of comprehension behind eyes that only stared back at her in blatant suspicion.

Noises from the street filtered up to the balcony. Somewhere in the distance—perhaps an apartment on the same level as hers—a musician was improvising through a medley of show tunes on a vintage piano. For Catherine, though, the world may as well have fallen completely silent, so strong was her concentration.

"I need to find him," she whispered so softly that it was nearly a private thought instead of a spoken statement. The hawk regarded her impassively, its only movement the outer feathers gently brushed by the April breeze.

Why am I even doing this? Catherine thought, chiding herself. Had she really expected this bird suddenly to start an intelligent conversation with her? Even as she considered it her heart was already supplying the answer, outlandish as it seemed. She wanted to find Kyle Falconer, and the hawk was somehow the key. She couldn't just give up and go back inside, not when her intuition was hotly protesting that the bird had not come to her balcony by accident.

"I need your help," she said, daring to inch her way closer, wondering if a wish spoken aloud held more clout than one kept secret.

With deliberate side steps the hawk returned to the corner, never shifting its attention from Catherine. "I'm not going to hurt you," she promised. "I just want to find Kyle."

The cold eyes stared back, acknowledging nothing. Only the faint sparkle of crystal imbedded in its chest offered Catherine any encouragement to continue talking.

"If you understand this at all," she found herself quietly pleading, "I have to talk to him. If there's someway that you could lead me . . ." For only a brief instant she forgot the caution she had fought so hard to maintain in her approach. Her spontaneous gesture of an outstretched hand startled the bird into flight.

"Wait!" she cried out, running to the edge of the balcony as it dipped below her sight, sunlight painting a pattern of shadows on the top of its graceful, arched wings. For a second it seemed to float, suspended on the cool breeze as it dropped lower and lower, finally alighting on top of a lamppost. And then, unexpectedly, it cocked its head and looked up at her, its eyes alive with challenge.

A less adventurous and perhaps more rational person would have let the incident go. To Catherine, however—grasping at straws and gambling on the most remote possibility—the action seemed much more than coincidence. Down below her, waiting as if in natural expectation for her to follow, the hawk struck a pose of placid resolve.

Catherine's mind raced with a dizzying mixture of hope and confusion. Hope because there was a chance that the bird *had* understood and was acquiescing to her request. Confusion because—if that were true—it certainly had to be one of her most bizarre communications.

Her determination to find the magician far outweighing her need to analyze the method, Catherine took one last look at the hawk before running back inside her apartment and down the hall to the kitchen. Her keys lay on the counter where she had tossed them. In one fluid motion she grabbed them up en route to the foyer and slid them into the pocket of her jeans. Propelled by an uncommon energy, Catherine pulled open the door, rushed into the hall, and found herself running headlong into Kyle Falconer's arms.

Reeling from the impact of their unexpected collision, it didn't immediately register with Catherine exactly who she had charged into. Instinctively her hands flew up in front of her, only to be pressed back into her chest as she hurtled against a black jacket that smelled of rich leather and sandalwood.

The arms that instantly had come up to catch her snugly encircled her waist, leaving no distance between their bodies. Only when Catherine had disengaged did she look up and into the face of the very man she had been seeking. "Are you okay?" he inquired, a shadow of amusement playing at the corners of his mouth. Protectively his fingertips still cupped her elbows, his head bent close in concern.

Flustered by his proximity and the uncanny timing of his arrival, Catherine could do little more than utter a monosyllabic response that was neither yes nor no. A languorous shudder rippled through her body, his touch upsetting her entire sense of balance.

Softly his breath fanned her face. "I seem to keep startling you," he apologized, his hands moving of their own volition from her elbows to her wrists. With a smile he inclined his head in a gesture of hopeful anticipation. "Can you forgive me?"

Distraction was evident in her every move as much as she tried to mask it. The questions occasioned by his appearance so soon after the departure of the hawk clashed with her physical response to his magnetism. His nearness was both disturbing and exciting; torn by reluctance, she withdrew her hands and clumsily thrust them into her pockets, agitated by his capacity to keep her emotions dancing in defense.

"I thought you had gone," she remarked, committed to maintaining a margin of composure under the stress of his scrutiny. *I probably shouldn't mention that I was just talking to a bird,* she decided, *much less trying to solicit its help.*

Irresistibly the mystery in his eyes beckoned to her as he replied, "Is that what you wanted, Catherine?"

Her quizzical expression probed for an explanation. He chose instead to ask if he might come in. "Unless you were on your way out . . . ?" he added.

Catherine stepped aside, silently bidding him formal entrance to the place that just last night had been his for the taking. And though he might have easily wandered past her and through the apartment with the familiarity of someone coming home, he surprised her by electing to wait until she had closed the door behind them.

"Are you sure I'm not interrupting something?" he inquired.

With a pulse-pounding surge of determination Catherine answered him. "I was on my way to find *you*," she replied.

"It looks like I've saved you a trip." The warmth of his tender smile echoed in his voice. "I would have come sooner if I'd had a better apology up my sleeve."

"Apology?" Catherine repeated, totally unprepared for the reply that followed.

"I overstepped my bounds with the review," he said. "I'm usually not that impulsive."

"*You* wrote it?" She gasped in astonishment. The revelation was so startlingly simple that for a split second Catherine wondered why she hadn't let herself be certain of it all along. Who better than Kyle Falconer would know how to write a self-review, especially if he had had a hand in the original text for the brochure? Beneath the matter-of-fact confession, though, still lay the recurring question that had become the cornerstone of their perplexing alliance.

"It was my fault you missed your deadline," he clarified. "Making it up to you was the least I could do."

"Why?" she blurted out, unsure of whether she should feel thankful for his help or angry for his intervention.

He studied her face before replying. "Because I don't want any part of my coming here to interfere with your life, Catherine," he said at last. An indulgent wink flashed in conspiracy. "I just hope the words weren't too far afield to lose you any fans."

Catherine had to smile in spite of her mixed feelings. "Not at all. They were exactly what *I* would have said."

"That was the idea."

"And what's the *rest* of the idea?" she countered. Without thinking, she had drawn her hands out of her pockets and onto her hips, a stance more defiant than she actually felt inside. "What is it you want?"

"Is that what you were going to ask me?" he queried, reminding her of her announced intention to look for him that afternoon.

"That and a *lot* of things," she replied. "Starting with *who*."

He put her persistence aside with good humor, enjoying the gentle sparring that only a woman of passionate intelligence could so effectively handle. "The 'who' is probably the easiest part," he said, chuckling. "I'm exactly who I said I am."

Catherine raised an eyebrow. "Merlin . . . as in Camelot?"

Without warning he touched her cheek in a wistful gesture. "I think Kyle suits this century a little better."

The sensuous electricity of his brief caress left her momentarily speechless, a void he chose to fill with a swift invitation to dinner.

"I don't know what to say," she hesitated, caught off-guard by what was evolving into the most normal thing he had done since they'd first met. Perhaps the *only* normal thing.

"Say yes." His eyes sparkled with promise, causing her pulse to quicken at the speculation of spending more time in his company. With a start she realized that they hadn't moved any farther into the apartment than the foyer but that he was now preparing to leave.

"Eight-thirty," he said, as casually as if she had already accepted. "I'll be wearing a tux."

"You haven't said where we're going," she quickly protested, as if the choice would make a difference at this point. Her fingers ached to reach over and touch his sleeve before he slipped out the door, if nothing more than to convince herself that his impromptu visit wasn't another dream.

Pleased by their temporary truce, Kyle Falconer's parting smile was as intimate as a kiss. "I'll meet you up on the roof."

Chapter Ten

UNQUESTIONABLY ONE OF the glamorous perks of Catherine's high visibility job was the opportunity to wear floor-length gowns and her best jewelry. Gallery openings and D.C. premieres more often than not required her to mingle before and after with the Washington elite; the sense of style she acquired from her mother imbued her with the confidence that the elegant impression she made was not one easily forgotten.

The flip side of an extensive wardrobe, however, was the dilemma she faced at ten minutes to eight: what to wear. Still wrapped in a velour towel from her shower, Catherine bit her lip as she surveyed the closet, trying to decide between extremes of conservative and exotic. His mention of meeting on the roof only served to complicate matters, obscure in its omission of where they were going after that. "Probably Mars," she muttered to herself, withdrawing a dark green silk from the center row. Like her mother, Catherine had a penchant for associating outfits with certain events. The green silk, for instance, represented a genuine coup in her profession—all born of a chance elevator ride with Mel Ahrens, the eccentric but brilliant Chicago sculptor who was reputed to hate critics with a passion bordering on violence. Unaware of her identity, Ahrens had engaged in idle conversation that led to a discovery of their joint fondness for Szechuan cooking.

Charmed by her personality, he sought her out during the crowded reception. Much to Catherine's surprise he had not only discovered by then who and what she was but made a point of monopolizing her time, a behavior that astonished his hosts. "I thought you didn't like critics," she reminded him.

"Only the ones who don't wear green dresses," he said, snorting in disgust. Three weeks later a box was delivered to her office as thanks for her insightful critique—an abstract, bulbous fortune cookie in bronze that at the right angle could be interpreted as rather suggestive. Someday she might even have the nerve to bring it out from behind the sprawling philodendron that conveniently camouflaged it. As her mother would have said, it was the thought that counted.

Well, she decided, if the green silk could inspire Mel Ahrens to conversation and spontaneous—albeit weird—art, maybe it could also inspire Kyle Falconer to lay his cards on the table, to trust her enough to share what smoldered beneath the surface.

Twenty minutes later she studied the image reflected back in her mirror, pleased with the soft drape of the Grecian-style gown that bared one shoulder and slit up the opposite side to expose subtly a shapely calf. She had deftly coiled her hair into a smooth chignon at the base of her neck, a style that accented her eyes and high cheekbones.

Watchful of the time, she stood on her toes to reach up on the closet shelf for her beaded evening bag, puzzled at first by the weight of something solid inside. There, right where she had left it after the last performance she had attended at the Kennedy Center, lay her mini-cassette recorder, an invaluable companion on assignment. She must have absentmindedly slipped the device back into her purse after transcribing her notes instead of returning it to the desk at the *Trib*. Just as she crossed to the dresser to set it down, an idea struck her.

"It's not as if I were sneaking an interview," she rationalized as she slipped a new a cassette into the compartment. The tape would simply be insurance against forgetting anything he said, not to mention a means of obtaining tangible proof of whether or not he was using hypnosis to manipulate her responses.

Satisfied with her strategy, Catherine applied a final pat of corn-silk powder to her nose before sliding her feet into the dark green pumps and making her exit, not at all sure of what waited three stories up.

• • •

It was cooler on the roof than she had expected. With an easy five minutes to spare, Catherine considered going back down for a wrap. And then she saw him.

There was an air of isolation about the tall figure who had been pensively looking out on the city lights, turning just as Catherine noticed him. Even from a distance his eyes sparkled, pleased by her arrival. The sheen of his black hair was enhanced by the lights from the rooftop wall, the crisp white of his shirt in competition with his smile of welcome. Catherine could not help but wonder what he had been thinking just before she got there.

If his arresting looks had taken her breath away before, the effect now was ten times more powerful. His muscular body moved with easy grace as he strolled toward her, devastatingly virile but seemingly unaware of his power.

"You look beautiful," he complimented her, producing a single red rose from the hand that she would have sworn had been empty a second ago.

Catherine accepted his praise and the flower with a nod of thanks, touched by a show of gallantry that was rare and unexpected in the twentieth century. Whatever his true origins, he had obviously been groomed in the fine art of courting.

"So where are we going?" she ventured to ask, savoring the delicate fragrance of the fresh bloom in her fingertips.

"Someplace you've never been," he replied, mischief dancing across his face.

"How do you know . . ." Catherine started to say, the words evaporating as her gaze followed the impromptu sweep of his hand to the far corner of the roof. Elegant in its simplicity, a table for two waited. Flickers of light reflected off the freestanding champagne bucket from the glow of the tall candles in their crystal holders. Two fluted glasses, properly chilled, graced the table's surface in classic accompaniment to the fine china and ornate silver.

"You've been busy," she remarked as he escorted her to the open-air dining nook that seemed to have materialized as effortlessly as the rose. An amusing speculation crossed her mind about whether or not he'd next turn mice into waiters and a pumpkin into a carriage. Obviously nothing the man did should surprise her, even though he constantly did. It's probably all illusion, she reminded herself.

Kyle Falconer gave a roguish shrug as he poured the shimmering amber liquid into both glasses. "Parlor games," he pleasantly insisted.

"Are you ever real?" she countered, laying her purse faceup on the white linen cloth, hoping the recorder was still running. The blunt approach had now and then broken down barriers with celebrities where other methods had failed; Catherine saw no reason not to try it on Kyle Falconer. With a keenly observant eye she watched for his reaction.

His features deceptively composed, Kyle handed her a glass, raising his own in a toast. "I'm as real as you *think* I am," he replied, the brief contact of their glasses producing a clear chime that seemed to echo in the stillness of the night.

Their eyes met over the rims of crystal, each studying the other with an intense look. Catherine was the first to back down, inwardly conceding that his ability to keep thoughts hidden were superior to anyone else she had ever met. As if he read her mind, he smiled tenderly, his index finger lazily trailing the length of the frosted chalice.

"You're still not convinced, are you?" he commented.

"Should I be?"

His free hand absently came up to comb through the wave of hair at his left temple in a gesture of mild frustration. "It *would* make things *easier*," he confessed in good humor.

"So would telling me what you're after," she challenged.

His expression was one of complete unconcern. "I can do better than that" came his response. "I can show you."

"When?"

"When would you like?"

In spite of her skepticism Catherine felt her senses stir, her curiosity aroused to a disquiet that she was averse to let him see. "How about right now?" she suggested as she set down her glass. To her surprise Kyle followed suit, offering her his arm.

"Oh, you won't need that," he pointed out as she reached for her purse. "We're only going over to the wall." Puzzled, Catherine left it where it was, hoping that they wouldn't be too far out of range for the microphone.

With gentle patience he took the rose from her hand and laid it on the waist-high ledge. "Close your eyes a second," he urged.

Behind closed lids, Catherine asked him why. "You'll see," he promised, the tips of his fingers barely grazing the inside of her slender wrist.

A breeze softly floated around Catherine's ankles, spiraling upward through the sensuous folds of her gown. Her face suddenly felt cool and moist. "When can I look?" she asked.

"Now."

Nothing could possibly have prepared her for the breathtaking sight that greeted her eyes upon opening. Down below her lay the long expanse of water she recognized as the Reflecting Pool, copied from India's Taj Mahal and, beyond that, the towering splendor of the Washington Monument bathed in the glow of golden spotlights. Intense astonishment covered her face as she realized that they were no longer standing on the roof of her apartment building but atop a structure equally high to offer the elevated view. Given the city's artistic symmetry and her knowledge of D.C. geography, that could only be one place.

"The Lincoln Memorial?" she murmured hesitantly.

He was standing close behind her, one hand lightly resting on the small of her back. "It's the best place to show you why I'm here," he replied, gesturing toward the marble pinnacle. "Look closely," he whispered.

Catherine strained to see what so strongly held his attention, his handsome face now squarely set in a look of reference and contemplation.

"I'm sorry," Catherine apologized, "but all I see is the Monument and the trees and the Capitol beyond that."

"The water," he instructed. "Look deep in the water and tell me what you see."

It was a phenomenon so common as to be overlooked without a second thought—the mirror image of the mighty column reflected in the pool, the surface so tranquil and smooth as to provide a flawless duplication. And yet, as Catherine turned her attention from the original to its liquid copy, her eyes picked out subtle distinctions between the two.

"Concentrate," she heard her companion gently coax as if from a distance. And as she did so, the image he meant her to see sharpened in clarity, causing her to catch her breath in the shock of its discovery.

Crisp and evenly tapered, the obelisk's face in the water now shone with the luster of polished metal rather than quarried stone, its sharp edges defined by gold borders. The previously shapeless cluster of trees near the Monument's base now formed a horizontal crosspiece, the hilt a mass of dark shadows punctuated by a cascade of reflected stars sparkling like diamonds. In the second it took Catherine to blink in disbelief, the image had disintegrated without so much as a ripple or splash.

As she quickly turned to him for answers, her eyes froze on the lips that started to move before she had even put her question into words.

"Excalibur," he said, his tone low and haunting, his respect for the vanished vision deeply evident. "It was stolen from my time and brought forth to yours." A muscle flicked angrily at his jaw, his mouth thinning with the first sign of displeasure she had witnessed since they had met. "Wherever it's hidden," he pledged, "I have to find it before it's too late."

Catherine barely touched her dinner, a tantalizing beef Wellington and Yorkshire pudding that was waiting on their plates when they returned from their journey—if indeed they had traveled at all.

"But it doesn't make *sense* for it to be here," Catherine protested, the image still sharp in her mind. "Why isn't it with Arthur?" Much to her own surprise she had been tossing off the king's name and others for the last half hour as familiarly as if they were neighbors down the street. By all accounts, the question posed was a logical one, for how could a sword of legend be stolen and yet still figure prominently in its own past?

"It *was* with Arthur," he replied, "up until twelve centuries ago." To clarify, he backtracked to the funeral rites that had marked the High King's passage from life into death. "In the tradition of warriors," he explained, "Arthur's body was laid out on a barge, Excalibur by his side. The barge was doused with oils and set aflame, cast out on a moonlit sea." As he spoke, Catherine could almost envision the tongues of bright orange and scarlet as they licked at the shrouded craft, the sizzle of burning wood as it struck the water, swallowed up moments later by black tides and pungent smoke.

"For three hundred years,"he continued, "the sanctity of their final resting place was preserved." A bridled anger surfaced in his voice. "Until that time I had no reason to leave the cave."

The statement sent a chill down Catherine's spine, and she found that in her lap she was digging her nails into the palms of her hands. "Why did you?" she said.

"Because of what Excalibur represents" came his reply. "For it to be found in the wrong century would be disastrous."

"The wrong one," Catherine ventured, "being *this* one?"

He was graciously refilling her glass, Catherine noticing for the first time that his remained nearly full. "That's why I need your help," he answered with soft insistence. "I think you know where it is."

So that was why he had sought her out. But to think that she could somehow help him—that she knew where to find Excalibur—well, the idea was simply preposterous. Her face clouded with skepticism. "That's ridiculous."

"Maybe in your eyes." He folded his hands together. "But in all the time I've known her, the Goddess has never proved to make mistakes." His warm brown eyes were full of expectation. "She's the one who sent me to you."

"What?" she asked in disbelief. "You're going to have to explain yourself."

"I can't, Catherine," he said, sighing. "If you're going to help me, it has to be blind trust."

She continued to press, but he begged off on further discussion until, in his words, she had had a chance to sleep on her decision. Once more she raised the same obvious, unanswerable question. "How do I know any of this is true?" she asked again as he lingered a moment in the doorway of her apartment, his masculine scent and tempting physique providing a distraction she found difficult to ignore.

Cupping her chin, he sought to reassure her upturned face that the final choice was hers. "If you choose *not* to help me," he promised, "I will accept it."

The kiss that she half anticipated did not come at all; instead he smiled as he took leave of her. With a pang of longing Catherine sensed that if she were to fling open the door again less than a second later, the corridor would be completely empty.

Her glance fell on her evening bag as she prepared to turn out the foyer light. "At least I know I didn't *dream* it," she consoled herself, withdrawing the recorder and noting that the cassette inside was still turning with steady precision.

As she stepped out of her silk dress in the middle of the bedroom, Catherine was seized with the desire to play back part of the tape before retiring, to hear the rich timbre of his speech as he spoke of people and places she had assumed until now were all fantasy.

Hers was the only voice the machine had recorded.

Chapter Eleven

THE RED ROSE on the ledge was all that remained by the time Catherine pulled on a sweatshirt and beat a hasty path back up to the roof. Gone were the chairs and table, the silver champagne bucket, and the dinner plates they had abandoned when he had proposed that they call it a night. Gone, too, was the cork she remembered accidentally brushing to the floor when she'd first set down her purse. Only the rose lay behind as evidence that their evening together had been real.

Once more, sleep did not come easily, though she had no new dreams on which to place the blame. Nor was it her admission to herself that she enjoyed being mesmerized by this man who wove tales of enchantment that kept her awake. A part of her *wanted* to believe that a world such as the one he painted had truly existed, even that it might one day exist again.

What continued to disturb her was the unmistakable void she felt in her life whenever they parted. Man or magician, she couldn't deny the way her heart leapt at his touch, the way her body longed to draw ever closer each time he was near. Since the first evening she had seen him she had wanted only for his arms to hold her, his lips to promise love.

How could she resolve this puzzle? If she chose to discount his story, he would be out of her life forever. If she accepted it as truth—that he came from a past that had long been dead—theirs was a union that could never be consummated.

Weariness enveloped her as she tried to concentrate, yet her eyes snapped open each time she pictured his face and replayed the words with which he had prefaced their good night. He had said the decision was hers and he would respect it. Why wasn't that comforting?

Again and again Catherine felt her senses tingle with unbidden memories. His reference to an omnipotent goddess brought to recollection her dream of the lake in the clearing and the lady's silver voice echoing as musically as the contact of the wine glasses in their rooftop toast. Hers was the voice that had also reverberated through the cave of crystal, urging with maternal firmness that her servant fulfill his mystical obligation. The same voice and spirit that he claimed had sent him across time . . . to find Catherine herself.

Yet now that he had found her, what was she supposed to do? His suggestion that she might know where the sword was hidden made no sense to her at all.

Still, the magnificent image of white and gold burned in her imagination. For only a fraction of a second she had experienced a bright jab of familiarity as the reflection in the pool came into clearer focus. Had she actually seen Excalibur somewhere in Washington, as he implied? And if she had, how could she have so easily forgotten?

Exhausted by confusion, Catherine cast yet another look at her bedside clock. At seven-thirty tomorrow morning, he said, he would be waiting on the wharf at the end of King Street in Alexandria. His index finger had gently outlined the lower portion of the lips she yearned to have him lean in and kiss. "If you believe me, if you trust me," he had whispered, "meet me there." And although he was a man who seemed easily accustomed to getting his way, there was an almost imperceptible hint of pleading in his eyes, as if what he feared most was that she might say no.

The hands of the clock inched their way toward daybreak.

Sunday morning dawned cool and cloaked in rain. Playful splashes of April showers against the window woke Catherine from her halfhearted sleep. The past few hours had done nothing to change her mind from its resolution to meet him. After all, who was she to say that she *didn't* have knowledge of things unearthly or magical? Certainly she had demonstrated enough imagination in her childhood to suggest an affinity for enchantment. Time and again her parents had gently dissuaded her views that animals could talk, that she could read her grandmother's mind, and that a unicorn periodically passed by her bedroom window at night. "She'll outgrow it, Karl," she'd often heard her mother say.

Largely to please them, Catherine *did* outgrow it, or at least relegate her feelings to a dark corner where they wouldn't be criticized as "weird." Yet in their short time together Kyle Falconer had unlocked that secret part of herself she had so strongly denied. Perhaps she was wrong, but the connection she felt toward him was something other worldly. And the alternative—letting him walk out of her life—felt worse than awful. Something about that choice struck Catherine as painfully wrong. And if he really did possess the power to unlock the secrets of Excalibur, the very least she could do was trust his judgment and offer her help.

Forgoing a hat or umbrella, Catherine slipped a windbreaker on over her turtleneck and slacks, letting herself out the door just as the clock struck the hour of seven.

Despite its prominent Southern heritage, Alexandria, Virginia, had fared far better during the Civil War than most other antebellum cities, largely owing to its early occupation by Union troops and subsequent isolation from the rest of the Confederacy. A thriving tobacco port just a hundred years before, the genteel township of the 1860s had all but ceased to engage in merchant trade as bitter war raged outside its boundaries and the railroads to the north began to assume the burdens of commerce. As if the countryside itself had swallowed it up, the crown jewel of Virginia's aristocracy slid from coveted prize to forgotten heirloom.

Not until Franklin Roosevelt's first term as president did the city enjoy a sparkling rebirth as a center of cultural and commercial importance. Along its narrow streets and ensconced in architecture that had not forgotten its Colonial origins, Alexandria bustled once more with taverns and galleries, fine restaurants, and shops. A stroll through Old Town could easily be compared to a journey back in time, its spirit most notably captured in the eastward view of the never-changing Potomac. Benches set out on the parallel shore beckoned would-be captains to sit and dream, to let the winds take their thoughts to the top of tall ships whose spinnakers billowed in the gentle morning winds.

Such may have been the thoughts of those few early risers who were already strolling along the wharf when Catherine arrived. They look like they're a hundred years away, Catherine silently observed. Her eyes, though, had already locked on the profile of the man whose thoughts went back much further. Without hesitation she hurried toward him, her heart hammering in her ears as he turned and saw her.

He was on his feet instantly, his lips parting in a silent greeting that made her pulse leap with excitement. Emotions conquering all sense of propriety, Catherine surrendered herself to the need for his touch as he stepped forward and clasped her body tightly to his.

The circle of his arms was firm and persuasive, his breathing warm and uneven on the back of her neck as she buried her face against his chest.

"I was afraid you weren't coming," he whispered into her hair.

"So was I," she confessed. Last-minute doubt had played havoc with her heart right up until the time she had stepped onto the wharf, taunting her with the idea that she might be motivated more by unrequited passion for the storyteller than by a belief in his story.

Her soft curves molded to the lean contours of his body as he gently rocked her back and forth, both of them oblivious to the rain that had started to send the less romantic river watchers in search of shelter.

Only with reluctance did she finally lift up her head and allow herself to be put at arm's length, his hands still grasping her shoulders with tender insistence. Drops of rain glistened on his jacket as Catherine studied him thoughtfully. "What's wrong?" she asked softly, aware of the tension that was clouding their reunion.

The look on his face was a mixture of gratitude and vulnerability. Even without words Catherine could sense an anguish that lingered deep within, a yearning to elicit a response of reassurance from her. The eyes that caressed her with trust brimmed with unspoken pain, sweeping over her face as if he expected her to vanish at any moment. His lips opened, but no words came.

Her hand slid up to lose itself in a thick wave of his hair, her heart resisting the urge to draw herself upward and cover his mouth with her own. Intuition warned her that a kiss would not be welcome now; patience and understanding would. "For what it's worth," she said, shrugging, lightly, "I'm willing to listen."

"*That*," he replied, "is worth everything."

For close to a century the wood-carved sign at Gallagher's Inn had proudly boasted the finest Irish whiskey this side of the Atlantic. Today was the coffee, though, that brought crowds inside from the Sunday rain. A rich aroma of amaretto permeated the walls and invited lazy conversation among the patrons.

There was still one booth available when Catherine and Kyle arrived, its high wooden back and no-frills design reminiscent of Early American simplicity. Pewter plates and tankards—salvaged from the building's humble beginnings as a rooming house—were lined up on high shelves and nestled in the nooks of period book-cases. To Catherine's delight a fire crackled comfortably in the stone fireplace against the far wall.

In spite of the cozy environment, however, she found it difficult to relax completely in her companion's presence. Having reconciled herself to an uneasy belief in his powers, she turned her attention inward to the dilemma of loving a man who could not be hers. Would it be better, she wondered, never to have met him . . . or to lose him to his own past once he found what he had traveled so far to retrieve?

"What are you going to do when you find it?" she asked aloud, dreading the answer she already suspected would come.

"I have to take it back," he said. "Hide it so that it will be safe until the next High King can claim it."

Catherine held off asking her next question until the waiter had set down two steaming mugs in front of them. "And what if you *don't* find it?" she asked.

The sense of conviction that was part of his character shone on his face. "How could I *not* find it, having you to help me?"

His show of confidence only served to mystify her further. "I still don't see how it's possible," she persisted. "How could I have seen something as incredible as what I saw in the water and not remember where it is?"

"Easily." He shrugged. "You didn't know what it was."

"You mean it's disguised?"

He shook his head decisively. "Excalibur's power makes it immune to change. Only time could alter its physical condition."

"How do you know that after twelve centuries it isn't a pile of dust?" A humorous thought came to her mind. "If *that's* the case, maybe I've been looking at it every day in my apartment."

In spite of his seriousness he allowed himself the break that laughter afforded, obviously appreciating her capacity to put him at ease.

"So why can't you use magic to find it yourself?" she continued. Certainly a man who could levitate over Mount St. Helens and vanish from a sealed coffin in a hundred feet of water could trace an Arthurian relic with little difficulty.

He hesitated with his answer, as if he were carefully weighing how much he could tell her. "Excalibur," he said at last, "wasn't brought here to be found easily . . . least of all by me. I'm afraid that explaining the reasons why would be as hard as describing how to travel across time."

"Which you haven't explained, either," she pointed out.

He regarded her with a smile of amusement behind his coffee cup. "I didn't know you were interested."

"*I* didn't know a *lot* of things," she replied quietly, her meaning cautiously secret. Three days ago she hadn't known that legends could be true. Three days ago she hadn't known the depth of her own heart to long for a stranger.

"Time is a series of circles within circles," he began. Catherine tilted her head in curiosity as he sketched on the back of his napkin. "All of the ages of the universe," he explained, "coexist on the same plane, just like a collection of songs all share the same flat surface of a record. Even though we can only play one song—or one life—at a given time, the others are constantly present, revolving at the same speed around a common core."

Catherine studied his drawing with a scowl. "I always thought time was linear," she protested

"Yes, that's the way it would look," he agreed, "if you stretched out the coiled groove into a straight line. It's the parallel nature of concentric circles, though, that makes the journeys of the soul possible."

"I think you've entered a subject that's not my best," Catherine sighed.

Laughter floated up from his throat. "I always *was* ahead of my time." He chuckled, his fingers just grazing her wrist as he underscored the words. "Let's say that you play the record through from beginning to end," he continued. "One song would lead to another and to another in what you equate to be a linear, progressive sequence."

"So far, so good," Catherine nodded.

His dark brows arched inquiringly. "What would you do, though," he proposed, "if you wanted to jump from the second song to the fifth?"

"Easy." Catherine shrugged. "You'd lift the needle up and set it down where you wanted it."

A grin tugged at the corners of his mouth. "A concept not far removed from the travel."

The simplicity failed to convince her. "Just like that?" She snapped her fingers.

"If it were just like *that*," he retorted with a definitive snap of his own, "there'd be more Merlins than the one sitting across from you."

Catherine wavered, trying to comprehend what she was hearing. "Easy enough said with a needle and a record," she admitted, "but how does it work with a person?"

Even as she asked, he was embellishing his sketch with what looked like a series of random railroad tracks oddly spaced within the circles.

"Windows," he remarked when he was finished. "The sensation of seeing something familiar or anticipating what will happen—"

"Reincarnation?" Catherine interrupted. "Is that part of it? Past lives?"

Again he hesitated before answering, his expression guarded. "*Some* of it," he said with a nod.

"What about the rest?"

"The rest," he went on, "are opportunities that people don't recognize for what they are." He indicated the series of vertical slash marks within his design. "In that blink of an eye we label as dèjá vu comes an alignment of open windows through which the soul can fly."

For an instant the memory of the hawk seared through Catherine's mind. "And a person could return again . . . the same way?" she ventured.

There was a ominous calmness in his eyes. "In exactly the same spot," he replied, "with no time having passed in his absence."

A concern that had preoccupied her earlier unexpectedly resurfaced in Catherine's imagination. Maybe it was just his choice of words . . . maybe something more. Whatever the case, she couldn't let it go without asking. "Two times," she reminded him, "you've said that Excalibur was brought here. Not sent but *brought*."

The dark eyes that only a moment before had projected warmth and trust now grew narrow, his expression a mask of stone.

"Yes," he answered gravely, his confirmation sending an awful chill through Catherine. "The one who stole it twelve centuries ago is here in Washington, too."

Chapter Twelve

ALL HER PREVIOUS apprehensions came rushing back to seize her. Catherine felt the color draining from her face as she cast an uneasy glance over her shoulder. Almost immediately her fingers felt the tender reassurance of his outstretched hand, his comforting touch a contradiction to the ragged uncertainty he had just aroused in her heart. She found she couldn't concentrate under his steady scrutiny as much as she tried to fathom the meaning of his ominous statement. What had the book said? Something about the existence of a power greater than his own? She attempted unsuccessfully to force her distracted emotions into enough order to resume their conversation.

As she paused to catch her breath, her fears were stronger than ever. "Who?" she asked in a whisper. Intuition completed the query. "Who are you afraid of?"

"An enemy." He sighed heavily, his voice laced with bitterness. "I should have suspected long ago that something like this would happen." His eyes flashed a gentle but firm warning across the table. "It's not going to be easy, Catherine. Finding Excalibur is only *half* the battle."

"And the other half?"

His response held a note of anxiety. "Getting it *away* from her."

His use of the female pronoun caught her off-guard. Catherine had been expecting his enemy to be another wizard or vengeance-bent warrior, presumably male. Her question was forced to wait though, preempted by his suggestion that they finish their coffee and start walking again.

The morning rain had dissipated to mist, a wisp of breeze scenting the air with a fresh sea smell. As they strolled up King Street, her hand in his, Catherine and Kyle easily could have been mistaken for casual tourists in search of Washington souvenirs. Little would random onlookers suspect—or believe—that the object of their quest was far more elusive, their conversation far more intense than their facial expressions conveyed.

Matching her pace to his, Catherine was oblivious to the appreciative stares of strangers as they passed. She was only aware of the exhilarating energy generated by his closeness. Never before in her life had she known a man who possessed all of the qualities of a storybook hero, yet remained just beyond her loving reach.

Her mother, of course, would have advised that the best things in life take time, especially relationships. Certainly her parents' own courtship had been testimony to the philosophy of patience, Catherine's mother having waited without complaint through World War II and Korea before her betrothed sealed his pledge with a gold ring in a chapel at Klamath Falls. "My mind was made up the first time I saw him," she used to say. Undeniably Catherine could finally relate to the words she had heard since she was a little girl.

It was also there, though, that all similarity ended, for time was not a privilege she'd be granted in allowing this love to blossom. Once Kyle Falconer had found what he came for, he'd be out of her life, never knowing the extent of her longing.

"I wish I knew what you were thinking," he suddenly remarked. Their walk had taken them off the main street and into the residential district that boasted some of the finest Virginia architecture.

"I thought you did," Catherine blushed.

His fingers tightened in an affectionate squeeze. "Only what you choose to tell me," he replied.

Quickly Catherine turned the conversation back to his story about Camelot. The details he revealed were consistent with what she had already learned. Gone completely was any suspicion that he had committed volumes of Celtic history to memory; his recollections were those of a man who had witnessed England's infant steps firsthand, and he had been a part of them.

"The job of king," he explained, "was probably never harder than when Arthur came to the throne. The old ways were being put aside, the new ways were black with corruption."

"The forerunner of modern politics?" Catherine quipped, encouraging him to tell her what the "old ways" had been like. Her question made him smile in reminiscence.

"Well, in the beginning," he said, "there was probably more civilization out in the woods than there was in the castles. That's where the Lake People lived."

"Lake People?"

"Nomads who believed in the worship of nature and the brotherhood of its children." A chuckle broke his reverent tone. "Maybe I should make that sisterhood," he said, correcting himself. "They called themselves the Daughters of the Goddess."

"The one who governed the earth?" Catherine asked, recalling his earlier reference. "The one who sent you here?"

"One and the same." He nodded. "She was worshiped as devoutly by her followers as the followers of Christianity have believed for two thousand years in their God. Sacrifices were made to appease her, prayers were sung to assure her guidance and all-powerful protection."

"And her daughters?" Catherine probed. "Did they have powers, too?"

The gaze he returned was enigmatic. Clearly he was torn between sharing his knowledge and respecting the secrets of a mystic cult. "Their talents were diverse," he said at last, "but all of their gifts sprang from a unity with the environment. Some were the psychics—the ones who could read the rivers and interpret the phases of the moon. Others were the healers. Their knowledge of herbs and the gentleness of their fingers gave them the power to restore life and mend mortal wounds. And some," he went on, cautiously gauging her reaction, "were empaths, capable of feeling the emotions and reading the thoughts of animals and plants."

"What about men?" Catherine asked. "How did they fit in?"

"There wasn't much opportunity or desire for contact with men or the outside world in general," he informed her. "And that's the way they preferred it."

"And yet they took an interest in the new king?" Catherine questioned. "It sounds like their society was too detached from the main-stream to really care."

"Separate," he agreed, "but still in need of a king's protection."

"From whom?"

"From the king's own warriors." His arm had casually slid around her waist, his thigh brushing hers as they walked. "The times I came from," he went on, "were dominated by the morbid fear of being conquered—first by the enemies they *could* see and then by the spirits they *couldn't* see. What had once been granted the right to flourish, undisturbed, grew to be viewed by the ignorant as a wellspring of evil. Much like your witch-hunts of Salem, the Lake People became the innocent victims of the new order of thinking."

"For someone who only arrived here ten years ago," Catherine observed, "you've done a lot of reading to catch up."

He acknowledged her compliment with a tilt of his head, con-tinuing his story as the first hint of sunlight sent dappled shadows across the tree-shaded sidewalk.

"There was pressure on Arthur to serve as a true Christian king," he explained. "Members of his court believed that, as such, there could be no room in Britain for pagan rites and worship."

"They wanted him to condone massacre?" Catherine gasped.

"Oh, but the didn't see it that way," he replied. "They saw it as a purification, a chance to rid the land of something they were afraid of."

"And Arthur stood up to them?"

"By virtue of Excalibur"—he nodded—"his first loyalty lay with the Goddess. His acceptance of the sword from her hand was an affirmation to defend her people from harm. In truth I suspect he was also reluctant to incur her wrath."

"I bet that didn't go over too well with his peers," Catherine commented.

"Arthur was High King." He shrugged. "They had no choice but to accept his judgment, much as they may have disagreed."

"Speaking softly and carrying a big sword probably didn't hurt, either," Catherine joked.

"Possession of Excalibur," he agreed with a small smile, "carried clout denied the average mortal."

"What made it so special?" Catherine inquired. "Besides coming from the Goddess?"

"That's more than enough," he said. "Excalibur had a power unlike any other weapon on earth. Sometimes I think that Arthur himself didn't even know the magnitude of its spirit each time he took it up in battle."

"You talk as if it had a personality," Catherine charged.

"Perhaps it did. In the hands of the right person—a person like Arthur—great good could come of its possession and strength."

"You're not biased in the slightest, are you?" Catherine teased.

"I'm not saying Arthur was the best," he justified. "I'm just saying that he was the best that his century had to offer under the circumstances."

"Maybe because he had the best teacher," Catherine remarked, raising her eyes to meet his.

"Not good enough, I'm afraid, to prevent the destruction of all that he loved."

"You're only one man," Catherine reminded him, surprised by his sudden look of amusement. "Did I say something funny?"

"No," he said softly. "Just something I'm not used to hearing."

"You started to tell me about Excalibur's power," Catherine urged, releasing him from the embarrassment her remark had inadvertently caused.

"Forged by the magic of the Goddess," he went on, "Excalibur's properties made its owner invincible against attack. While Arthur was a fine enough swordsman in his own right, his skill with Excalibur made his conquests legendary. A single blow, however slight, was lethal."

"How did he die, then?" Catherine ventured.

His prolonged silence made Catherine's throat tighten. She realized she had just asked him to share something that would be painful in the telling.

With a resigned shrug he related the story of Arthur's last days. "Those who survived the slaughter at Birdoswald told of the final confrontation between the High King and his son, Mordred. Arthur dealt the first blow with his war spear, sending Mordred to the ground. As he fumbled to loosen Excalibur from its bloody sheath and finish the job, Mordred had just enough strength left to level

95

his own sword at Arthur's head and let it fall. With Excalibur out of Arthur's hand at the moment it happened, no magic of this world or the next could rescue him from death."

The swell of his pain was beyond tears, his expression one of mute wretchedness. Instinctively Catherine moved into his arms, wanting to absorb the pain he was feeling for the loss of the friend he had raised since birth.

"Maybe if I had been there . . ." He sighed, his words trailing off. "Then again, a feeble old man wouldn't have been much use, would he?"

Catherine regarded him with a critical eye. "I don't think I can get used to that," she confessed.

"Used to what?"

"Have you looked in a mirror?" she suggested.

Flattered but unmoved by her quick retort, he reminded her that his present image was only temporary. "Once Excalibur is restored," he said, "I'll return to the way I was."

Catherine regarded him with somber curiosity. "You still haven't told me who has it," she insisted, or what she wants with it."

"The answer to that," he said responding to the second question first, "is anybody's guess. I've never thought that she wanted it for herself. More than likely she stole it as an instrument of bargain, which makes it all the more dangerous."

"'She' being . . .?"

"Her name is Nimue," he said. "An incorrigible child in a woman's body. She could have used her talents to preserve the good. Instead she chose the path of darkness."

"You sound like you know her pretty well," Catherine pointed out.

"I should. She was my protégé, the one I hoped could carry on after I was no longer of value. At the start she was nothing more than an enthusiastic diversion." He paused, his eyes becoming shadowed with pain.

"Go on," Catherine said gently.

"You see, to pacify his court as amends for his protection of the Lake People, Arthur informally agreed to start thinking more for himself. Up until then he had asked my advice on everything from how many stags he should kill to whether he should banish his half sister for seducing him." Catherine's raised eyebrow didn't escape his notice. "Morals," he interjected, "were not exactly the highest."

"And?" she prompted.

"I had time on my hands and no one to listen . . . until Nimue." His voice grew taut with anger. "In our days together I taught her almost everything I knew. Who *wouldn't* have been flattered by the attention of a beautiful woman."

Catherine felt a surge of jealousy, her imagination churning with unwanted thoughts of what his relationship with Nimue had been. "You called her an enemy," Catherine said. "Why?"

His eyes conveyed the seething contempt within. "Because," he replied, "it was she who brought about my downfall."

Chapter Thirteen

THEY HAD PAUSED to rest in a lush common that separated two Jefferson-vintage estates, the low brick wall offering a place to sit away from the main avenue. Moisture still clung to the trees like the crystal prisms of a chandelier. Rejoicing in the return of sunlight, the birds filled the stillness with melody. To Catherine their lively refrain was an ironic contrast to the magician's story of betrayal.

"In all the years I was raising Arthur, teaching him to be king, I never rewarded myself with companionship," he explained. "Divided loyalties had no place in a country where war could start at the drop of a gauntlet."

"Divided loyalties?"

"If I loved someone—a woman," he said, "her concerns would preoccupy me, her safety would supersede that of my king."

"But wouldn't Arthur have understood?" Catherine protested. "After all, he had someone himself."

"Not the most fortunate of liaisons. Don't take me wrong," he quickly added, "but I thought Guinevere was a mistake from the beginning."

"Couldn't you have warned him? I thought you could see into the future."

"Into the future," he sighed, "but not as easily into a human heart. I guess in a way it's probably better I *wasn't* there to see the end." He shook his head in dismay. "He may as well have said 'I'm giving up England for the woman I love' for what it cost him to take her side against his own law."

Lost in thought it was a long while before he returned to his narrative.

"After I met Nimue," he said, "I thought she was the fulfillment of a prophecy."

"In what way?"

In response, he backtracked to his childhood. "I used to see things," he explained, "visions that I knew made me different from other children. One of the earliest visions was a bonding with a daughter of the Goddess. And although I never saw her face, I always sensed that she was beautiful and caring." He turned to study Catherine in thoughtful reflection. "The vision told me that she'd one day bear my only son, and that even though my own powers would be gone by then, his would be the magic to keep the world safe."

The breeze blew a black wisp of hair across his forehead, and Catherine suppressed the desire to reach over and brush it back.

"For years," he continued, "I put the vision out of my mind. If such a woman existed, I rationalized, I would have met her in my prime, long before I agreed to raise in secrecy the son of Uther Pendragon." Lazily he doffed the jacket that was no longer needed for warmth, laying it between them on the wall. "Arthur had just barely come to power when a sensation started to overtake me that changes—drastic ones—were in the wind. I think I really felt it the first time at his coronation, so strongly that I took ill later that day and raged with a fever for three weeks. Even after I recovered, I still couldn't shake the uneasiness that danger was close by, waiting."

"Was Nimue the danger?" Catherine asked.

"Oddly enough," he replied, "she was the distraction that took my mind off the premonitions. I started to feel at peace when I was around her," he recalled. "Too late I found out that letting my guard down was a mistake I'd live to regret."

As they resumed their walk—his jacket roguishly slung over his shoulder and his free hand entwined in Catherine's—he related the story of how they had met.

She was painfully shy at the start, he explained to her. For the first few months he wondered whether she could even talk or whether—like most people—she was afraid to initiate any contact with a man purported to be an offspring of Lucifer.

"She'd leave me herb cakes and flowers," he said, "always slipping away before I had a chance to thank her . . . or to ask her what she wanted."

His description was that of a fair-skinned girl just midway through her teens. "Her hair was the color of summer wheat," he said, "and fell past her waist, unadorned save for a single ivory-and-tortoiseshell comb." Her clothes, he went on, were those of the Lake People— coarse black fabric that not only concealed any suggestion of a figure but enabled them to move through the shadows, invisible on the outskirts of the king's territory.

"And then one day," he continued, "I heard someone singing just before dusk. There was something sad and haunting about the sound. Having nothing better to do, I followed it."

There, in a clearing, he came upon the same girl. "My arrival startled her and she ran away, too fast for me to follow. The next dusk, however, she was back again, as if she had known I'd return. This went on through a full cycle of the moon," he said. "A cat-and-mouse game that always ended with her running away whenever I came close."

His handsome face had become brooding, and Catherine inwardly questioned whether she should stop him from continuing. Curious as she was about the course of their relationship—and the depth of it—an uneasiness pervaded her heart. Gradually she was beginning to sense that his detachment from romance had its roots in an experience far in the past. Either Nimue still held claim to his feelings or else she had destroyed them beyond resurrection.

"I returned one night," he was saying, "to find a harp had been left for me. I took it as an invitation that she was getting used to an audience and was willing to request accompaniment to her ballads."

Catherine shuddered, the memory of her second dream burning clear in her imagination. The harp music she had followed in the caverns, the jagged sobbing after the instrument had tumbled from the darkness.

The music, he explained, had been the beginning of their trust and friendship, a common bond they had with the ways of the Ancient Ones. Little by little she began to share more of her life with him and accompany him on his travels.

"I was flattered," he confessed. "It was like having Arthur all over again—someone young to teach and impress with the things I could do. Unlike Arthur, though, she was a quick study, committed to learning all she could in the pretense of assisting me."

"But why did you teach her magic?" Catherine inquired. "I thought magicians kept secrets to themselves."

"What good is a secret," he said with a shrug, "if you're too old to use it? I'm not sure where I got the idea—maybe from Nimue herself—but I began to see that an apprentice would be valuable if Camelot were to survive. There was also the matter of the vision," he added.

"The one about you and a mate?"

"It all began to fit." He nodded. "From what little I knew, Nimue could have been the one I was meant to find. My memory was so weak by then, any memory of the details was foggy at best. For the first time in my life I felt truly wanted, truly loved."

Catherine tried to swallow the lump that lingered in her throat, her mind already anticipating the story's conclusion.

"She led me high into the hills of the Summer Country one night," he said. "By then I was so obsessed with her that I don't think I could have resisted even if I wanted to." Heat stole into his face, the shame still apparent even from having let his trusting nature seal his fate.

"The last sound I remember," he recalled, "was her flaunted pronouncement that she was as barren as Arthur's queen, that no son would come from her joining that night." His mouth dipped into a frown. "What might have been a bittersweet consolation—the knowledge that a child could succeed me—was wiped out by her laughter. The next thing I knew, I was trapped in a cave of crystal from which there was absolutely no escape."

"If there was no escape . . ." Catherine challenged, her muscles tensing.

His voice was calm, his gaze serene. "I said I taught her *almost* everything," he replied. Despite her pleas, he would offer no further explanation.

By the time they returned to her apartment, Catherine had run through an exhaustive list of the places she had been since her move to D.C. None of them impressed her as a feasible hiding spot for Excalibur.

"What if it was a prop in some play I reviewed?" she argued. "Or stuck in a box with a moose head at a garage sale? It could be *anywhere!*"

"No," he countered. "Nimue would never have let that happen. Odds are that even if someone else physically *owns* it, she's never that far away from claiming it at her leisure. Her lust for control is too strong simply to let it go."

"Well, I give up." Catherine shrugged, tossing her windbreaker over the back of the couch. "too bad the Goddess wasn't more specific about how I'm supposed to lead you right to it.

"She has her reasons," he replied. "We just need the key to unlock what those reasons are." He had strolled to the étagère, once more regarding her photographs with a tenderness that touched her.

"I really wish I could help you," she said quietly. "I just don't know what you expect of me."

"Maybe more than I should." He turned to face her, the energy gone from his eyes. For the first time Catherine saw him weary with defeat and felt the crushing reality of her own inadequacy to erase his disappointment.

The question that had played on her lips from the start could no longer be contained. "I know you said it has to be found," she repeated. "And that terrible things could happen if it's used out of its time."

"Yes."

"What will happen . . ." She hesitated, torn between her need to know and her desire to keep her fantasy alive. "What exactly will happen to you?"

He drew her gently down to the couch, his hands clasping both of hers. "For ten years," he said softly, "I've been away from my own century. As you can imagine, the journey itself wasn't without great risk. The longer I remain here, the greater the chance—" His fingers stroked hers lovingly. "That I will die."

Catherine lowered her eyelids to conceal the tears that had built in her realization of a truth too bitter to accept. Without her help Excalibur would be lost forever. And without Excalibur, so would he.

"Could you *make* me remember?" she whispered at last, her eyes conveying a new confidence in him. Certainly a regression to scan the recent past wasn't beyond the realm of possibility.

"I can't *make* you do *anything*," he replied, nonetheless moved by her offer. "My power is limited to illusion."

"But what if I *wanted* to?" she contested. "Couldn't you do something to make me dream about the last time I saw it?"

"I don't know," he said. "I've never tried it."

Catherine scowled, reminded of the dreams she still attributed to his hypnotic intervention. "*I'm* willing to try," she insisted, the trust apparent in her liquid green eyes. "It's worth a shot, isn't it?"

For only an instant she saw a veil of fear darken his expression. "Are you sure you'd want to do this?" he probed.

"What I'm sure of," she replied firmly, "is that it might be our only hope."

He laid her back on the soft cushions, elevating her head with the extra throw pillows. Her dark hair fanned out over their surface like a feathered halo, her hands neatly folded across her waist. As she lay watching him, he drew the drapes against a sky now cloudless and bright.

"What do I have to do?" she asked when he returned to kneel on the floor beside her, his fingers plucking to retrieve the crystal pendant from its resting place against the black curls of his chest.

"Just concentrate," he said soothingly. "Concentrate on the image you saw in the water last night . . . try to drift back to the last time you might have seen it."

As the focus of her eyes moved between the clarity of his face close to hers and the shimmering shadow that rhythmically passed back and forth between them, Catherine felt her eyelids grow heavy.

"When does it start working?" she murmured.

"Think of Excalibur," he replied. "Think back . . ."

His voice became a reverberating echo, her sense of balance slowly spinning, gradually picking up speed. For an instant she sought to call out his name but the sound wouldn't come. Desperately she clung to the white-and-gold image in the Reflecting Pool, repeating to herself his instructions to keep it firm in her mind and not let go.

Even with her eyes tightly closed, she could still see flashes of light swaying in front of her like sparks of playful electricity. The image began to ripple, as if a stone had been cast into the water. Catherine's eyes ached now from straining to see it as, around her, the world became velvet black.

In alarm she realized that his reassuring voice had become faint, drowned out by the pounding thunder of approaching horses.

Chapter Fourteen

CATHERINE'S FIRST IMPRESSION was that something was definitely wrong. Dust clogged her throat as she opened her eyes to find herself in the middle of a dirt road, its surface scarred by deep ruts such as a wagon would leave. The vegetation on either shoulder was sparse; what little there was lay dry and brutally crushed. Certainly this was no place she recognized as within D.C. borders.

She had only a second to consider her surroundings, turning just in time to see three riders on horseback bearing down on her at breakneck speed. Either oblivious to her presence or indifferent to her safety, they came straight at her, leaving her the singular choice of literally diving out of their path. In a cloud of brown dust they were gone, never once looking back at where she lay.

Shaken by the encounter, Catherine unsteadily scrambled to her feet, spitting out the dirt she had swallowed in their passing.

The low vantage point had afforded her only a quick look at the horsemen and barely a glimpse of the silver that hid their faces. The definitive clank of metal had accompanied the sound of hooves and the snorting of the giant beasts as they were ruthlessly driven onward by their masters across the open field.

Catherine shielded her eyes as she looked up the road to see. The trio was becoming tiny in the distance, bent on speed to reach their destination. It was the sight beyond them, though, that made her catch her breath, so striking in its stark simplicity.

Against a sky of pastel blue rose the spires of a mauve-colored castle, its foundation spreading deep like claws into the treacherous promontory on which it was built. A road crudely carved into the cliff's face twisted its way up the side, disappearing into a thicket of dense trees. It was there that the riders were headed, the distant sound of a mournful horn already announcing their arrival.

So distracted was Catherine for the next few minutes by their laborious climb up the side of the hill that she failed to hear the lazy canter of two horses approaching from behind her.

"There's a sight I'll never get tired of!" a young man's voice rang out as the steed drew to a stop. Startled, Catherine wheeled around to see two riders in the path, the one on the right proudly beaming as he pointed at the hilltop fortress.

He looked little more than twenty-one, though his unruly mop of red hair and boyish freckles easily could have camouflaged another decade without betrayal. The broad shoulders and chest tapered down to a trim waist; powerfully built thighs and calves hugged the sides of the chestnut stallion that pawed restlessly at the sun-baked earth.

His clothes were well worn but still serviceable. A thick tunic of rough cloth ended just above the knee, layered over what seemed to be a shirt woven from indeterminate fibers dyed a deep reddish-purple. Coarse tights encased the legs that disappeared into a high boots of blackened leather whose soles were thick with mud.

Dominating the image, however, was his confident bearing. His manner disclosed both a cavalier ease with the surroundings and an unspoken expectation of hospitality from the castle on the headlands.

He decisively swung one leg over his mount and dropped soundlessly to the road. To Catherine's surprise he was striding toward her, his eyes fixed straight ahead, yet not seeing her. Only as she jumped aside to see him move through the space she had just occupied did it occur to her that she was invisible. That, of course, would explain why the earlier riders had nearly trampled her. They thought the path was empty.

"Gawain and Agravain might serve well," he announced. Catherine gathered that this was the continuation of a prior discourse with his companion. "Out from under my sister's thumb they just might learn to be men." Hands planted squarely on his hips, he surveyed the land that lay ahead. "The other twin's too scared of his shadow, of course—not much use to us here. Same for the babe." He frowned a moment, his eyes level under bushy, drawn brows. "For the life of me I can never remember the name of her oldest."

"Mordred" came the sullen reply from the second rider, his flat response drawing Catherine's attention away from the unkempt but likable youth.

The speaker was cloaked from head to toe in a hooded black cape embroidered with silver stars and crescent moons. Only his hands—arthritic and a bluish pale—were visible as they barely held the reins of the smaller black mare.

"Merlin," Catherine whispered hoarsely.

"There's something about the little viper," the younger man continued. "Did you see the way he stared at us up and down like he was witless? Small wonder she wants him gone from Orkney!"

"And closer to the breast of her enemy," the old man murmured.

The remark must have fallen on deaf ears, because the man on foot abruptly changed the subject. "So what does the Sight tell you about my homecoming?" he inquired, barely able to control his enthusiasm.

"Meaning?"

The youth's ruddy cheeks blushed from the indelicacy of the query that followed. "She missed me in her bed, don't you think?"

"I wouldn't doubt it," the older man said with a sigh.

"Well?"

"Well, what?"

"Do you think that tonight—" the redhead ventured, but his companion was already dismissing the implied suggestion.

"Every time you ask me, Arthur," he reminded him, "and every time I tell you the very same thing."

"You've been wrong before," the young king snapped.

"When?"

Exasperated, Arthur declined to answer, putting forth instead his prediction that a lustful romp with his queen would summarily produce a strapping son in nine months. "Wait and see," he boasted.

"Believe what you will." The magician sighed. "I happen to know better."

In one brisk motion the king had remounted his stallion, bringing their debate to a perfunctory close. Only as he turned his horse did Catherine finally see what lay slanted in its sheath on the opposite side of the saddle, its jeweled hilt gleaming magnificently.

"So are you coming along or not?" Arthur inquired with an edge of impatience that could have been fostered either by the length of their journey or by the outcome of their argument.

The hooded figure shook his head. "There's somewhere else I've promised to be," he replied.

Split between which one to follow, Catherine watched them part company—the king headed toward the castle she now assumed to be Camelot, the magician galloping in the opposite direction. Sunlight turned the sword into a sizzling bar of gold and white as the High King sped away from her, its bobbing radiance still visible from a distance.

To the south, the second rider was bound for the forest, the green branches and cool breezes beckoning after tiresome travels.

Again sensing a strange connection to him, Catherine found herself eager to speak with the magician. She started in pursuit of the black-robed figure, but all trace of him had vanished by the time she entered the woods. Her optimism quickly shrank to despair. Ignoring the mocking voice inside that told her she was chasing ghosts, Catherine pressed ahead, her eyes and ears alert and receptive to any sign that she was not alone.

The presence of an unexpected brook reminded Catherine of her thirst. She knelt down to dip her hand into the running water. Clear and clean, it was as cold as mountain ice, dancing over streambed stones as smooth as disks of polished marble.

Catherine leaned in to cup her hands and drink. She was completely unprepared for what happened next.

The reflection she saw through her fingertips startled her, so that she was compelled to let the water trickle down her wrists as she bent farther in. Before she could assimilate what she had just seen, her eyes caught a fleeting glimpse in the water of the sweeping black shadow closing in on top of her. With an inhuman scream the figure toppled Catherine forward, strong hands pushing her head down toward the rocks while its weight sought to immobilize her.

Gasping as her mouth and nose filled with water, Catherine struggled to free herself from her attacker. Her resistance seemed only to incite more violence, the thrusts downward fueled by an energy that seemed superhuman.

The lean fingers found their way to Catherine's throat, the nails digging deep across her windpipe and causing her to choke. As furiously as Catherine attempted to pry them loose, her attacker became that much more determined to hold tight.

With a burst of adrenaline Catherine rolled her weight to the side, hoping to throw her assailant off-balance. An icy splash rolled over them both as they fell into the river, Catherine seizing her chance to squirm away.

Relentlessly the black figure struck out with lightning speed to grab hold of Catherine's hair, yanking her straight back and into the water. Before she could get up, a slippery blackness enveloped her, the heavy fabric of her assailant's robes now drawn tight across her face, covering her nose and mouth.

Catherine struggled to pull it free, aware that her head was completely submerged in the cold water. Her attacker's full weight was straddling her chest and pinning her down.

Arms and legs flailing against her zealous adversary, Catherine felt as if her head would burst from the lack of oxygen. Her strength was giving way, her heart pounding erratically. Mercilessly the hands of her unseen foe pressed downward in cold-blooded fury . . . again and again.

Was it her imagination or did she now hear something? It sounded like shouting, hollowly pulsating through ears filled with water. A feverish anxiety that rescue was on the way provided the impetus to garner what little strength she had left. She vigorously set her hands to slashing out at the body that loomed above her.

Her nails made contact with cool flesh and a tangle of hair. Half crazed in her semi-drowned state, Catherine took frenzied hold of the heavy cloth her fingers met and gave it a vicious tug. The cloth fell away, flooding her eyes, nose, and mouth with stinging bubbles of freezing water that made her wince in shock. Blindly she tried to focus on the face that lingered over her, but the water imposed a mottled screen that blinded her sight.

Rough hands grabbed her shoulders and threw her back with brute force into the streambed, causing her to strike her head against an outcropping of rock on the embankment. Gulping for air as the sensation of hot, sticky liquid exploded at the back of her skull, Catherine squinted once more to see the face of her killer. The image began to fade, and she fought for consciousness, screaming as her eyes adjusted on the dark-haired man who sought to restrain her on her living-room couch.

"Catherine!" he shouted. Kyle's face was as white as a sheet, the terror in his eyes closely matching her own. Disoriented, she tried to pull away from him, her jaws clenched tight in fear and her fists coiled in defense. "What is it?" he demanded, his hands holding tight to her wrists. With a gasp Catherine stared up at the thin line across his cheek that was starting to turn red, her eyes and throat giving way to a floodgate of hysterical sobbing.

Spontaneously he gathered her up in his arms, cradling her head against his chest. "I'm here," he whispered, stroking her hair. "I'm here, Catherine.

As gently as a feather, she felt his lips graze her forehead, heard him repeat her name over and over. With trembling limbs she clung to him, longing for the crushing warmth of his body to erase the intensity of her nightmare.

"Don't try to talk just yet," he urged, the color slowly returning to his face. "Take it easy."

"How long was I out?" she attempted to ask, her words cracked and dry.

"Only a few minutes," he replied. "When I realized you were having a bad dream . . ."

But Catherine was dismissing his answer with an emphatic shake of her head. "It was longer than that," she insisted. "I was doing just what you told me. I was thinking about the sword, and then things started to spin." The words tumbled out carelessly over each other. "I woke up in this strange place that—" She scowled in anger, the details already slipping away from her memory. Fresh tears choked back her words as she gingerly reached toward the ugly scratch on his cheek, the one left by her own hand. "I didn't mean—"she started to say. His smile protested that apology was unnecessary.

"I should never have agreed to it in the first place," he said, his voice curiously guarded. "We'll just have to find Excalibur some other way."

The mention of the name sharply triggered her subconscious and she blurted out what she anticipated would please him, the revelation that at least the mystical sword had been part of her dream. "What doesn't fit," she argued, "is that you told me to think back to the last time I—" The words died on her lips as she read the sudden and unmistakable look of entrapment reflected in his eyes.

In stark horror came her first chilling suspicion that she had followed his instructions more precisely than she dared imagine.

Chapter Fifteen

CATHERINE REFUSED TO be pacified by his excuse of subliminal suggestion, his observation that everyone, from time to time, felt the sense they had lived before and dreamed accordingly. "You've been absorbing so much about Arthur lately that—" His explanation was cut short by her insistence that external influences weren't the cause.

"There's something you haven't told me," she accused, her eyes flashing with renewed fire. *"None* of this was by *accident."* Not their meeting. Not their subsequent involvement. Not his request for her help.

"Nothing ever is," he replied, at a loss to dispel the thick wall that had come up between them. "Whatever it is that you think you saw—"

"What I *know* I saw," she said, correcting him. There were still gaps in her recollection but not enough to dissuade her from the belief that she had caught a glimpse of an earlier incarnation, an existence he seemed just as earnest to deny. "Why won't you tell me?"

"I've told you the only things you *need* to know, Catherine." Hunched forward, he rested on his elbows on his knees, absently staring at the pattern in the Oriental rug. "More than that would only complicate your life."

"I think your *arrival* took care of that," she replied impatiently. "Complications are becoming commonplace."

"This obsession about the dream you just had—"

"Which wasn't really a dream," she said, interrupting. Before he could continue, she seized on a question to test him. "What color was Arthur's hair?" she asked.

"Why?"

"Just tell me what color Arthur's hair was."

With reluctance he replied that it had been red, that Arthur had inherited the same fierce coloring as all the prior Pendragons.

"There's no way I could have known that!" she maintained. "I could only know that from seeing him for myself."

It was a heated argument that continued for the next half hour, with neither of them relenting. Even his advice that the violence she had suffered in her sleep would best be forgotten, failed to shake her supposition that she had relived a death from a past life at the hands of a black-garbed enemy.

"For that matter," she hotly retorted, "it could have been *you*." Even as she said them, it was too late to grab the hurtful words back. Her face flushed with humiliation and anger at herself as she watched his jaw tighten and his luminous eyes widen in blunt astonishment. With fearful clarity she realized that her barbed annoyance had propelled her into a distrust that was neither healthy nor warranted. Certainly if he meant her harm, there had been more opportunities in the past few days than the isolated incident of the regression she, herself, had urged him to conduct. Maybe the startled look she had read in his face had only been anxiety for her well-being, as he claimed, and not an admission of guilt.

Wordlessly she stared across at him. Her eyes filled with tears of frustration as she placed a tentative hand on his forearm. "I shouldn't have said that," she apologized, the accusation still sour in her throat.

He regarded her with a cool neutrality that had a far more devastating effect on her than the anger she would have expected. Her hand slid to the couch as he stood up, her mind racing for the words to make him stay should he start walking toward the door.

Heart pounding, she watched as he stood there, immobile. And in that moment she saw more than a wizard whose intentions she had challenged. Here was a sensitive man whose pride she had wounded with a too hasty remark. No matter what he professed about his tenure in her century or his single-minded mission to find Excalibur, his human side was clearly vulnerable. And possibly also frightened.

The next words that fell from his lips were neither a rebuttal nor a show of forgiveness. "Why are you afraid of me, Catherine?" he asked quietly, piercing the distance between them with a look that told her he had known her misgivings from the very start. "Is it because of my power as Merlin?"

"It's not Merlin the magician who scares me," she replied, summoning the courage to reveal to him what her heart had been trying to convince her of all along. She was already destined to lose him, she rationalized. To let him go without a single word would only prove a torment in the years to come, wondering if the truth might have made a difference.

His face softened slightly, an eyebrow arched in query. "Who, then?" he asked.

Her voice was steady in its conviction. "Kyle Falconer . . . the man," she replied.

Her answer puzzled him. "Because he's an illusion?"

She looked up and beheld deep brown eyes that genuinely wanted to understand her cryptic meaning.

"Because he's just real enough to hurt me far worse than any dragons or abracadabras." Resolutely she rose to her full height. "Maybe you *shouldn't* have come into my life," she said, her eyes glistening with moisture, "because now I can't picture it without you."

Tender surprise washed over his face. He murmured her name, and as his fingers reached out to catch the fresh tear that hovered on her left cheek, his touch was almost unbearable in its softness. Then, as if the gesture suddenly seemed insufficient, he swung her into the protective cradle of his arms, his nearness overwhelming her with desire.

"I'd never let *anything* hurt you," he whispered, his voice simmering with barely checked passion as he pressed her head close to his chest, stroking her hair in soothing reassurance. "Especially not myself."

Lightly he fingered a loose curl at her neck, his breathing sporadic and warm as she tilted her head back to look at him. Both of them simultaneously yielded to the unspoken need to draw closer to each other.

Catherine felt her knees weaken as his lips slowly descended to meet hers, caressing her mouth more than kissing it as his grip tightened at her waist. Sensuously he massaged the hollows of her back as his tongue traced the soft fullness of the lips that hungered to be taken. Like an awakened river, Catherine felt the blood course through her veins as the delicious sensation of his mouth covered hers, smothering it with a savage intensity that invited more.

His touch was a pleasure, pure and explosive, his indelible kiss hurtling her beyond the point of no return. Yet as he raised his mouth from hers, the eyes that searched Catherine's face were curiously asking for pardon, not for permission to claim what she willingly longed to give.

"I think I'm the one who should say 'I'm sorry,'" he said, caressing her cheek with his fingertip.

Catherine opened her mouth to protest, but he was already releasing his hand from where it had traveled to her hip, his face reflecting a self-conscious turmoil she was unsure how to quell.

"Maybe it would do both of us some good," he proposed, "to put Excalibur aside for the afternoon . . . go out for a change of scenery."

"And do what?" Catherine asked. She wondered if his suggestion could be tied to a graceful break from a situation that had rapidly grown too intense for either of them to handle.

"This is your time and your city," he said softly. "Is there anything special you like to do when you need to unwind?"

The question made Catherine smile, reminding her of how little of the mundane they really knew about each other—his favorite color, her favorite meal, which books they both read, whom they'd support in politics. In retrospect she had learned all of those things and more in the first three hours she had dated Nat. Largely owing, of course, to Nat's fondness for talking about himself.

As for Kyle Falconer, Catherine had a suspicion that even in the full course of a lifetime she'd still never know all of his secrets.

"I used to go to plays and galleries to relax," she said with a chuckle. "Of course, now that I get paid to do it for a job, it's not quite the same." In amusement she recalled how she had attended a show case of one-acts as a casual spectator and ended up throwing the cast and director into a panic that she had shown up unannounced to review them. "Definite drawbacks to a byline with my picture under it," she added.

"What else do you like to do?" he asked her tenderly.

"Well, I guess a mainstay from my childhood is going to museums." Catherine explained that it was her father who had first introduced her to the serenity of strolling from exhibit to exhibit. "My earliest memory," she said, "was riding on his shoulders and looking at covered wagons that brought people to the West for gold."

"You mean, they couldn't conjure it up by alchemy?" he teased, obviously enjoying her reminiscence. Wanting to please her, he inquired whether there were any museums nearby.

Catherine had to suppress a laugh. "Are you kidding? This is Washington, D.C., the museum capital of the world!"

For reasons still a profound mystery to mankind and Congress, the entire estate of James Smithson had been magnanimously willed to the United States government in the 1830s. An English philanthropist, Smithson himself had never set foot on American shores, but with his death he had provided the financial backing to establish the institution that would proudly bear his name.

The Smithsonian was, in fact, not just one museum but many, all charged with the purpose of increasing and diffusing knowledge in accordance with Smithson's master plan to educate humanity.

First ladies' ball gowns and dinosaurs, space capsules, and Impressionist art took center stage in the buildings that graced either side of the two-mile-long mall between the Lincoln Memorial and the Capitol. "I think you could spend a month in any of them," Catherine observed, "and still not manage to see everything."

Faced with the decision of which one to visit, Kyle deferred to Catherine's judgment, cocking his head in interest at the choice she pointed to on Constitution and 10th. Home to a host of reconstructed Ice Age mammals, meteorites and the 45½ carat Hope Diamond, the Museum of Natural History was a multilevel microcosm of the planet's evolution. "I used to come here a lot when I first moved to Washington," she explained, extolling the power of natural phenomena to reduce life's trials to trivialities by comparison.

Her enthusiasm prepared him for the sight that always astonished tourists upon entering the magnificent rotunda—a charging African bull elephant preserved by taxidermy and substantially dwarfing the spectators who posed at its platform for pictures. "The first time I saw it," Catherine told him, "my theory was that they must have brought back the elephant, set him up in the middle of the park, and build the museum around him."

Hand in hand they strolled past dioramas that chronicled the origins of man and beast, Catherine drawing his attention to the pieces she especially liked. Without question she had inherited an insatiable curiosity and appreciation of the past.

"What a wonderful thing it must have been for you," he remarked as they stood together before the glass case that displayed the world's most precious gems. "Having a father to share his wisdom is something no child should be without."

His words touched a chord of loneliness in her, and she looked up to see him enviously watching a young father hold his son up to the exhibit. "I think yours would have been proud of you," she offered softly. "*Whoever* he was . . ."

Each absorbed in their private thoughts, they continued on in silence for the length of the hall. Fervently Catherine's imagination replayed the dizzying intensity of their kiss, her heart longing to shatter the shell of his resistance that had been centuries in the making. In bitter acknowledgment she saw all too clearly that her predecessor's act of seduction had immunized him against any second chance at love. *Her* love. As ravenously as his lips had devoured hers and his hands had explored her soft curves, she instinctively knew then—as she knew now—that he would never again allow himself to feel anything beyond Platonic friendship.

Not a word more had been exchanged about her dream or its perplexing content. Hard as she tried to remember, her mind refused to be jogged on exactly what had struck her as so shocking at the stream's edge just before the brutal attack. Somberly she weighed the considerations of bringing it up now in a neutral setting, reluctant to let more time slip away lest it take further details with it. The worst he could do, she decided, was say no.

They had paused at the elevator, Kyle having casually suggested a moment before that they grab something to eat in the downstairs cafeteria.

"There's something I need to talk about," she began, hoping her voice concealed the anxiety she felt inside. "I've been thinking about the dream. . . ."

In confusion she realized that he hadn't heard her. Instead, there was a look of alarm in his eyes as they lay fixed on the exhibit of ancient weapons that stood twenty feet away.

Chapter Sixteen

"BUT IT CAN'T be," Catherine contested as they both stared at the sword on display between a blackened iron mace and a Turkish scimitar. "It doesn't look *anything* like what you showed me."

Rusted and devoid of jewels, only fourteen inches of the sword's shaft remained beneath the twisted hilt. The rest was jaggedly broken off. All but obliterated by the trials of time and war were the roughly engraved suggestions of the letters *W, V,* and *R.*

"Whosoever draweth this sword from the stone . . ." he murmured, his face a study of reverent humility as he gazed through the thick glass at what he had come so far to find. A chill raced down Catherine's spine as he recalled aloud the Goddess's prophecy. "It was in plain sight, as she said it would be, Catherine. And you led me right to it."

"But how can you be certain?" Catherine challenged, puzzled by the ugly metal that bore no resemblance to the glorious original. "You told me that its appearance couldn't be changed."

"Only by time. What you're seeing is the result of a journey that never should have taken place."

"I still don't see how it—" Catherine cut her sentence short as an older couple and a serviceman meandered in from the left to get a better look at the exhibit they were blocking. Impatient for them to move on, Catherine's eyes roamed over the display once more, taking in the calligraphy plaque that identified the weapon only as ENGLISH, LATE FIFTH CENTURY. It was the inscription below, however that seized the larger share of her attention, its content attesting to the anonymous donation of the sword to the Smithsonian exactly ten years earlier. The same amount of time that Kyle Falconer had spent looking for it.

As the trio of visitors exited past the case and she turned to share her discovery, Catherine experienced a rush of panic. The magician was raising his palm and moving it slowly toward the glass. In all of their discussions about searching for Excalibur the question had never been brought up of exactly *how* he was going to go about stealing it back. Certainly a theft in broad daylight in a public corridor flanked by two security guards didn't seem a wise strategy, particularly if he vanished and left her to explain.

She parted her lips to question him, then stopped, shocked to see him suddenly wince with pain and withdraw his hand as if it had just been burned by a hot surface. "What is it? What's wrong?" she blurted out, spontaneously taking the fist he was kneading in anguish. Tender red blisters dotted his fingertips as well as the heel of his hand where it had barely touched the transparent wall.

"Even *here* she's using magic to protect it," he muttered, his eyes searing with fresh hatred.

"Nimue?" Catherine started to ask, uneasy about the attention his brief outcry had attracted. One of the Smithsonian guards was already starting to stroll in their direction.

Swiftly Catherine linked her arm through Kyle's, urging him to walk away from the exhibit with her. It was all she could do to keep him from peering back, intuition telling her that the guard was probably watching them. "Trust me," she whispered. "We know where it is, at least. But that guard's not going to let us get within ten feet of it right now." Her mind searched rapidly for a solution. "Let's take a break and go downstairs to the cafeteria for a few minutes. I promise you, after all that commotion, there's no way that sword's going to go anywhere in the next half hour."

Glancing furtively at the guard, Kyle agreed reluctantly, his mind still not entirely sold on the idea.

"Why would she have to use magic?" Catherine asked as they settled into a corner table along with two sodas and a bag of chips. "If it really *is* Nimue, why would she bother to use some kind of spell? As far as she's concerned, you're not even *here*."

"She knows the Goddess," he replied. "She must have anticipated—even when she stole it—that it would be only a matter of time before someone would be sent after her." He was still favoring his injured hand, the surface skin obviously still smarting as much as his ego.

"I guess that leads to an obvious question," Catherine remarked. "Why did the Goddess let her get away with it to begin with?" His stories of an omnipresent spirit indicated that nothing was outside the reach of her power. How, then, could she have missed an act of destructive mischief being plotted by one of her own followers? By all logic she could have prevented its removal . . . and yet didn't.

"To answer that," he replied reluctantly, "I'd have to tell you what became of Nimue after my own downfall in the cave of crystal."

"Something tells me," Catherine observed, "that you don't really want to."

"Maybe because every minute of its telling is a minute lost from the time where Excalibur belongs."

"True, but if it's got some kind of"—she shrugged in confusion as she searched for the right word—"what is it? A spell? If she's the one who put it on, she's probably the one who'll have to take it off. Your rushing back upstairs isn't going to accomplish anything." She reached across the table, lightly resting her fingers on his wrist. "I just thought if you could tell me more about what she did, we might be able to figure out some kind of plan."

"We?" he repeated, a smile teasing his lips. "I'm afraid I can't let you get any more involved than you already have been. Helping me find it—"

"No!" Catherine objected, her anxiety rising that their time together was no longer being measured in weeks or months, but hours, maybe less. "I *want* to help, I'm a *part* of this, much as you may want to deny it."

"I appreciate the offer," he said, nodding, "but I don't think you have any idea what you could be getting into."

"Meaning what?"

"Meaning that it seems you've already forgotten what I've told you about Nimue protecting what's hers. If she's somewhere in the building . . ." He hesitated, his eyes imploring. "I don't want you anywhere near here if there's a confrontation."

119

Catherine's expression hardened, implacable in her determination to stay with him as long as possible. "That's not our decision to make," she informed him, tilting her chin in a show of defiance. "Are you going to tell me or not?" she persisted.

"A promise first," he countered.

Beneath the table, Catherine crossed her index and middle fingers, a gesture from her childhood that silently canceled out any pledges made under duress. "Okay," she said, "I promise."

"Long before her path crossed mine," he began, "it was already destiny that Nimue would become High Priestess—a mantle she wore with cool dignity and unquestionable satisfaction. Unfortunately the respect she demanded was backed up with heavy threat. Nimue's penchant for making her own rules raised the ire of the Goddess and the resentment of her followers."

"So what did the Goddess do?" Catherine inquired. "Could she demote her . . . like maybe to a tree?"

"I'm afraid it wasn't that simple," he explained, "desirous a solution as that might have been. You see, the troubled times were well in force by then. The Lake People's numbers were dwindling, their members marked for annihilation by a society that Arthur as king could no longer reasonably influence. In a desperate measure to carry out what was right and just, Arthur implored the Goddess to provide an adviser such as I had been. Who better for her to send than my own student?"

"But if she was so impetuous," Catherine argued, "wouldn't that only make things worse?"

"No," he continued. "Even Nimue would see the importance of preserving the kingdom. Without Camelot's protection—limited as it had come to be—the worshipers of the Goddess would eventually be driven from the Earth." Across the table, he winked at her. "Not much different, I suppose, from putting the school bully in charge of the classroom and watching him instantly reform under his new found power. Perhaps the Goddess secretly hoped the burden of responsibility would change her unruly daughter for the better."

"Apparently the idea didn't work," Catherine pointed out. "Camelot fell, anyway."

"Who's to say," he said with a shrug, "that it wouldn't have ended sooner had she not been there? At any rate, it was her presence within the castle at the last that ultimately led to the greatest treachery of all."

His eyes reflected a bitter distaste for what had transpired. "To Nimue's credit," he went on, "she remembered my warnings about Mordred—that the illegitimate offspring of Arthur and his half sister, Morgause, would one day spell the end of a golden kingdom, that kingdom being Camelot. In spite of our warnings, Arthur was put in the position of finally having to acknowledge the boy as his only heir."

"But why?" Catherine asked. "So far it sounds as if no one up to that point paid much attention to laws or etiquette."

"Arthur might not have paid much attention, either," he agreed, "if it hadn't been for his own memories of a country plunged into turmoil without a king. I'm sure, deep down, he was only doing what he thought was best for Britain, assuring his people that a son would succeed him if death should come in his war against Lancelot."

"What did Nimue say to that?"

"It wasn't what she *said*," he replied, "but what she claimed later to have *done*."

"Which was?"

"Substitute Excalibur with a fake."

"What?" Catherine gasped. "You mean the one he used in the last battle, the one that was laid next to him on the barge—"

"No," he said in a low, composed voice. "Although at the time that is what Arthur's followers thought. But Nimue only *claimed* to have switched them. She used the coincidence of Arthur's tragedy at Birdoswald as false evidence of her sincere but foiled attempt to keep Excalibur from being stolen by Mordred and transferred to him after his father's death."

"Mordred?" she repeated. "How does *he* fit in?"

"As a convenient scapegoat for what must have been her master plan from the very beginning. He was thought of so despicably by almost everyone who knew him that one more black mark against his name presumably would never be questioned."

It was the time frame now that puzzled Catherine. Unless she was wrong, there was still a gap of three hundred years for which he had yet to account.

"The actual switch," he explained, "took place on the night of

Arthur's funeral. Nimue knew full well that once the sword slid beneath the waves in the channel of Avalon, all chance of seizing it would be lost. She waited until just before the oils were lit by flame to approach Arthur's battle-weary contingent with her carefully rehearsed confession."

"And they believed her?"

For a second he seemed lost in thought, his brow furrowed as if trying to recall something important. "As mortals, they had little choice," he finally replied. "If her own people feared her powers, you can imagine what it was like for ordinary men. They knew who she was and had seen her too often in consultation with the High King to challenge her motives. Arthur's death had stunned them to the core. Nimue's attribution that the duplicate sword had been the cause persuaded them to relinquish it in exchange for what they believed to be the real one."

"But why did she hold off so long after that to make her escape?" Catherine wanted to know. "What was she waiting for?"

"Initially," hew speculated, "it would have been to avert suspicion of wrongdoing. Her sudden disappearance would raise too many questions. Second in her mind—and the one that would soon after swell in importance—was the legend that a new king would one day come to power and need Excalibur's magic. Naturally she saw her possession of the sword as a golden chance to dictate the direction of the fledgling regime. What king wouldn't be indebted to her for handing it over and teaching him its power?"

"Where was the Lady of the Lake all this time?"

"Do you mean, did she know what was going on?" In thoughtful deliberation he rolled back his cuffs, exposing the thin layer of silky black hair that started above his wrists. "She'd be a poor excuse for a goddess if she didn't," he remarked. "But like a patient mother who time and again forgives her child's transgressions, it was her choice to allow Nimue every chance to come forward voluntarily."

"I guess after three hundred years went by"—Catherine smirked—"she figured out that it wasn't very likely."

"Time passes differently among our kind." He smiled. "It was not so long as to be forgotten but just long *enough* to pose a threat of danger. The Goddess at last called together her council and ordered Nimue to produce Excalibur for its proper return to the sea. Instead

Nimue decided to escape with it, using one of the same tricks she had begged *me* to teach her back in the days of innocence."

Once more his brow creased. Catherine could feel his preoccupation even as he was talking to her. His abrupt query of what time the museum closed rekindled her concern that desperation would compel him to act rashly.

"About an hour and a half," she replied, shaken by the firm order that followed her response.

"I want you to leave, Catherine." The cold dignity with which he spoke made a stony mask of his features.

"Leave? What do you—"

"It's going to be too dangerous for you to stay here." Strong hands grasped hers matter-of-factly, squeezing them tightly. "You're going to have to let me do this myself." Clearly a plan had taken shape in his mind, even as they sat talking, a plan he had resolved to put into effect immediately.

"I don't understand," she protested, searching his face for hidden meaning. "You need my help. What could be so dangerous about my giving it to you?"

"You have to leave," he repeated. "If not right now and at my request, then by the museum guards when they start the evacuation."

"What are you talking about?"

A gleam of resurging confidence shimmered behind the dark riddle of his eyes. "Upstairs, in about twenty minutes," he said knowingly, "there's going to be a fire."

Chapter Seventeen

THE IMPLICATION OF his announcement sent a flush of anger across Catherine's face. Through clenched teeth, barely above a whisper, she challenged that the importance of Excalibur couldn't be put above the safety of the museum's visitors and staff, not to mention the loss of priceless artifacts. "I can't let you do that," she flatly informed him, not at all sure how she'd even begin to go about stopping someone as powerful as she knew him to be.

"Do you really believe," he said, "that I'd do any serious harm to something that you treasured?"

"I think that a fire," Catherine pointed out, "falls into the category of 'serious harm,' don't you?"

"Not if it's only an illusion." Gone was the steely edge to his words. It was replaced by a tender insistence that he knew what he was doing. "She's afraid of it," he said, recalling to himself and to Catherine an old memory of Nimue's dread of flames. "To any creature of the forest," he continued, "fire represents a force, a power, beyond even magic."

"I thought the idea was to draw her out, not scare her off."

"Excalibur," he replied, "is the one thing she'll risk her life for. If I know her as well as I think I do, her priority will be to get the sword as fast as she can and remove it from danger."

"You mean, she won't know the fire isn't real?"

"Not until it's too late. By the time she realizes it, I'll already be gone."

Swallowing the pain that rose in her throat, Catherine looked up at him, unable to accept the dull ache of foreboding. A stab of guilt assailed her senses at the bitter truth that at this moment she'd rather jeopardize the world than face tomorrow without him. "You'll really be leaving . . . as soon as you have it?" she forced out the words.

"I have to," he whispered with grim resolve. "I've known that ever since I arrived."

In resignation Catherine nodded, mindful of the blunt honesty that had pervaded their conversation on the night she imagined he had scaled her apartment balcony to seduce her. Kyle Falconer had always kept in the foreground his determination to do what was expected of him.

"If it's not a real fire," she tried once more, "I wouldn't be in any real danger."

He bent his head to study the slender fingers that gripped his in feverish anxiety. "It's not the fire you'd be in danger of, Catherine."

"You can't mean Nimue, then. She doesn't even *know* me!"

The soft brush of his palm on her cheek make her long for the protectiveness of his arms and the sensuous vitality of his body.

"She'll know that you helped me," he replied. "That alone will be enough to make you a target of her wrath. And without me here to protect you . . ." He shook his head. "It's better this way. For both of us." Taking a deep, unsteady breath, he withdrew both hands and pushed back his chair. Catherine was on her feet as quickly as he was, fearful for the moment that had come.

"I want to be with you," she whispered, her voice edged with tears.

His hands slipped up her arms, bringing her closer. "You always will be," he promised, his breath hot against her ear. "Remember that, Catherine."

The urgency of their parting and the shiver of her own wanting drove her to lock her arms around the back of his neck, pressing her body as closely to his as she could, oblivious to the sounds and sights around her. His grip tightened as she buried her face against his throat.

The heady sensation of his mouth against her cheek demanded a response, and she parted her lips as his own claimed hers with savage mastery. Whatever calm she might have had in reserve was explosively shattered by the hungry, exploratory message of his tongue and the tantalizing tenderness of the hands that intimately encircled her waist.

Passion pounded the blood through her head and chest, her heart screaming for the privacy to finish what they had begun. Her desire for him outweighed everything else, fueled by the awareness that he, too, was physically responding to the unspoken but powerful message that bound them as one.

When he abruptly removed his mouth from hers and held her away from him, Catherine felt that her very flesh was being stripped away.

"I have to leave now," he said, softening the blow with a heart-rending gaze and a sweet disclosure. "Much as my conscience tells me I'm going to regret this good-bye . . ."

Only their fingers prolonged his departure, interlocked in a sensual vow that said more than words.

"Will I ever see you again?" Her voice quavered, her body fighting its own battle of personal restraint.

His reply was neither an encouraging affirmation nor a blunt denial. "If it's the will of the Goddess," he answered, his eyes drinking in the memory he would carry back with him to another time and place. "She's the only one who knows."

Even through his fingertips she could sense his supple muscles tensing as he reminded her to leave as soon as she heard the alarms go off in the upper corridor. Catherine swallowed hard and squared her shoulders as his hand slipped from hers. Without moving, she watched him walk away, hesitating only as he reached the cafeteria exit. Her heart caught in her throat as she anxiously waited for him to turn around for one last look. Instead he kept going, leaving Catherine to the sensation of desolation and grief that swept over her.

Trembling as she stood there, her eyes stinging with hot tears, Catherine knew then—as she had suspected all along—that there was only one choice she could make. "Forgive me, love," she murmured to herself. She hurried toward the doorway with the decisive stride of a woman who knew what she wanted.

A child's bloodcurdling scream for his mother pierced the librarylike quietude of the second floor as a literal curtain of red and orange flames sprang up, clear to the ceiling, just left of the weapons exhibit. Within seconds the hall was a cacophony of alarms, loud shouting, and pounding footsteps as visitors scrambled for the exits. From an alcove just around the corner from the elevator, Catherine watched as the crowd blurred past her in the rush to safety. Her eyes strained to find the magician as he lay in wait for his enemy.

Visitors from the higher levels clattered down the stairs, prodded on by the guards who yelled to make themselves heard above the crowd. Menacingly the inferno's scarlet fingers teased the wood and glass, coiling themselves like liquid serpents around the nearest displays. All except one.

Above the din, Catherine heard shouting that demanded to know why the overhead sprinklers hadn't gone on. Across the corridor she could see two guards fumbling to fling open a metal door behind which lay a blinking circuit board. Her gaze traveled upward to the sheet of fire that danced along the high ceiling, inches from the valves that would release water on the room below at the first hint of smoke. If there *was* smoke. In the rush of confusion only Catherine was aware of its startling absence and the lack of accompanying smell that a fire of such magnitude would generate in the wake of its destruction.

Mesmerized by the skill of Kyle's deception, Catherine continued to watch, shrinking back against the wall only when she feared discovery by the guards intent on the efficient rescue of a frightened public. And then she saw her.

At first glance the blonde in the navy linen suit blended with the frenetic crowd that moved past Catherine toward the stairs. Her blazer insignia identified her as a museum employee yet, unlike her peers, she moved quickly among the evacuees without making a single helpful gesture or offering a word of encouragement to them. In the flash of profile Catherine glimpsed a complexion as flawless as porcelain and golden hair swept back in a style that added several years to a youthful exterior. She was shorter than Catherine but was possessed of a body that, even attired in a professional ensemble, suggested a sensuous and alluring physique.

Catherine watched intently as the woman moved with trepidation toward the case that protected Excalibur, tossing a glance over her shoulder as she approached the glass. Only then did Catherine see the naked fear written across the woman's face.

Catherine crept forward, barely daring to breathe, lest the slightest sound—even masked by the din of chaos—betray her presence. A fat woman, her sides already heaving from the exertion of descending one flight of stairs, jostled into her, throwing her off-balance against the wall.

"This way, ma'am," a stern voice barked in Catherine's ear as a guard caught her elbow and tried to steer her into the mainstream of people. Resourceful thinking prompted Catherine to thank him and briskly move along with the crowd, extricating herself from them as soon as possible and slipping back into the corridor. Her point of exit now left her without a place to hide should the woman she now sensed beyond doubt was Nimue turn around.

The magician was nowhere in sight, and Catherine gulped back the fear that her intervention in a conflict not her own might hinder rather than aid his recovery of the legendary weapon. Even as she forced herself to dismiss such negative thoughts, her complete focus was drawn now to the trancelike posture of the golden blonde, whose left hand extended toward the case that reflected in its glass the sparkling brilliance of the crackling fire.

Fear and anger knotted inside Catherine, the latter gaining in momentum as she silently relived the anguish of Merlin's descent into shame. Before her stood the woman whose insatiable greed had deceived the wizard for his secrets and Britain's own people for the one symbol of its unity. A sheer black fright swept through her as she remembered his praise of the weapon's power . . . its malevolent destiny in the hands of the wrong person, a person of Nimue's choosing. Catherine bit her lip as the blonde's fingertips made contact with the glass, effortlessly proceeding to pass straight through it. An ice-blue light set the hand to glow that emerged on the other side, the fingers squeezing hold of Excalibur's tarnished hilt and lifting it from the velvet pedestal, the entire display ablaze with an iridescent radiance that matched the fire in its intensity.

All around them the hysteria continued, yet Catherine was aware only of the drama her frightened eyes were witnessing. With measured caution Nimue was withdrawing the sword from the case as though from an unseen slit, the metal's blue gleam vanishing as it

128

came in contact with the air outside the case.

Still the magician hadn't appeared. Catherine felt her temperature rise in response, a desperate feeling permeating her soul that she had to take some kind of action, any action, to prevent Nimue from escaping.

Suddenly, as if the flames themselves had spoken, Catherine knew where he was. And in that moment she knew exactly what she had to do. Another second would be too late. The nearest guards were furiously breaking out fire extinguishers to battle the unexplainable inferno in their midst.

Summoning all of her strength, Catherine ran full force at Nimue just as she turned. The impact of the blow sent them both sprawling to the museum floor.

"I'm awfully sorry! Here, let me help you!" Catherine dramatically sputtered in the pretense of an accidental collision. To her relief the sword had been thrown out of Nimue's hand, clattering to the ground just inches from the curtain of flames.

With a ferocity that better suited an animal of the wild than a human, Nimue ruthlessly pushed Catherine aside, scrambling to see where her prize had fallen. Annoyance was immediately replaced with outraged shock as she wheeled around to see the black-haired man rising from where he had bent down to retrieve the sword.

Despite her fears, Catherine felt a hot and awful joy as she realized the plan had been a success. With a guttural snarl the blonde lunged at the figure whose silhouette was framed by the fire, shrinking back as he parried the jagged point in warning.

"You!" the woman screamed, her knuckles glowing white in anger as she stared in dumfounded horror at him. For what seemed an eternity, neither of them moved, trapped in a standoff of iron wills. Then he began to lower the sword, his eyes blinking as if blinded by dust. Terror-stricken, Catherine realized what was happening, her quick glance falling on the sardonic grin that was spreading on Nimue's face.

"No!" Catherine yelled out, the noise shaking him from the trance in which his enemy sought to ensnare him. In alarm he looked in her direction, as if he were startlingly aware for the first time of her presence. "Go!" she yelled again. "Now!"

His own hesitation clutched at her heart. She felt a fresh surge of panic that he would risk his own escape to protect her.

"Go," her lips silently pleaded. "It's what I want. . . ."

The hot, yellow tongues enveloped him as he stepped back into their fiery brilliance, the broken tip of Excalibur disappearing last. With a scream Nimue turned her full fury on Catherine. "Get him back!" She snarled, her copper-colored eyes viciously impaling her new quarry.

Stunned by their face-to-face exchange, Catherine momentarily recoiled, shaken by the violent impact of recognition, the electrifying knowledge that she had seen those very same eyes before.

Like a cat stalks its pray, Nimue circled, her fingers curled to attack. Too late Catherine discovered that Nimue had maneuvered her into a vulnerable position, blocking off escape to the corridor.

"What are you going to do now, little girl?" Nimue sneered, her left hand raising like a evil talon, her lips curled back in hatred.

The flames were hot at Catherine's back. Yet their warmth gave a strange comfort, for they were a product of the man she trusted above everyone else. "They're only an illusion." His words floated back to her. "The one thing she's afraid of . . . an illusion of fire . . . she won't know until it's over . . . illusion . . . illusion . . ."

"There's no escape for you." Nimue laughed wickedly, drawing back her poised hand as if to hurl a thunderbolt.

With a rush of adrenaline Catherine hurled herself through the curtain of crimson flame. Her last recollection was that of spiraling downward through an abyss of crystal-lit stars.

Chapter Eighteen

Two DEER BOUNDED out of the thicket, the buck's magnificent antlers matching in color the silver-limbed beech that grew at the forest's edge. Sweet honeysuckle tickled their soft brown noses and the doe dropped behind her mate, her silky ears twitching appreciatively at the familiar sounds of dusk's approach. It had rained steadily all afternoon, turning the mossy earth moist and painting the massive tree trunks wet and shining. Only in the last half hour of daylight had it finally stopped, with the slate-gray clouds dissolving into feathered wisps of pink and amber on the English horizon.

Food had not been plentiful that spring, forcing the wildlife farther down from the hills than they were accustomed or comfortable. The scent of man was prevalent here, heightening the caution of the two tawny creatures as they crossed a crystalline stream to the enticing bounty of junipers and coralberry on the opposite side.

The doe drank long and deep of the water, mindful of her mate's telepathic communication to be wary in this part of the woods. Hunters with ugly crossbows and deadly arrows could be anywhere, ghoulishly delighting in reducing their herds as if for heinous sport. It had been different in the Old Days. Much different.

A crackling underbrush prompted them both to freeze, the buck bracing to give the signal for his lady to run. Unspoken as always was the sacrifice he would make of his own life for hers, for the horned crown upon his head would make him well worthy of a gamesman's pursuit, enabling her to flee to high ground. His nostrils flared in puzzlement, for it was not a human scent carried on the breeze but that of an animal foreign to him. His mate cocked her gentle head as if to ask him what it was, slowly following his gaze to the low branch of ash leaves that barely rustled to their right.

Tentatively a bright point of gold poked through the foliage, followed in turn by the snowy-white forehead of the beast who owned it, its china-blue eyes blinking back through long black lashes at the two creatures from whose stream it wished to drink.

The doe—her manner customarily polite—could not help but blatantly stare at the new animal as it emerged from its hiding place, its dainty goat-like hooves leaving not a single mark upon the rain-washed soil. Never before had the deer seen anything quite like this. It was smaller than the horses they had watched the hunters ride. Its mane and tail were unlike a horse as well, falling into thick curls like white, sculptured marble. It was the horn, though, that fascinated the doe most, for in full view now she could see that it spiraled out from the center of the animal's head, ending in a point that sparkled as if by magic.

Have you ever seen one of those? she wordlessly asked of her mate, fearful of taking her eyes off their enchanting visitor lest it vanish.

It's one of the Old Ones," his thoughts replied after carefully assessing the distinctive attributes and drawing the only conclusion possible. "Who'd have guessed there were any left."

In silence they watched the creature drink. The milky-quartz of its smooth skin glistened with the droplets of water it had acquired beneath the umbrella of trees.

It looks so tired, the doe observed, wondering if this delicate creature could understand their language, their noiseless exchange of curiosities about it.

The same who hunt us, hunt it, he observed grimly, suddenly edgy that the animal's very presence might bring along unwelcome company. *We'd better move on,* he bluntly announced.

I thought we might try to talk to it, the doe ventured with earnest hope in her eyes. *Maybe it needs a friend. . . .*

Warning flashed in the buck's narrow face, his attitude disdainful of his mate's flippant challenge to his judgment. *It isn't our place to offer its kind a friendship that would endanger our own lives.*

Before the doe could reply, a soft musical voice cut into both of their thoughts. *It's all right,* the unicorn quietly reassured them, raising its noble head. *Thank you for allowing me to share your stream.* Plucking its way up the lush green embankment that rose from the water's edge, it paused only a moment to consider which direction it should take, its lithe body then cantering into a full gallop as the doe and her mate looked on.

We should have asked it to stay, the doe reflected wistfully. *It seems safe enough here, doesn't it?*

Not as safe as it used to be, he grumbled, annoyed at her persistence. The buck turned his attention to the fragrant flowers that had brought them this far to begin with.

It didn't seem very young, the doe continued. *Then again—*

Their kind never age, he retorted chewing on the juniper leaves. *That's the way it is.* Or so he recalled from the legends he had heard as a fawn.

Do you think it has a mate? the doe queried, unable to fathom what it would be like to travel the world alone.

I rather doubt it, came his unconcerned reply. *It's a wonder it's lived this long itself.*

But if creatures like that never age— she started to argue, abruptly distracted by the hint of lavender fog that had started to rise from the marshy earth closest to the stream. *Oh, my!* she exclaimed, her eyes widening as she studied it. *What do you suppose that is?*

The buck raised his head, his senses now prickling with an inexplicable fear. Long fingers of ethereal mist teased the tender shoots of grass, caressing them with a translucent blanket that frothed purple and white at its base. A cold draft of north wind slid across the ravines causing the doe to shudder. *What's happening?* she asked him anxiously, her graceful limbs trembling from the unexpected gust.

His reply was interrupted by a dull thud from beyond the triad of fire-scarred oaks that symbolically represented the east boundary of forbidden land. Forbidden in that certain death awaited at the hands of its predominantly human population.

What do you think made that noise? the doe inquired. The sound had been too light for one of their own, yet too heavy for a stone or branch. From the corner of her eye she watched the mist that swirled among the thistles as if playing tag with itself. It didn't *seem* all that harmful and its color was actually rather pleasing.

The buck's nose quivered as the first scent of trouble reached him.

Beneath his breath he cursed the horned creature for the disruption its arrival had caused.

Are we leaving? the doe asked hastily, perplexed by the harsh order her husband was silently shouting. In obedience she fell into a run beside him, breathlessly pursuing the reason behind his sudden change of mood.

Human, he muttered as, in unison, they easily cleared the hurdle of rotting stump that blocked the darkening path back to safety.

I didn't hear anyone coming, she said. *All I heard was that thump.*

His keen eyes fixed ahead on the forest's road, he found himself loathe to admit that *he* hadn't heard anyone coming, either.

Icy spasms of pain pinched every muscle of Catherine's body, contorting her legs and causing her midriff to twist and writhe in fiery contractions. A dissonant hum assailed her ears, brought on by a complete loss of equilibrium. Futilely she tried to block the sound with her palms, twisting her head in frustration that the steady noise was amplified from within. Her eyelids were heavy and she tried to will them open, aware that she was in a netherworld somewhere between slumber and wakefulness.

Visions of a mirrored corridor flashed in her imagination, flickering at exaggerated speed as if lit by a strobe. In her mind's eye she could see herself somersaulting helplessly in midair, propelled forward at phenomenal speed. Chords of music collided and swelled, the velocity of her flight making it impossible to discern a recognizable melody. The wind blew cold in the chamber through which she traveled, numbing her to the bone. Then, suddenly, it stopped altogether. She tried to find her voice as she felt her body mercilessly plummeting toward the inky blackness that lay below, flailing her arms in the hope of grasping hold of something, *anything*, to halt the perilous trajectory.

The impact of landing knocked her breath away and sent a sharp reverberation up her spine. Damp earth clogged her nose, causing her to cough. Her eyes still stinging with cold, Catherine blinked, then hesitantly squinted them open, dazed and disoriented by the sight that greeted her.

Mud and grass thickly cloaked the sunken place where she lay on her back, its craggy walls and depth suggesting a rain-washed gully.

Four feet above her she could see what looked like a twilight sky through the sprawling branches of a blackened tree. With difficulty she struggled to turn and sit up, experiencing a subsequent shock for which she was completely unprepared. Gone were the clothes she last remembered wearing, her creamy, bare skin exposed and streaked with fresh mud.

Her spontaneous reaction was to back as far as she could into the wall, hugging her knees close to her chest. Panicking, her eyes darted around the floor of the crevice, but her clothes were nowhere in sight. The spirit of resourcefulness that caused her to scan the gully for some kind of covering went unrewarded, and she shivered at the prospect of having to stay where she was.

The *where*, of course, loomed as large as a major question to be answered. The fact that she was outside was a given. So, too, was the assumption that it had been raining.

Her conscience sought to impose order on her jumbled thoughts. "What was I doing last?" she asked herself. With a jolt of recognition her memory seized the image of Kyle Falconer withdrawing into a fire, wielding a jagged shaft of rusted metal. Quickly the image was replaced by a glimpse of blond hair and curved fingers that lashed out like an angry cat. And then, as if a curtain had been briskly shut, the world had turned black.

A dribble of pebbles down the side of the wall quickly turned Catherine's attention upward, her glance just catching the shadow that furtively ducked out of sight.

Catherine remained huddled where she was, reluctant to call out. A second trickle of earth a few minutes later near the same spot indicated that whatever it was hadn't left. Catherine held her breath, watching.

To her astonishment and relief it was a child whose head cautiously peered over the edge, quickly pulling back as before.

"Hello?" Catherine called up softly. "Are you there? Hello?" Impatiently she waited for a reply, yet none was forthcoming. Just as she had resigned herself to a long night without shelter or clothes, the child's head once more appeared, innocently staring at Catherine as if nothing were wrong. Catherine offered a gentle and encouraging smile. "Hello," she repeated, but the child didn't respond.

The girl looked to be three or four years old, her matted hair unkempt and dirty, her complexion the palest pink. Pudgy fingers hugged the earth as she crouched over the side, her burlap shift stained with grass and berry juice.

"Can you understand me?" Catherine asked. Suddenly the child was on her feet, the snapping sound of broken twigs emphasizing her frightened scamper away from the shallow ravine.

With a sigh of defeat Catherine again withdrew into a ball, at a complete loss as to what to do next. Her limbs aching and her fair skin pimpling in gooseflesh, Catherine wearily laid her head on top of her knees as a screech of owls split the silent sky that was surrendering itself to evening.

A plan, she told herself. *I need some kind of plan.* She was forcing herself to concentrate when the sound of something hitting the ground just a few feet from her made her jump. In the shadows of night and earth, her eyes picked out a rounded, unmoving shape. A stirring from above brought home the fact that she was not alone.

It was hard to tell whether the taller of the two silhouettes rigidly poised at the mouth of the opening was a man or a woman. The smaller, fidgeting shape instantly reminded Catherine of the child. Her hopes brightened that the little girl had understood enough of her plight to fetch help.

"Hello?" Catherine whispered, her greeting bluntly ignored as before. After a moment the taller figure finally moved, its long arm swinging downward and pointing in her direction. Curiosity overriding her fear, Catherine interpreted the gesture to mean the object that lay on the gully's moist floor. Slowly she crept forward, her fingers making contact with what felt like coarse cloth tied up in a bundle with thick cord. Above her, the two figures awaited in mute expectation.

Gratitude washed over Catherine's face as she unrolled the package, her hands eagerly discovering a round hole at the top and long sleeves at both sides. In feverish haste she pulled the dark garment on over her head and stood up. Its ragged hem trailed well past her ankles, the material rough and scratchy. To Catherine, however, it was heaven-sent, its warmth quickly spreading over her skin.

"Thank you," she started to say, but the two ghostly silhouettes had vanished.

Spurred on by the new freedom her attire now afforded,

Catherine stood on her toes to look over the ledge, dismayed to see only bushy clumps and towering trees. From somewhere close by came the melody of rippling water, reminding her of how thirsty she was from her subterranean sojourn.

Fortunately the interior wall was not a smooth face, nor a straight, vertical one. Adventurously she attacked crude pockets in its surface with her fingers and toes and hoisted her way out, wriggling on her stomach as she reached the top.

The fragrance of honeysuckle permeated the night air, and she drank in its sweetness, groping her way toward the sound of the babbling water. With thanks she sank to her knees when she reached it, splashing the refreshing liquid all over her face and neck. Preoccupied with ceaseless questions of where she might be, the bobbing torches that approached from the broad expanse of meadow might have escaped her notice had it not been for the swell of garrulous shouting that broke the night's tranquillity. Scrambling to her feet, Catherine peered into the distance. Her gaze barely made out the half a dozen horsemen whose presence was swathed in an eerie orange light from their flaming beacons.

It was a sight that immediately revitalized her senses, for whoever they were, they represented civilization and shelter. She could hear the pounding hoofbeats of their horses now, the entourage on a steady course that would take them right past the stream.

With courage and determination she crossed the streambed in order that the riders might see her better. They were almost within hearing distance of her voice, and she stepped forward to wave her arms, too distracted to have ever anticipated the iron hand that clamped over her mouth from behind and toppled her to the underbrush.

Chapter Nineteen

THE MUSCULAR BODY THAT pinned her down was like a deadweight, one hand remaining on her mouth while the other pressed at the back of her head. As Catherine squirmed to try to free herself, she could feel the ground at her ear vibrate with the thunder of the approaching horses. Panicked, she realized that they were going to pass straight by without seeing her, leaving her at the dreadful mercy of her attacker.

The body around her suddenly tightened like a steel vise, completely restricting all of Catherine's movement as a spattering of dirt and pebbles pelted them from the riders' vigorous crossing. The clanking metal conjured in Catherine's mind a similar memory, one that she couldn't quite place. Even in their brief passing, the strong smell of liquor and overpowering sweat permeated the night air.

As the haunting sound of hoofbeats began to die, Catherine felt her attacker's grip slowly release and the weight withdraw from her back. Unnerved by the sudden change, she rolled on to her side and squinted up into the darkness at the tall shape that was now standing in front of her. Catherine's mind was spinning with bewilderment, her presence seemingly forgotten as she determined that the figure was intently watching the bobbing cluster of orange light making its way up the hill. Logic told her that now was the time to make her escape. But it also told her that she probably wouldn't escape very far in the unfamiliar terrain, particularly from someone she couldn't help but sense was more comfortable with the night's cloak of shadows than the stark illumination of the sun.

A soft gasp escaped her as the figure turned and dropped down to eye level. Catherine found herself face-to-face with the most unusual woman she had ever seen. *Handsome* was a far more suitable adjective for her face than any feminine description. Pale skin the color of the moon was pulled taut over the high ridge of her cheekbones, her piercing, dark eyes startling against so fair a complexion. The aquiline nose gave her an aristocratic look; her generous mouth neither smiled nor frowned. Although her straight black hair was mostly concealed by the hood of her heavy cloak, a prominent widow's peak dipped down the smooth forehead, nearly meeting in the center the dramatic ebony brows and scar in the shape of a half crescent.

Her pearl-black eyes quickly scanned Catherine's face and body, and then, as if satisfied by what she saw, she abruptly stood up and extended a long-fingered hand to help her rise. As she effortlessly drew her up, Catherine noted with awe that the woman was a little over six feet tall. The woman wordlessly pointed at the orange glow that was all but gone and shook her head in a deep scowl. Only then did Catherine begin to understand that the woman hadn't meant to harm her but to protect her from others who would.

"Who were they?" Catherine started to ask, but the woman was already striding away from her.

Intrigued by their encounter and sensibly dubious about spending the rest of the night where she was, Catherine hiked up the folds of her cumbersome gown and proceeded to follow.

Velvety soil caressed her bare feet as they wended their way through the forest, whose leaves gently rustled on the breeze as if talking to one another. Now and then the crunch of twigs or shaking branches caused Catherine's heart to leap in her throat. Unperturbed, the tall woman leading the way seemed not to notice, never breaking her pace as she led them deeper and deeper into the woods.

Only once did Catherine happen to look up, puzzled to see a latticework of tree limbs above her that struck her as comfortingly familiar. Beyond the rise of a distant hill, a full moon that blushed dusky rose was peeking up through the silhouettes of mighty oak. In reminiscence, Catherine frowned, for only a few nights ago in Washington there had been no moon at all. How could it now be coming up full unless—

For her own sanity, and survival, she shook away the thoughts that had been nagging at her and concentrated instead on following her briskly moving silent guide.

139

They had entered a small clearing whose forest floor was bathed in a pale rosy glow. The scent of sweet flowers perfumed the air. Catherine hoped that they might stop to rest for a while before moving on. As if she had sensed Catherine's thoughts, the tall woman paused in the clearing's center, tossing back the hood of her cape and freeing the thick tumult of blue-black hair to fall well past her waist.

As Catherine eased herself onto a flattened tree stump to catch her breath, she was startled to see shadows cautiously emerging from all around her. Her eyes adjusted to the dim light, and she could see that they were women dressed exactly as she was. There had to be at least three dozen of them—little girls, withered crones, and others at every age in between. Their faces were pale and their large eyes reminded her of deer.

Catherine watched in fascination as the tall woman's hands animatedly flickered, prompting several of the younger women to withdraw into the darkness, returning a moment later with lumpy bundles in their hands. Under the silent direction of their leader they proceeded dutifully to unwrap the parcels on the forest floor, revealing apples, berries, and hunks of a doughy substance that resembled homemade bread.

Drawn by the food, the others came forward and sat down in a circle to share the communal feast. Catherine looked across at the tall woman who had remained standing. Palm upward, she swept her hand from Catherine to the food, nodding her head.

Two women on the ground moved apart to make room for her, one of them tearing off a piece of the parchment-colored dough and thrusting it at her, pantomiming that it was something to be eaten.

The sweetness was a flavor Catherine couldn't identify, its texture closely similar to French bread. Realizing how hungry she was, Catherine devoured it, graciously accepting the handful of blackberries that followed. Across the impromptu picnic spread of food, her eyes made contact with the child who had proved her salvation from the damp gully. Embarrassed by Catherine's attention, the little girl shrank back behind an older companion.

In spite of their numbers, not a single one of them spoke, relying instead on facial expressions and a sign language that was clearly of their own invention.

"Does anyone here speak English?" Catherine ventured at last, startled by how loud her voice sounded after the interminable stretch of silence. Brows knit in confusion, the women stared at Catherine, then sought explanation from their leader, who remained apart. Patiently the tall woman went through a sequence of touching her lips, pointing to Catherine and sensuously spiraling her hand upward toward the stars. Satisfied with a reply that completely mystified Catherine, the women returned to their eating.

"Now I know how Dorothy felt in Oz," Catherine muttered to herself, her voice failing this time to elicit even a raised eyebrow or a stare. Wherever this place was, she decided, it was definitely not Washington, D.C.

Their meal complete, the women proceeded to retire in small groups to the edges of the clearing, tightly curling up on the ground next to each other and gradually falling asleep.

Catherine looked at the tall woman for a clue as to protocol and responded to her unspoken instruction to take a spot by herself beneath the overhanging limbs of an oak. Maybe by morning, Catherine consoled herself, she'd be able to learn more. Then again, maybe by morning she'd have awakened in her own bed after a very weird dream. Her eyelids heavy with sleep, she caught the reassuring glimpse of the tall woman keeping watch over her friends, a rigid sentinel against the night's enemies. If any among the group could explain to her what was going on, Catherine reasoned, obviously she would be the one. Curiously content that no harm would befall her, Catherine fell asleep.

By the time she opened her eyes again to the first hint of daybreak, her companions of the previous evening had all disappeared, leaving behind no evidence they had ever existed.

Perplexed as she was by their vanishing act, Catherine's waking thoughts were dominated—as they had been in slumber—by the magician. Over and over during the night she had replayed in her mind those final awful moments in the corridor of the Smithsonian. Her memory was permanently engraved with the image of the flames swallowing the last of Excalibur, and then, less than a minute later, closing in around her.

Her first impression following the spasms of cold pain had been that she was dead, that this was what it felt like for the soul to be wrenched from its protective human shell. If she were truly dead, though, she reasoned, there'd be no cause for feeling embarrassed or fearful or curious, emotions she felt as strongly now as those she remembered from being alive.

That, then, left another possibility, one that up until a few days ago she never would have dared imagine. What if, she asked herself, a little magic had remained behind that had propelled Kyle Falconer back into the past, *his* past? What if in stepping into the curtain of flame, she, too, had tumbled backward in time?

She closed her eyes, trying to recall their conversation at Gallagher's Inn and his sketch of circles. What had he said about windows? She dimly recalled a phrase about the passage being prompted by the sight of something familiar. What, then, had been so familiar to provoke a time journey of her own—if that indeed was what had happened?

She might have spent the entire morning debating the issue had it not been for a flurry of screaming starlings bursting out of a bush at the far edge of the clearing. A low rumbling noise vibrated through the trees, accompanied by what sounded like laborious, dragging thuds.

Catherine was barely on her feet when across the narrow clearing she saw two slender trees roughly split apart, as if shoved aside by the hands of an unseen giant. Grunting sounds came from the forest, the branches shook violently, and suddenly a purple-and-green scaly snout emerged that might have belonged to a crocodile had it not been at least ten times larger in size and the height of a full-grown oak.

Catherine lost no time in scrambling toward the woods, aghast at what she had just seen. Behind her, the heavy trampling continued, the grunts escalating in intensity and speed. Onward she ran, not having any idea where she was going, concerned only with escaping the giant—whatever it was.

Branches smacked sharply back against her face as she plowed through them. Encumbered by the length of the gown, she tripped twice, gasping for breath both times as she struggled back up. The massive predator was not far behind, its hot breath turning the air putrid and nauseating.

She was at the point of collapse as she reached a fork in the path, uncertain of whether she was making any progress or running in crazed circles. *"This way"* came a voice on the wind. About fifty feet up one of the paths stood a creature that Catherine thought was a white horse, until she saw a straight gold horn protruding out of its forehead. "This way," the little voice urged again. "Hurry."

In the absence of a better plan Catherine hiked up her skirt and started running as fast as she could. The dainty white creature took the lead. Behind them both, the grunting sound grew even louder.

Just when Catherine felt as if her legs could carry her no farther, the same voice was telling her to turn left at the next outcropping of blue rock. *"You'll be safe there,"* it reassured her.

To Catherine's surprise the creature with the golden horn remained on the path as if to taunt the monster in pursuit. *"Duck down now so it won't see you,"* the lyrical voice instructed.

Catherine did as she was told, biting her lip as she watched the animal nonchalantly prance in circles as it waited for the behemoth to catch up. In a quick kick of its cloven hooves, it was off again, Catherine looking up in time to see the long swish of a lizardlike tail disappearing after it through the trees.

Exhausted and drained of energy, Catherine was shaken by the near-death confrontation and the selflessness of the pretty animal that had intervened at exactly the right moment. It was a long time before she was able to move. Which way now? she asked herself finally, wishing more than anything for a pair of red shoes she could click together to transport her back home.

Wearily she looked down the slope behind her, where there was a grassy carpet descending into a meadow. At least it would be cool, she decided, perspiring from her extemporaneous sprint from danger.

Leaves of bright green and yellow blocked the morning sun as she came upon a little used path, the soft earth crisscrossed with twigs and branches swept down from a recent storm. Up ahead, the sound of moving water drew her onward, reminding her of her thirst.

Even before she reached it, Catherine felt her pulse begin to race and her mind begin to reel in anticipation.

There in the clearing, just as in her dream, stood the shimmering lake of iridescent blues and greens, its surface as smooth as fine crystal. Mute with wonder, Catherine approached, barely able to control her gasp of surprise as a melodic voice cut into her thoughts.

"Yes, my daughter," the silvery voice said, *"you've come home to us."*

Chapter Twenty

A HUNDRED QUESTIONS flew to Catherine's mind at once. Impatiently she tried to pull her thoughts together, facing an admission of truth dredged from a place beyond reason or logic. All her loneliness and disorientation melded into an upsurge of powerful yearning for answers, answers she had somehow come through the fire to discover.

There is no need for words, Catherine, came the voice from the serene depths of the glassy pool. *You have only to* think *things here and they will be known.*

"My name . . ." Catherine stammered out loud. "How do you know my name?"

I know that it is the name you are called in the century from which you just came, the lake replied. *Unless you would prefer to be called something else—*

"What century is *this?*" Catherine interrupted, running both hands through her disheveled hair. Certainly the two creatures she had witnessed on the forest trail weren't from recent age.

"It is the time of the New King."

"Arthur?" Catherine asked. "Is *that* what all this is about?"

A playful ripple broke the surface as if its occupant were amused. *Arthur Pendragon has been gone from us for three hundred years now,* the waters spoke. *A new king rules Britain today . . . sadly, a man not of our choosing.*

Catherine scowled, trying as hard as she could to remember a remnant or two of English history. What was this voice trying to tell her?

Such thoughts, the soothing voice broke in, *are not necessary. That which you have forgotten will come back to you if you let it.*

"I'm sorry," Catherine confessed in exasperation, "but I don't understand *any* of this."

Perhaps if is because you still fight to communicate in the ways you were taught in the future.

"You mean talking?" Catherine frowned. "What other way is there?"

The same way you're hearing me talk to you the Lady of the Lake calmly explained.

"But your voice—"

My voice is only heard within, Catherine, just as I trust there were times when only you heard Merlin's inner voice.

A shiver came over her as she silently recalled their first conversation in the restaurant, and her tortured suspicions that he had exerted a power over her to infiltrate her senses and read her mind.

No, my child, spoke the lady with gentle clarity in response to Catherine's private recollection, *it was never Merlin who had the power to read your mind, but rather you who had the power to read his.*

Once more Catherine's head felt as if it would burst from the barrage of puzzles and doubts that were crashing down around her. "How can it be?" she started to ask, but a splash of cool water leapt up just then to tickle her left foot.

There will be time enough for answers, the lake announced maternally. *For now, let me cleanse the marks of the forest from your skin and scent your hair with the fragrance of spring.*

Catherine cast a quick glance over her shoulder, reminded of the sacrifice the animal she could now easily label as a unicorn had made only moments before. Had it made it to safety? Would the lizardlike monster come back and trace her scent down to the lake?

To answer your second question first, the lake spoke up in reassurance, *even dragons know better than to violate a place that is sacred. You are more than safe within my liquid embrace.*

"And the unicorn?" Catherine inquired anxiously, shedding the crude fabric and allowing it to slip to the ground.

Perhaps, the lake whispered in the manner of riddles of which she was most fond, *it is the manifestation of your own courage and belief in magic.* Lovingly the waters turned warm and swirled around Catherine's ankles. *For as long as courage and magic exist in the world, so, too, will my unicorns . . .*

Not until she was submerged up to her neck in the massaging currents of the lake did Catherine give in to the fatigue that had been with her since her arrival. The caressing eddy of sensuous whirlpools enveloped her in a soft cocoon as she let her thoughts drift. Tenderly the lake's fingers combed through the tangles of her hair, setting it to glisten to a polished mahogany sheen.

When Catherine at last crawled out of the water and onto the cool, mossy embankment, all concerns about where she was—and why—had faded. Sleep was now all that she longed for. *"You will need your rest for what lies ahead, little one,"* the voice of the lake whispered in her ear. And with that she wove her spell of enchantment that Catherine might build her strength and dream uninterrupted for the next two days.

They were walking hand in hand, she and Kyle, through a park that reminded her of Virginia. A thin shaft of sunlight struck his hair, and it shone like black sable as he bent his head close to hers.

"I always envied Arthur for this." He smiled, both hands cupping her chin as a contentment natural and pure settled in his face.

Catherine felt her own hands slide around his waist as she drew closer, his proximity lulling her to euphoria. Burying her face against his neck, she breathed a kiss there, drinking in his tantalizing aroma of sandalwood.

"And you don't regret what you had to give up?" she murmured, her last words smothered by the ravenous press of his lips.

"Not in a hundred years"—he groaned huskily—"or a hundred times that." Reclaiming her moist mouth, he crushed her to his chest, passionately draining all of her doubts and fears. "I love you, Catherine."

Like an echo chamber, her name rang over and over again in her ears until she realized that it was not the magician's voice that was coaxing her out of slumber but the cool words of the Lady of the Lake.

Momentarily confused by her surroundings, it took Catherine a few minutes to adjust her eyes to the lakeside cove that was just beginning to stir with the signs of a cloudy daybreak. Directly above her, two chipmunks were playing tag in the trees, sailing like miniature acrobats from one branch to another. Screeching blue jays heckled the late sleepers, their brilliant teal wings a pleasing contrast to a pale gray dawning. Across the lake, two deer paused for refreshment, indifferent to the wisps of fog that hovered just above the water's surface.

To her surprise Catherine found herself in a clean cloak. On the ground to her left lay a neat pile of blackberries, dark cheese, and round disks that resembled rice cakes drenched in honey. Before Catherine could open her mouth to ask, the lake was explaining that they had been left for her by the silent ones. The remark touched a chord of remembrance.

"The women of the forest—"

The last of my followers, the lake replied, her voice laced with unmistakable sorrow. *Perhaps Merlin already explained to you their plight . . .?*

"The Lake People?" Catherine asked, biting off a piece of the sticky cake. "Is that who they are?"

They travel in the shadows now, as well they must, the lake explained. *By day there is too much danger.*

"I tried to talk to them," Catherine recalled. "But none of them answered."

For nearly two centuries, the lake went one, *they have kept to their vows of silence, communicating only with each other and the forest. Strangers, as they have learned, bring only trouble and death.*

"But they helped *me,*" Catherine pointed out, puzzled by the thoughtful silence that then punctuated their discussion.

How much, the lake finally continued, *did Merlin tell you?*

"You mean about Excalibur?"

What I mean, the lake gently corrected, *is about yourself.*

The remark was enigmatic, causing Catherine to frown. Even before she could ask the lake why it wanted to know, the waters were shifting from periwinkle blue to deep heliotrope, their lower depths slowly churning.

Why have you returned? the silvery voice inquired.

"I didn't *know* I was returning *anywhere*," Catherine blurted out. "All I wanted at the time was to get away from Nimue."

I see, the lake said. *And that was your only reason?*

Catherine hesitated, forgetting as she did so that no thoughts could be kept secret from the spirit that dwelled in the magic pool.

For there to be love, the lake announced matter-of-factly, *there must first be honesty. He's told you, of course, of what must happen once Excalibur has been restored?*

Catherine swallowed hard and lifted her chin. "He's told me that he'll have to return to the cave," she said woodenly.

Has he told you that you cannot join him there?

Catherine only stared ahead, biting her lip to hold back the sob that otherwise would have come.

Yet in spite of this, the lake observed, *you were willing to follow him, knowing that even if you were to find him in this place, you would not have a lifetime together?*

Her question, though not harsh, was a challenge flung in Catherine's face. She narrowed her eyes at the surface that now foamed opal and emerald green. "Maybe a single day with the one I love," Catherine replied, her voice barely above a whisper, "is worth more than a lifetime with anyone else."

As quickly as it had built, the foam subsided, leaving once more a tranquil surface that reflected the gathering clouds above.

You must ask that he tell you the rest, the waters commanded at last. *For it would not be wise for a journey of so many years to end without truth.* These last of her words wavered and faded, forcing Catherine to strain to hear them.

"Why can't *you* tell me?" Catherine protested, disturbed by what appeared to be an abrupt dismissal. "What is it I'm supposed to know?"

The lake gave no reply.

Her appetite gone, Catherine pushed aside the remaining food and tried to peer into the transparent waves that lapped at the shore, surprised that in spite of their pristine clarity, she could not even see the ground that lay beneath.

"Since I have to find him," she said out loud, "the least you could have done was tell me where he's gone."

There was no response. Overhead, the branches began to rustle as a breeze swept through the meadow, carrying through their leaves what sounded like the hushed echo of a name. Catherine tilted her head to one side, critically appraising the umbrella of towering trees.

Desperation overriding her innate skepticism, Catherine closed her eyes and concentrated on her one-word question.

Avalon, came the eerie whisper of the wind. *Avalon.*

Her confidence strangely rejuvenated, Catherine scrambled to her feet and gingerly started back up the path that had brought her to the lake, willing to let intuition and an unexplainable sense of telepathy guide her to the man she loved. Onward she climbed, pausing now and again to listen to the clues the forest was mysteriously providing. *This way,* it urged. *No, no—that way is too steep . . . it's less rocky down here . . . watch out for that crevice over the rise.*

When at last Catherine came upon a winding brook, she felt as if she had been hiking for hours. It was difficult to tell how far she had come, for all the terrain was beginning to look alike. Perhaps her admission of love for the Goddess' servant had created animosity. Maybe the forest's whisperings were nothing more than a cruel hoax to send her screaming back to her own century. With a wry smirk Catherine realized she wouldn't know how to get back now, even if she wanted to.

Acquiescing to the need for a cold drink and a brief rest, she knelt down where the water seemed the most shallow and cupped her hands. For only a second a vibrant image flashed before Catherine's eyes and she closed them to try to recapture it. She opened them again, barely in time to see the sweeping reflection of black shadow descending on top of her.

Chapter Twenty-one

POWERFUL HANDS WRENCHED her up from the brook's edge and roughly turned her around. What started as a scream of fear in Catherine's throat exploded into a sweet cry of recognition, for the muscular arms that held her were those of Kyle Falconer.

Surprise mixed with anger on his unshaven face, leaving him speechless, save for the husky gasp of her name. As if she were weightless, he brusquely swung her into the coarse folds of his jet-black tunic, his hands possessively locked against her shaking spine. Yet what Catherine had deemed a prelude to a joyous reunion was quickly shattered by the abrupt thrust of her body away from his. "How did you get here?" he demanded, his eyes dark with menacing suspicion.

Catherine inwardly flinched at the bitter tone of his voice and its dramatic contrast to his brief display of physical longing only a moment before. "I followed you," she replied, meeting his penetrating gaze of accusation. "Through the fire."

His hand involuntarily started to move upward, toward the crystal he still wore around his neck, curtailing the action as he crisply reminded her of her promise in the cafeteria at the Smithsonian.

Catherine recoiled at his display of anger and choked back her tears of disappointment. "I crossed my fingers. The promise didn't count," she replied with a challenge.

Distrust chilled his eyes with reserve as he denied her the warm smile she had almost come to expect from past experience. "I'm sending you back," he announced in a hardened voice.

Catherine stiffened as though he had struck her, staring at him in disbelief across the sudden ringing silence. "No," she said flatly, keenly aware of his stark scrutiny. A dim blush of pink raced across her proud face.

"No?" he repeated, arching his left brow. "You don't belong here, Catherine."

A surge of strength came to her, her despair lessening as the cryptic words of the lake floated back to elevate her beyond his intimidation. Her voice was firm now. "According to the Goddess," she countered, "that's not entirely true."

"You've spoken with her?" he probed cautiously, unsure of where her admission was leading.

"Yes," she replied, sustained by the unsullied honesty of her statement. "We talked quite a lot."

"And what did she say?"

"I think what's more important," Catherine answered, "is what *you* haven't said to *me*." For an instant his glance sharpened, outwardly betraying his guard. Tenderness softened her speech as she used the name by which he was known in his own time and world. "You're the one who told me, Merlin, that every act is dictated by a prevision beyond our understanding." She paused, broadcasting an ethereal certainty in the tilt of her head and the cool green of her eyes. "My coming here might be all a part of that. Shouldn't I at least know what it is before you send me back to where you say I should be?"

A permanent sorrow seemed to be weighing him down, and he shook his head regretfully. "My own fingers weren't crossed," he said, "when I promised I'd never hurt you. To tell you what you ask, Catherine, would break that vow."

"Would it be any worse than the wedge between us from *not* telling me?"

His eyes slid past her to the swift-flowing brook, and his brow pulled into an affronted frown. "Back in Washington," he said, "I told you that you'd be putting yourself in danger."

"Yes . . ."

"Here on Nimue's familiar turf"—his voice hardened ruthlessly in concert with his cynicism—"you'll be at even greater risk. She'll use you as my liability, Catherine. Even with Excalibur, I can't promise I could protect you."

It was the first time he had mentioned the sword. Catherine's attention was drawn now to the opaque black sheath strapped to his waist and trailing to just past his knee. Mesmerized by the thought of what it held, she only half heard the remainder of his argument.

"What did you just say?" she asked quickly.

"Only that I don't want to lose you." This time, though, his repetition omitted the one word she had seized on as a careless slip of the tongue. "Catherine?"

"You said 'again,'" she informed him excitedly, her heart hammering wildly against her ribs. "We *were* together before, weren't we?"

A shadow of alarm swiftly spread over her face, all of her nervousness slipping back to hold her in its icy grip as he sharply turned from her, his jaw angry and tight with strain. For what seemed an eternity she waited, watching the broad shoulders that were heaving as he breathed. Finally, in desperation, she called to him, longing to end the impenetrable masquerade that was keeping them apart.

At his next words the heavy weight of tension slipped from her heart; a dizzying wave of recognition and relief swept over her, forcing her to steady herself against the nearest tree trunk. "Yes, Catherine," he murmured in resignation. His voice faded to a hushed stillness as he stared off into the grove of silver ash and swaying beech. "You *were* in my life before."

At his suggestion they took leave of the brook, an idea met with little resistance by Catherine, whose sixth sense imbued her with the prickling uneasiness that its shallow depths held danger. Without hesitation she accepted the hand that reached out to steady her way over the rocks, warmed by the consolation that at least he didn't withdraw it once they reached level ground.

"I was already old by the time I met you," he began, "nearly a full year before the Dance of the Giants." Her puzzled expression caused him to smile. "Looking in your eyes," he explained, "it's sometimes easy to forget how much is no longer a part of your memory."

The breeze that laced through the high grass made Catherine thankful for so heavy a garment as her benefactors had provided. Overhead, the sun had slipped between the caress of two smoke-colored clouds, dimming the meadow as subtly as houselights for the start of a play.

"Perhaps its common name is more familiar," he continued, proceeding to describe the circle of bluestone megaliths in southwest England known to moderns as Stonehenge. "It was built as a monument to the dead," he reminisced. "A bitter recompense of war waged by Arthur's uncle, Ambrosius."

Grief-stricken by the Saxon massacre of over five hundred unarmed Britons during a truce, Ambrosius had sought to raise a temple on the Salisbury Plain befitting their memory. However, his vision of a towering spectacle to forever mark his loss of warriors left his best builders scratching their heads in frustration. "Even if it had been possible to quarry that much bluestone and safsen in Wales," Kyle explained, "the distance was far too great to move it across the Channel, much less transport it that far inland."

"So what did they do?" Catherine inquired, mentally comparing their challenge to the feat of the Pyramids.

"To put it in the modern vernacular," he replied, "they looked in the Yellow Pages under M for 'magic.'"

"And 'Merlin'?"

They had reached what once seemed to have been a road out of the forest, its width now overgrown with messy dandelions and muddied tangles of ivy. Old memories brought a wry and twisted smile to his face. "It was a time when men still had the faith to consign their dreams to a higher power and the optimism to believe that the foundations they laid would last forever."

Catherine's eyes followed his pensive gaze toward the craggy promontory that rose in the distance as if it had been pulled straight up from the earth and left to harden. Blackened chunks of stone and twisted iron lay in careless heaps down the cliff's sides and along its base, the remnants of whatever proud structure had once graced the rocky pinnacle. In sudden recognition Catherine knew all too clearly what his place had been. The magician confirmed with a grim nod that they were indeed traveling on the same road she had passed in her dream. "In a few more centuries," he said with a sigh, "Richard of Cornwall will claim the hill and start to build Tintagel, erasing the last of a great legend under the weight of its gray towers and walls."

Catherine felt his arm come around her waist and linger, his head bend momentarily in respect for long dead ghosts and glory. As soft as cats' paws, a light rain began to fall, prompting the resumption of their walk and his story.

"So you're the one who built Stonehenge?" she asked, still wondering why the magician was recounting this particular feat.

"I'm afraid I can't take the credit for its formation." He smiled humbly. "Or even for *thinking* of the idea." Mystery flickered across his face. "I owe all of that to a little girl I met one day in the woods."

In her most outlandish dreams Catherine never would have imagined the secret his chronicle was to reveal.

"You were a child of the lake," he explained gently. "Even before you could speak, you were gifted with the power to read the thoughts of the wind and the deer and to know their recollections as if you had lived them yourself."

The color drained from Catherine's cheeks, and she felt her legs start to give way, her mind frozen in a limbo where all actions and decisions were impossible. Strong hands reached out to steady her as, beneath his breath, he bitterly cursed the choice he had made to share the truth.

"I'm okay," Catherine insisted, emphatic that he continue with his story.

It was beginning to make sense to her now, hard as it was to assimilate all the pieces. The Goddess' remark about Catherine's capacity to read the magician's mind brought back the memory of their previous conversations. Was it possible, then, she wondered, that what she had mistaken for dynamic storytelling was in fact the application of her own talent to "see" the past literally as he told it? With a shiver Catherine realized that the haunting dreams as well had not been a product of his magic but an empathy of her own, gleaned from their brief encounters.

"You must have been three or four," he went on. "A beautiful child with a stubborn chin and a wild streak of independence." Another memory danced back in her mind, the image of him standing in front of the étagère and looking at her pictures. What was it he had said? Something to the effect that she hadn't changed.

"You didn't run from me like other children were wont to do," he recalled in admiration. "You just keep on playing with a pile of flat rocks as matter-of-factly as a modern little girl would play with dolls . . . a self-assured child who in some strange way made me feel as if I had met my match."

The rain started to fall now with a steady regularity that reminded her of the harbor at Alexandria and the cozy warmth of Gallagher's. It occurred to Catherine that by the measure of time in her own world less than twelve hours had passed since she walked out of her apartment to meet him.

"Without my saying a word," he related, "you knew what was weighing on my mind—the dilemma of how to appease Ambrosius without breaking the backs of his workers. You pointed to the circle of vertical stones and flat lintels you had built and told me that across the sea I could find their copies."

"Across the sea?"

"Ireland," he said. "Legend had it that a vanished race of Gaelic giants had moved them from Africa and that ordinary water poured over them became magic and healing. What better tribute to both the dead and the living than a complex of stones whose origins dwelt in the mystic past?"

"And so you moved them?"

"Yes." He nodded. "Into the exact configuration shown to me by a child I knew to be special."

A low rumble of thunder underscored his words and his eyes quickly combed their surroundings for shelter. Catherine, however, was too swept up in the story to notice the impending storm.

"Did you see me again after that?" she asked, hopeful that he would say yes.

"I sought you out when I returned from Ireland," he went on. "I even brought you a trinket I thought would please you." Before Catherine could ask what it was, he added that she had seem quietly disappointed, perhaps longing for something different. "When I asked you what was wrong," he said, "you told me that one day you'd like to see the new High King for yourself. Mind you, I was surprised, given that Uther hadn't yet died nor acknowledged Arthur as his son."

"How did you know I didn't mean Uther?"

"For one thing," he said, smiling, "he had been king too long to be considered 'new' by anyone. For another, you referred to my ward by name." He shook his head. "You couldn't have known

Arthur was even with me unless you had read it in my thoughts. No one knew of Arthur at all until two years later when he came forth."

"So *did* I?" Catherine asked. "See Arthur, I mean?"

"Not an easy task," he admitted. "Your people rarely emerged from the dark of the forest, and Arthur—well, I doubt Arthur would have gone into the woods for the sole purpose of seeing a child."

"So what happened?"

"I made you invisible for the hour that I knew Arthur and I would be passing on the road to Camelot. I told you that by the time you returned to your own people, the spell would have worn off. The vision that you had of seeing Arthur and me, Catherine, was a memory from the last day . . ." Kyle hesitated.

The sky was nearly black now, illuminated only by sharp flashes of lightning.

"The last day of what?" Catherine's lips trembled.

"Your life," he quietly replied.

Chaper Twenty-two

IN THE SECONDS followed his response, a drenching cloudburst sent both of them running toward the refuge of a stout, leaning tree. Overhead, the swiftly moving shadows of sky swirled like dark liquid in a blender, their very presence a fearful portent that the worst of the storm was still yet to come.

The line of his mouth tightened as he pointed to a small, low building in the valley, barely visible from where they stood beneath the tree's dripping branches. "Do you think you can make it as far as that cottage?" he inquired, prepared to carry her if need be.

"Whose is it?" she asked, her eyes fixed on the wisp of smoke that curled from its sagging roof.

"Hopefully," he replied, "someone with a kind enough heart to let us in."

As they neared the crude dwelling Catherine became aware of the other hovels near it, their dilapidated exteriors camouflaged by vegetation left to grow wild and unkempt.

Her eyes scanned the muddy parcels of land that surrounded the pitiful community, dismayed to see no evidence of harvest or livestock. With sinking anguish the thought came to her that this, too, might have been a part of Camelot's tapestry and a sorry reminder of its degradation.

Catherine tensed at the sound of a heavy iron bar being flung back behind the gnarled oak door and obeyed the magician's whispered instruction to keep close to him. Ominously the door creaked open to reveal the grotesquely fat woman who lived within. Piggish eyes peered out in suspicion beneath a shock of dirty hair the color of rotting pumpkin. Her foul-smelling shift bore the signs of recent meals and restless nights. Her pockmarked jowls rotated from side to side, reminding Catherine of a cow chewing cud and causing her to wonder whether their arrival was interrupting the late-afternoon meal.

Kyle's voice was polite, yet edged with a rim of authority that prompted the woman to glance down at the covered weapon that hung at his side. "My lady and I seek lodging," he said, smoothly adopting an accent thick with brogue. The woman stared at them with a dumb look until, with one fluid gesture, Kyle extended his right hand and opened his palm to reveal a bright gold coin. Hungrily the woman snatched at it with grimy fingers. The magician, however, was quicker. "Lodging?" he firmly repeated, withdrawing his hand.

With an unintelligible grunt the woman stood aside as she opened the door farther and bade them enter, locking out the storm behind them.

The cottage interior was dark in spite of the fire, owing to the clumps of packed straw stuffed in the windows to keep out the rain, and a floor comprised of dark earth that over the years had absorbed the smells of human and animal inhabitants. Flames licked the bottom and sides of a black cauldron; across the room came the aroma of burning pork. An uneven table against one wall was littered with hunks of black bread, broken bowls, and a dirty harness and oxen yoke, both long retired from service. Even when times had been better, Catherine suspected, the standard of living had probably not been significantly different from what lay before them here.

Laboriously shuffling under the burden of her size, the woman led the way to a low door near the back of the cottage and shoved it open. What little light spilled from the fire shone through to a smaller room with a corner hearth and raised wood box that seemed to be a rustic excuse for a bed.

The temptation of a second gold coin elicited a yellow, gap-toothed grin, and the woman ambled across the room to procure a stubby candle.

"She's also going to give us food," the magician murmured, an announcement that, even under slightly cleaner conditions, might have made Catherine feel that their luck was improving.

The wan smile that lit Catherine's face as she surveyed the cramped room caught Kyle's curiosity.

"I always wanted a bedroom with a fireplace," she said with a sigh. "Although this isn't exactly the way I pictured it."

Left alone while Kyle went for kindling, she tentatively explored the shabby but dry quarters, ending with the bed that presumably belonged to their hostess. Scratchy but thick blankets were tucked in around a lumpy surface that her inspection revealed was straw. A misshapen brown sack through which poked an occasional goose feather quill constituted the bed's only pillow.

As she sat down on the edge to stretch her aching legs, Catherine's glance fell on the long, black sheath propped up against the wall. In her preoccupation with the room she obviously had failed to notice the magician unstrapping it from his waist and leaving it just inside the door.

The diversion of his story and the impact of the thunderstorm had pushed Excalibur far into the background. Alone with it now, inquisitiveness overcame her and she crossed to pick it up, astonished by its unexpected weight. Certainly the weapon that Nimue had effortlessly wielded at the Smithsonian had appeared to be much lighter.

With her pulse hammering in anticipation, she laid it across the bed. Nimble fingers unlaced the drawstring top from which only the hint of a handle was visible when worn. With her right hand Catherine grasped hold, sliding down the sheath with her left.

The shock of discovery hit her full force. She could only stare, tongue-tied, at the gleaming shaft of gold and white, as perfect as she had witnessed it in her imagination. Below the jeweled hilt could easily be seen the engraved destiny of a redheaded boy whose strength and virtue had enabled him to withdraw its full length from a prison of stone.

A quick intake of rasping breath to her left caused Catherine to jump. She turned her head in time to see the fat woman send a bowl of bubbling stew clattering to the floor as her grubby hands flew up to her mouth in horror. Almost immediately Kyle appeared in the doorway behind the woman, one arm laden with wood. His sharp eyes assessed the situation and his free hand shot up to grab hold of the woman's wrist.

"You've seen nothing," he said in a harsh, raw voice that caused the woman to whimper. "Nothing."

She was all too glad to take leave of them, pulling the door closed behind her as Kyle and Catherine regarded each other in a frozen tableau. Dumfounded by both Excalibur's appearance and Kyle's veiled threat, Catherine found that the words of apology were wedged in her throat. Her body stiffened in expectation of seething reprisal. To her surprise he proceeded to go about laying a fire, turning to address her only after its ignition by magic began to color the room with the warm glow of pink and orange.

"The road to Avalon," he said quietly, "is too long to take chances." With an almost clinical detachment he slid Excalibur back into its covering, not once making eye contact with her.

"What happens when we get to Avalon?" she asked.

"When *I* get there," he emphasized, "I'm committing it to a barge as it once lay for Arthur's funeral and sending it out to the heart of the channel. Once the barge has burned, it will join Arthur as it was meant to at the beginning."

"The way it looks—" she started to say, but he was already answering.

"Excalibur has been restored to its proper time and place," he replied. "The magic that protects it will keep it looking exactly the same until it's found again by the king for whom it's fated." Not until he had finished lacing the strap did he look over at her, softness replacing his previous look of black-layered censure. "I'll have to send you back in the morning," he calmly asserted, as if prepared for her exclamation of protest.

"Is it because of what happened just now?" she asked, her stomach churning with frustration.

Pausing, he gazed at her speculatively, two deep lines of worry appearing between his eyes. "It's because of what *could* happen that I'm most worried," he admitted. "Knowing that at least you're safe in your own world . . ." His hands came up to squeeze her shoulders, an action that prompted him to change the subject. "You're soaked through," he observed. With gentle fingers he pushed back the wet tendrils of hair that clung to her forehead and neck. "You'd better get out of that gown and into bed. If I hang it by the fire, it'll be dry by morning."

Catherine felt the blood surge from her fingertips to her toes, only marginally aware of the cold she should have been feeling by now from their time out in the rain. His appeal at that moment was devastating. She felt as though she were losing herself in the erratic current of passionate emotions that swelled within from the gentle grip of his very touch.

"I'll see what I can do about more food," he said, politely affording her the privacy to which he felt she was entitled. With that he slipped out the door, leaving her to undress in silence and tortured longing.

The three decisive knocks that came a few minutes later found her swathed in the coarse fabric of the bedclothes and sitting upright against a pillow that felt surprisingly comfortable against her bare back. His voice came through before he did, inquiring whether he might enter.

"I hope this is an improvement," he offered, setting down a tray of dark broth and cheese by her side, his eyes discreetly averted from the creamy shoulders that poked out at the top edge of the blanket.

Catherine's nose wrinkled in puzzlement at the enticing smell of garlic and chicken coming from the badly cracked dish. "Is it safe?" she inquired.

"She had a little help," he explained, a conspiratorial wink sealing his remark.

"Aren't you going to have some?" she asked as he withdrew to attend to the fire.

"Maybe a little later."

For an instant Catherine felt a tinge of embarrassment not her own. With a start she realized that what she must be sensing was his own discomfort with her unclothed state beneath the covers. The words of the Goddess once again teased her with their haunting reality. It was more and more evident to Catherine that she did indeed possess remnants of the power of a prior life to read the emotions of others. With a half smile as she brought the bowl to her lips, she savored the bittersweet feeling that he, too, was as affected by their circumstances as she was.

With meticulous care he was hanging her gown on a hook above the hearth, squeezing water from the garment as he did so. A golden light rippled above his profile and she ached for the fulfillment of his body next to hers. Despite his closed expression she could sense his vulnerability and his simmering ambivalence between honoring his duty as a magician and satisfying his desire as a man.

"My compliments to the chef," she said with a nonchalance contradictory to her true feelings, her spirits revived by the thick liquid that trickled down her throat.

"There's more if you're still hungry," he advised as he sat down on the hearth with his back to the fire, pulling off the thigh-high boots that covered the long expanse of thickly knit tights beneath his tunic.

Only then did she finally venture to remind him of the answer he had started to give just as the sky unleashed its turbulent fury.

"Is it really that important to you?" he asked after a thoughtful silence. The green eyes that met his confirmed without words that it was.

"The day you saw Arthur on the road," he said slowly, "I returned to the forest afterward, to make sure that the spell had worn off. As many times as I had rendered Arthur and myself invisible to others, there was always that slim chance that something could go wrong." His fingers absently flicked at the mud that had collected on the heels and across the top of the dull leather. "You were too important for me to trust to assumptions of a flawless reversion."

Catherine laid aside the bowl, drawing up her legs and resting her chin on her knees as her fingers intertwined on the outside of the blanket.

"I waited at your favorite spot for you to appear," he went on, a quiver of remorse evident in his voice. "Sunset melted into sunrise, and still there was no sign of you."

The image of the twisted brook danced through Catherine's mind, though whether from her violent dream or a thought of his own, she couldn't discern. "The water," she spoke up, superimposing the image with the brook where he had found her. "It has to do with the water and the brook, doesn't it?"

Sad eyes glistened in the sparkle of the fire as he nodded and paused. "It's the place," he replied finally, "where Nimue murdered you."

Chapter Twenty-three

A BRILLIANT FLASH of copper-colored eyes and pointed nails that lashed into her throat like talons made Catherine scream out in the middle of his secret, an explosion of memory bursting inside her brain like a blood-red display of fireworks. In her mind's eye she was reliving the impact of ice-cold water flooding her nose and mouth, the snarl of hatred that creased the contorted face she had glimpsed only once above her body before a welcome wave of blackness enveloped her. The face of Nimue, her cheeks scratched during her victim's last attempt to break free . . .

In three powerful strides he was next to her, crushing her head to his chest as both arms sought to still her spasmodic shaking. Sobs choked back the questions that assailed her, and she dug her fingers tightly into the broad back that had slowly begun to sway. "I'm here, Catherine," he repeated over and over, his hands firmly massaging the taut muscles of her silky back as his lips grazed her ear, whispering reassurance.

With a shiver Catherine found herself now recalling with vivid clarity the reflection she had deemed so disconcerting in her dream, the one she had been unable to remember earlier. As she had leaned over the brook it had been her own image as a child that had blinked back and not the adult she had expected.

"W-why?" she asked, stammering, hot tears trickling down both cheeks. "Why did she kill me?" The convulsing sobs that rocked her body caused the top blanket to fall away as she pulled back, exposing the rosy peaks of her breasts. Swallowing hard as he glanced downward only long enough for her to retrieve the fabric, his reply was as shocking as the disclosure of her death itself. "She knew what you would one day mean to me," he replied. "Like a dog in a manger, she chose to deny me what she did not even want for herself."

Catherine's breath was coming in short, uneven spurts as she grasped to take hold of the hands that were smoothing her hair. "I've got to know the rest," she insisted, her tear-streaked eyes pleading for his confidence.

In a weary voice that seemed to come from far away, he confessed that he hadn't learned the answer himself until the night of his own downfall in the cave of crystal. "I didn't even know she had killed you," he said, his words trailing off in remembrance of the pain. "Although I always wondered whether she had told the truth about the comb she claimed to have found . . ." His narrative replayed his gratitude for Catherine's contributive influence with Stonehenge and described the ivory and tortoiseshell comb he had returned with from Ireland as a gift. "How was I to know," he said, "whether or not your disappointment had been sufficient motive to toss it aside one day in the woods?"

"I can't picture myself *ever* parting with something that came from you."

"Maybe if I had listened more closely to my heart," he said, sighing, "I would have known that."

His first encounter with Nimue had not come until many months after Catherine's disappearance, the passage of time lessening his surprise at her possession of the bauble he had brought to please the little girl. "The first time she let me speak with her," he said, "I asked where she had gotten it, contenting myself with her casual reply in the absence of any hard evidence to contradict it."

Across the room the fire sputtered and sent shadows across the low ceiling as he recalled the details of Nimue's final and shameless treachery. "She flaunted your death in my face," he continued, his misery obvious and acute.

Catherine bit her lip, unable to bear the sight of him in pain without breaking down herself. "Forgive me," he said hoarsely, his head bowed over the two slender hands he kissed and pressed tightly between his own.

His nearness kindled feelings within her as hot as the fire. She stretched toward him, impelled by the intensity of her passion. Beneath the tunic, his muscles suddenly hardened like steel as she felt him pull back. Anxiously she searched the face that was still etched with torment. A lock of black hair fell forward as he bitterly shook his head. "No Catherine," he said his voice raw with unutterable declarations of grief and guilt. "Much as I'd—" He abruptly chose not to complete the thought that Catherine's heart longed to hear. Her spark of hope was quickly extinguished as he rose from the bed and urged her to get some sleep for her journey in the morning.

Catherine felt herself flounder in the agonizing maelstrom of his concurrent yearning and rejection, unable to account for his abstention from an intimate union with someone whose feelings were so readily apparent. Aching with an emptiness beyond description, she let herself slide down under the rough covers, her youthful happiness fading as she watched the tall silhouette lower himself once again to the hearth to keep company with the flames instead of company with her.

Her voice longed to call out to him; her arms yearned to open and pull him close next to her. In defeat she realized there was nothing she could say or do that would change who they were or what would happen the next day. Her eyes blinked back fresh tears as she watched him over the edge of the coverlet, memorizing every detail of the sculptured cheekbones and firm mouth that she hungered to smother once more her own with tantalizing kisses.

Even in the darkness his black hair gleamed, reminding her of the striking and sensuous impression he had made in a tuxedo on the night of their rooftop rendezvous. With a scowl she realized that she couldn't even remember which night it had been. Last night? The night before? A week ago? Their time together—brief as it had been so far—all melded into one memory, incapable of ordinary measurement. As she had known in her soul from the very beginning, theirs was a history that spanned centuries and one that would take as long to forget once it was over.

Catherine's eyes flickered in and out of sleep, determined as she was to stay awake and watch the magnificent man who would own her heart for as long as they both lived. Her body stiffened in astonishment as she saw now in the amber glow of the fire that he had shed his own clothes to dry, apparently satisfied that she had at last fallen asleep.

Her gaze traveled down the rich outline of his back, its muscular width tapering to tight, round buttocks the same pale color as the rest of his body. His sinewy thighs and calves were lightly covered with fine black hair; his arms moved with an easy grace as he pensively jabbed at the coals with the iron poker.

Catherine's heart swelled with unrestrained love for him, his sensuality threatening to draw her like a helpless magnet to his side, her lips tingling in remembrance of his touch. Then, through her torrid thoughts, came the peaceful voice of the Goddess, as clear as if she were standing at the foot of the bed.

"Patience, Catherine," she told her. *"It is not yet the time to obey your heart."*

Catherine opened her mouth to respond, quickly shutting it in the realization that the slightest sound from the bed would call attention to the fact that she was observing him.

So what do I do? she forced her torturous thoughts to answer in silence.

A silvery laugh betrayed the Goddess' amusement. *I see you're relearning the old ways of communicating,* she commented. *I knew it wouldn't take long.*

That doesn't answer my question. Catherine felt her mind snap back in mild annoyance, wondering how long the unseen visitor had been present.

Doesn't it? she said. *You've always known him better than anyone. Whatever he's thinking now shouldn't be that hard for you to figure out . . .*

The air around her grew still again. Through their exchange the magician hadn't stirred from his spot by the fire, his eyes still wide open and unblinking, the short stubble of unshaven whiskers giving the lower half of his face a distinctive shadow.

Catherine inwardly quivered at the Goddess' suggestion, comparing it to an indirect form of voyeurism. *Then again,* she considered, *maybe he's not thinking of me or of us at all. Would it really be that wrong to concentrate for a few minutes in the interest of finding out?*

She shifted her head on the pillow, closing her eyes tightly in pretended sleep just in case he should look over. After enough time had passed for him to have directed his attention back to the fire, she cautiously opened one eye, satisfied with the new position from which to study him.

In feverish excitement she let all thoughts but those of the magician empty her head, focusing her exclusive concentration on what dwelled within the rugged profile in front of her.

Playful fingers coaxed the straps of her camisole from her shoulders as his lips traced a sensuous path down her throat. Slowly his hands moved downward, skimming either side of her body as he mumbled his desire into the soft cleavage of her breasts.

"Are you sure we have time?" She laughed, tousling the waves of thick hair that were descending almost to her waist now.

"We have all the time in the world," he announced, locking both arms tightly around her thighs and lifting her into the air, her hands grabbing hold of his shoulders for balance. Tucking her curves neatly into his own virile contours, he seductively let her slide down his chest, his hands tenderly cupping her buttocks as he tilted his head back to part her lips with a moist kiss. "Have I told you how much I love you?" he murmured as he eased her on to the feathery softness of the four-poster bed.

"Not in the last five minutes," she replied teasingly, unbuttoning his shirt with lust-arousing diligence and kissing the nipples that beckoned her through the matted swirls of curly black hair.

Instinctively her body arched toward him as he peeled away the half-slip and tap pants, lovingly admiring the shapely beauty who lay back against the smooth sheets, desiring him.

With an urgency matching his own, Catherine caressed the planes of his back, sliding her hands under the elastic waistband of his shorts and expertly pulling them down as his body moved, partially covering hers.

"Do you suppose they'll be upset if we don't show up at all?" he proposed as his hand seared a fiery path down her abdomen and between her legs. The touch of his bare skin against hers exalted her, the heat of his body coursing down the entire length of hers as a moan of ecstasy slipped through her lips.

"They'll have to live with it." She sighed, yeilding with a cry of delight to the burning sweetness that consummated their love and passionate fidelity. Again and again they surrendered themselves to each other's masterful seduction, collapsing at last in the drowsy warmth of embrace and completeness.

In the soft coolness of moonlight streaming through their window, his loving voice stirred her from her a half sleep. "I've thought of the perfect name," he said, his fingers lazily tracing circles on her shoulder.

"You mean if it's a boy?" she whispered, snuggling up and draping her arm across his chest.

"Of *course* it will be a boy!" he insisted, as if it could be nothing else.

"What, then?"

"Arthur," he replied with satisfaction. "What do you think?"

"I think," she said, sliding her hand down the outline of his hip, "that we should wait and see if it's a boy first."

"It's a boy," he repeated knowingly. But she had already fallen back asleep.

The dream had been so real that Catherine expected to roll over and find him next to her. Instead she lay by herself in a room dimly lit by cracks of sunlight coming through the straw. It was already morning. For a moment she experienced a feeling of panic as she saw that the magician was gone. Just as quickly her fears were quelled by the outline of Excalibur leaning against the wall closest to her. He'd be back for it. That was a given.

Swiftly Catherine pulled on the gown—now dry—and hesitantly opened the door. Their hostess was nowhere in sight, presumably outdoors somewhere by the looks of the cottage and the main door that had been left ajar.

Though Kyle couldn't—or wouldn't—have gone too far, Catherine's mind raced about what to do with Excalibur. Instinct told her she should take it with her, even if she were only going as far as the front of the house.

With the sword nearly dragging on the ground because of its length, Catherine almost collided in the doorway with the woman who had loaned them her room.

"Good morning," she said pleasantly. In response the woman stared down at the black shape at Catherine's side. Instinctively

Catherine tightened her grip on it. "Have you seen my husband?" she inquired, hoping to extricate herself.

With a disdainful grunt the woman pointed outside and continued about her business. Grateful for the limited bit of information, Catherine stepped out into the morning air.

To her dismay, Kyle wasn't in plain view. The only signs of life, in fact, were two men in the distance with crossbows. Catherine shrank back against the shadow of the cottage, finally determining that either they hadn't seen her or else were too absorbed in their hunting.

The aftermath of the storm had littered the valley with broken branches and limbs, some nearly the size of the very room in which she and Kyle had passed the night. With a quiet prayer of thanks she silently expressed gratitude for shelter appearing as fortuitously as it had.

A shadow across the sky suddenly commanded her attention. She shielded her eyes, trying to determine what it was. With a cry of delight she beheld a familiar bird of reddish-brown, gracefully circling above the trees. With a smirk of irony Catherine realized how drastically her perceptions had changed in so short a time, how easily she now accepted his ability to change form. Whimsically she found herself wondering if he could change her into a bird as well, that they might fly to the ends of the earth and never come back.

Her daydream was suddenly shattered by what sounded like a thin whine of metal across the valley. In horror she let loose an ear-piercing scream as she watched the sailing black arrow embed itself in the falcon's chest, sending the feathered body spiraling downward in a comet of blood.

Chapter Twenty-four

BY THE TIME she reached the crumpled heap of feathers, the ground beneath it was already stained with rust-colored splatters from the gaping wound at the front of its left wing. The lethal arrow, still protruding from its mark, had entered at an angle and emerged out the back, grotesquely pinning the shoulder arch into an unnatural bend, as if an inhuman force had cruelly twisted it backward. The impact of the arrow's contact had also split the chain around the falcon's neck, hurtling the crystal several feet from where the bird lay with its head contorted in strident screams of agony.

Catherine dropped the sword to the ground and fell with a cry to the bloodied creature as it tried in vain to right itself with its good wing and its diminishing strength. "I'm here." Catherine sobbed soothingly. "I won't let anything happen to you." She hoped that her voice concealed the unspeakable and ghastly alarm that she was experiencing at his perilous condition. Blood continued to ooze from the gory cavity that his thrashing had enlarged. Her limited knowledge of such subjects told her that she'd somehow have to remove the arrow if she hoped to rescue him from the open and attend to bandaging what she could.

In her preoccupation with the hawk's life, she had nearly forgotten about the instigators of his accident, bristling as her sudden glance fell on the two hunters whose strides had now brought them to within fifty feet of where she hunched on the ground. Crossbows slung over their shoulders, they looked to be little more than young teenagers, though so rigorous a century would easily have categorized them in the ranks of mature men. Amused by what they had found, the two were distracted enough by their own exchange of ribald remarks and bawdy speculations not to notice the fingers that were rapidly unlacing Excalibur's sheath. When next they looked up to resume their approach, Catherine was withdrawing the shaft of gold and white, her eyes flashing icy contempt for their deadly sport.

The braver of the two continued to walk forward, his face quickly blanching when he saw the slender woman grasp hold of the hilt with both hands and lift it with surprising ease, as if she had been doing it all of her life. Both boys gasped, whether from fear or recognition, as sunlight danced off the razor-sharp edge, setting it to glisten with an aura that in the dark might have been fluorescent.

"Go!" she yelled, her knuckles white with rage as she felt a peculiar reverberation of power quivering from the sword's tip all the way down its hilt and up her own arms. The fury and implacability of her aggressive stance left no doubt as to her intentions should they defy her order. With only one backward glance between them, they turned and ran, releasing Catherine at last from the pose she had tapped all of her courage to maintain. Not until much later would she pause to reflect on how weightless the weapon had felt when swept up in defense against a hostile opponent.

For now, all her attention returned to the fallen hawk whose curved beak was opening and closing as it struggled for breath. Panicky, Catherine saw that it had given up the fight to roll off the twisted wing, its little remaining energy reserved for simply taking in air.

"I won't let you die," Catherine whispered, sliding her hand gently under its back, where her fingers encountered matted feathers saturated with sticky blood. "I promise." The bird squirmed and shrieked in anguish as her hand found the speared end, along with almost three inches of the thin wood shaft. As carefully as she could, she tried to lift him partially on to her lap so that the weight of his own body wouldn't cause any more damage than had already been done. His very size, though, made her plan impossible, and she was forced to lay him gingerly back on his side, desperate for a miracle to alleviate his pain.

"When I was little," she began conversationally, in short, rapid breaths, her knee sliding in to balance him, "I used to hate taking off Band-Aids." With both hands side by side she firmly grasped the back half of the arrow. "And so you know what my mother used to do?" Squeezing her eyes shut, she gave a quick snap of her wrist and felt the shaft break cleanly. "She used to say we'd count one-two-three. She made it a game—we'd count together—" She was close to hyperventilating now, her left hand moving once again to the hawk's bloody back as her legs gently straddled it. "And so we'd starting counting—" Catherine continued breathlessly, her knuckles closing around the scant three inches above the point. "And she'd tell me she'd peel it off—her fingers could not have gripped it any tighter—" when we reached the count of three—"

Catherine's free hand rested as firmly as she dared on the entry wound, primarily to see that the broken shaft end followed through when the time came. "And so there I'd be," she said panting, "—expecting it to come off on three—and instead Mama would say 'one, two.' " Catherine held her breath and pulled firmly from the back, completely drawing out the bloody death-missile as the hawk emitted a curdling scream.

The worst, however, was not yet over, and an angry flood of bright red erupted from the torn skin. With furious haste Catherine used Excalibur's sharpness to rip a substantial portion of cloth from the front of her own cloak, swathing the writhing creature whose eyes now rolled in delirium.

"You're going to be all right," she repeated, trying to keep her composure as she nervously watched the gushing wound almost instantly saturate the coarse layer of material. "I'll get you out of here—you're going to be fine—" Panic rioted within her as she cradled the bird in the crook of her left arm and stood up. The hawk's magnificent head fell back limply as it tried to twist, but no sound came forth from its parted beak. Sunlight caught the sparkling flash of the crystal pendant in the grass. In that moment Catherine sensed that the weakened bird was trying to tell her not to leave it behind.

Awkwardly she leaned over to scoop it up, stuffing it into the folds of fabric that encased the bird. Fearful of laying him down for even a second, she fumbled to retrieve the black sheath and the sword, dismayed to find that it had returned to its former heaviness. Unsure of what awaited her next—or where she was going at all, for that matter—she chose to forgo disguising the weapon as before. Chances were that she might not be as lucky next time. Excalibur's sight alone was enough to ward off attack; prudence dictated that she keep it at the ready.

Over her shoulder in the distance, she could see the fat woman's bulk trudging around the cottage. Even with the protection of Excalibur, Catherine felt uncomfortable with the idea of returning. For all she knew, the hunters might even come back.

No, she determined, the forest would be the best place—the safest place—to go. Surely she could find her way to a stream to wash his wounds. Dragging Excalibur along behind her, she hurried from the valley into the forest. There was no more time to waste. Pressed close against her breast, the bird now barely moved or breathed, the signs of life slowing ebbing from its body.

The front of her cloak clung moistly to her left breast, and in horror she realized that it was the falcon's blood that had penetrated through. With trembling fingers she stroked the feathered head that flaccidly sagged into the hollow of her shoulder, her heart longing to will the closed eyelids to flutter open and reveal the same startingly bright intensity that had once mystified her. "Please," she begged. "Please don't die."

Weariness enveloped her, reducing her to hot tears in the frustrating knowledge that she had been walking in the woods for what seemed like hours without result. Cramps throbbed in both legs, her shins smarting from the brutal exposure to prickling branches that the open rip of her gown readily permitted. Aching with their double burden, Catherine's arms felt as though they might fall off at any moment. *Concentrate on something to take your mind off being tired,* she told herself. *Think about work. Think about the apartment. Think about the last concert you reviewed.*

Such memories seemed so far away now. Thoughts of the past week, even of Larry Mitchum, all swirled and melted into a blurry gray montage on which she discovered it was impossible to focus. With a start she found herself trying to recall the date and year of her birth. On an even more desperate level, her scrambled thoughts sought to remember what her last name was. The answers refused to come.

Drained and hollow, her muscles screamed from the physical and emotional strain to which she was being subjected. She was oblivious to all reason, save the only one that mattered: She couldn't let her precious cargo die.

Onward she wandered, intent on her feverish quest to notice something familiar, to find something with which to treat his deadly injury. Hope even flickered that she might run across one of the Lake People, in spite of the Goddess' disclosure that they kept to the shadows and the safety of darkness. "Why couldn't I have been a healer instead?" she muttered to herself, perceiving such a gift as infinitely more valuable under current condition than the bizarre talent for mind reading that she still couldn't quite refine.

Without provocation the memory of her attempt to use it on Kyle last night slipped back to haunt her. Had such thoughts truly been his? Or had sleep and her own erotic dreams of desire intervened before she even had the chance to concentrate fully?

The dizzying ecstasy of his lips in both real life and in her fantasy retained a prominent hold on her, as did her response to the pulsating seduction of a passion that paralleled her own. Hers was the heart he had come across time itself to find; his was the life she had deserted her own future to share.

At least a hundred times since the Goddess' words of gloom, Catherine had secretly insisted that there *had* to be a way. How could they *not* be together when they had come through so much already? If the Goddess was as all-knowing and as wise as Kyle had claimed, the depth of their commitment couldn't be that difficult for her to see.

Fragments of the dream once again floated back to cheer her, for the more she considered it, the more convinced she grew that it *had* been a projection of his own wish, his need to be loved and cherished as much as she did.

It was the setting, though, that still puzzled her, as it had then. The details of white eyelet sheets and rose-colored draperies filled her with peace, as did the scent of his freshly showered body. Clearly it was a vision that belonged to a modern century, yet not one that she recognized. Where had they been going? Why had he talked so much about naming someone Arthur?

Most of all she wondered why the Goddess had told her to resort to mind games in the first place, when it would have been so much easier to speak her heart out loud to the brooding silhouette that watched the evening fire.

In anger she faced the bitter truth that if she had been stronger and ignored the nagging voice in her head, at least maybe the night would have been theirs. Maybe he wouldn't have gone out early that morning—

Her head spun with a myriad of what-ifs and possibilities, but her thoughts kept coming back to the same simple philosophy; that everything happened at exactly the time and in exactly the way that it was supposed to. Even death.

A movement in the lower branches of a dense hedge caused Catherine to tighten her grip on Excalibur's hilt. Her sharp eyes scanned the foliage as her imagination playing havoc with speculation of what it could be. Tension gave way to blessed relief as two squirrels tumbled out of the leaves, embroiled in a fierce game of tag and totally indifferent to their audience.

"Only squirrels," Catherine started to say to the bundle in her arms, quickly choking back a tormented cry of discovery as her stare now beheld the cradled falcon, its eyes wide open.

Without warning, death had come swiftly to claim him, even as the loving circle of her arms had sought to carry him safely in rescue.

"No!" she screamed, dropping to her knees, frantically trying to feel for a sign of a heartbeat in the bloodied chest. Deep sobs racked her insides as she pleaded for him to come back, her breasts rising and falling under her labored breathing. "No!" she repeated over and over, the anguish of her loss viciously ripping apart her heart.

In despair she flung out her hands, accidentally knocking the crystal from where it lay near the hawk and sending it rolling toward the bushes. Her grief peaked to shatter the last shreds of her control, and her body violently lunged forward to retrieve on hands and knees the one symbol she had left of his memory.

As her fingers stretched out to grasp it Catherine was stunned to see a dainty pair of white-and-gold cloven hooves patiently facing her on the other side of the hedge.

Chapter Twenty-five

THROUGH BLINDING TEARS Catherine raised her head and blinked in rapt astonishment as the delicate animal she had seen once before gracefully emerged from the emerald hedge, its polished horn gleaming in the light.

Trembling, Catherine rose to her feet, the crystal clenched tightly in her right hand. She now saw that the equine creature was much smaller than she had originally perceived in the woods, its head reaching only as high as her shoulder.

Behind long lashes that fluttered as gently as butterfly wings, the unicorn's bright blue eyes regarded her with curiosity. *"Is something wrong?"* it asked at last, its sweet, melodic voice lilting flutelike on the air.

It turned its beautifully sculptured head to where Catherine was pointing, sighing in heartfelt compassion as its gaze fell on the pathetic remains of a fellow beast. The unicorn drew closer, dismayed that yet another senseless act had claimed one of the forest's own. There was too much of that these days.

Its silent thoughts reached out across the abyss of Catherine's loneliness to render comfort. *What a wonderful thing to be loved at the end with so pure a heart,* it said, the curls of its mane falling in a fluffly cascade down its slender neck.

The innocent observation caused Catherine's senses to reel and her eyes to well up with fresh tears. "How do you know about love?" she asked.

A laugh as light as a silver bell prefaced the unicorn's answer. *One doesn't live as long as my kind without learning something,* it replied. *The very air around you dances with love's energy. That,*—it nodded,—*was how I knew.*

In thoughtful resignation it watched as Catherine knelt down to touch the blood-soaked feathers, its heart wincing in sympathy as the floodgates of her grief poured open and she wrapped her arms around the lifeless body.

Is there anything I can do? it inquired, unable to stand so much pain in one so young and pretty. As an errant breeze teased its porcelain-white fetlocks, the unicorn anxiously glanced about at its surroundings. Intuition was subtly warning that danger might be close at hand. Its voice urged Catherine in whispered caution that it was not safe for them to stay in one place so long. *Perhaps you should think of moving on . . .* it recommended, tactfully implying that distance would assuage the evident sorrow.

The kind and well-intentioned words of advice, however, were falling on a distracted mind. Somewhere, Catherine recalled, she had read something about unicorns, a legend about their magical power to heal. Had it been something to do with the golden horn? She couldn't remember.

Even magic has its limits, the sweet voice interrupted, tossing its snowy curls in despair. Catherine looked up as the unicorn completed its hesitant delivery of bad news. *I'm afraid it's too late.*

The forlorn expression that tightened on Catherine's face was so upsetting that it was virtually impossible to ignore or dismiss. *Well,* the unicorn said, sighing, *I suppose it wouldn't do any harm just too look.*

Catherine moved aside as the elegant beast stepped forward and lowered its head, the spiraled horn barely grazing the falcon's torn chest. With heart pounding and nerves quaking, Catherine waited for the unicorn's verdict. Unexpectedly the velvety smooth muzzle of pale pink wrinkled in puzzlement. *How very strange,* it remarked, cocking its head to one side as if to study the bird from a different angle.

"What's strange?" she asked.

Without lifting its head the unicorn inquired what manner of enchantment was in place. *I sense that life is gone,* it said, *and yet it's not.*

A sudden surge of hope coursed through Catherine's veins. Was it possible that somehow she had been mistaken?

Oh, it's quite dead, the unicorn said, reading her mind, and hastily corrected her rush of false hope. *It's just that I feel a spirit here that by the laws of nature should have already left. Whatever this creature was,* it speculated, *its death is certainly not as it seems.*

"That's because—" Catherine began, vacillating between telling the truth and perpetuating a lie.

Because what?

With quiet firmness Catherine chose to confide in the pretty animal whose courage had already saved her once from harm. "It's Merlin," she said.

The pale brows above its blue eyes arched in questioning surprise. *Merlin?* it repeated. *As in the Merlin?*

"You know who he is?" Catherine asked excitedly, longing now for the security of a kinship with one from the magician's past.

Who doesn't?

The unicorn shrugged its shoulders. A hint of disapproval colored its remembrance. *He left us some time ago and never returned.*

"It wasn't his fault," Catherine quickly defended, hoping that she had not made a mistake in sharing the secret. "A lot of things happened, things that he's come back to fix."

I see. The unicorn nodded, its tail swishing up and against its hip to dispatch efficiently a crimson dragonfly. *That would explain, I suppose, what you're doing with the High King's sword.*

The casual reference to Excalibur was the unicorn's first mention of it since their encounter, though surely it had not been because of any failure on the animal's part to see it.

Impatiently Catherine turned the conversation back to the hawk. "There must be *something* you can do," she insisted. "You said yourself that it didn't feel right to you."

Feeling that something isn't right and proceeding to take action, the unicorn gently pointed out, *are two entirely different things. However deeply your heart aches in sadness, there comes a time when acceptance is all that remains.*

Catherine shuddered at the unicorn's blunt counsel, stunned and sickened by the knowledge that nothing could bring back the one she loved. She covered her face with trembling hands, the crystal sliding to her lap as she gave vent to the bitter emotion raging in her soul.

The sudden vibrancy of the unicorn's voice caught her off-guard. *May I see that, please?* it asked, its withers quivering as its head bowed forward.

Uncertainly Catherine extended the crystal in the flattened palm of her hand. The luminous blue eyes widened in astonishment, its face now shining with a steadfast peace. *Of course.* It nodded. *I should have suspected . . .*

"What is it?" she demanded, both excited and aggravated by the unicorn's gift for abstraction.

There is only one who can explain such things, it announced with finality. *You must go to the Goddess.* It curiously studied Catherine's peculiar reaction. *The idea doesn't please you?* it inquired.

Catherine stiffened, momentarily abashed in her recollection of the blame she had silently laid at the Goddess' doorstep for denying her what she most desired. "We disagreed about something," Catherine confessed vaguely. "Well, not *exactly* disagreed. I guess it was more a lack of communication. To go to her now—"

Would be the wisest choice of all, the unicorn said.

"Even if . . . even if I still think she was wrong?" Her voice had drifted into a hushed whisper.

It would not be the first time her judgment has been questioned. The silky black lashes blinked in earnest concern. *You must not let your anger destroy your faith in the ways of the Goddess, for she is most powerful.*

"Powerful enough to bring him back to life?"

If it is meant to be, the unicorn replied. *Nothing occurs in the Goddess' world that is without a reason.*

"How do you know?"

Absently the unicorn pawed at the grass with an exquisite hoof. *I know because it simply is. Since the beginning of the forest and until the end of the stars, the Goddess knows all that will come to pass and directs all creatures to fulfill her plan.*

In spite of her tears a smile tipped the corner of Catherine's lips. "Merlin said the same thing."

Perhaps, her companion demurely suggested, *he learned it from a unicorn.*

Catherine dabbed at her red-rimmed eyes with the ragged edge of her cloak. "How far from here is the lake? She sniffed, closing her fingers around the crystal that the unicorn had found so interesting.

If I carry you— it began, but Catherine interrupted with a vigorous protest.

"Your size," she said, hoping not to offend the animal's feelings of generosity. "It would never work."

A sweet laugh rippled the air. *If your love for this man of magic is as strong as you say,* it replied, *my back and my legs shall be just as strong to carry you where you must go.*

Little by little the warmth began to creep back into Catherine's body. On a day that now seemed far in the past, she remembered that Merlin himself had called the maternal spirit the giver and taker of life. Whatever was going to happen now, she quietly resolved, it was no longer in her hands but in those of the mysterious waters.

The unicorn's sharp intake of breath caught Catherine's attention. "What's wrong?" she exclaimed, alarmed by the flaring pink nostrils and its ears, sharply pricked forward in heedful caution. Newly perceptible on the breeze came a whiff of pungent sulfur, a sickening odor she remembered smelling just recently.

Quickly! The unicorn snorted in fear. *Climb upon my back!* Like a camel kneeling down, it lowered itself so that she might straddle it without difficulty. *Hurry!*

The urgency of its tone set Catherine to picking up the falcon and wrestling with Excalibur's weight in her free hand. Beneath her feet, the forest ground began to tremble as the aroma grew stronger.

"How can I hold on?" she lamented, not entirely convinced that even with both hands unencumbered she'd make a skilled equestrian.

Press tightly with your knees and thighs, it breathlessly instructed as it rose again to its diminutive but stately height. *And keep your head down when we come to trees.*

"But what—" Catherine started to ask, her words smothered in a frothy cascade of leonine curls swept back as the unicorn burst into speed, its hindquarters barely escaping the jag of bright green flame that ripped through the underbrush.

Young saplings shivered and fell at the forest's path, parted by the bulk of reptilian scales that passed between. The oily black tongue flicked out like a snake as the ugly head emerged in the clearing, yellow clawed feet sinking into the soil and leaving deep indentations. The magic flames sizzled into putrid smoke as the dragon's full body now occupied the very spot that only a moment before had been a scene of peace.

The slits of the malevolent beast's copper-colored eyes narrowed in anger that her human quarry had once more escaped. For the time being . . .

How long and how far they rode, Catherine could not tell. The unicorn's hooves trailed weightlessly over the terrain. *Courage!* it whispered each time Catherine felt as if she were going to fall, her legs aching from the pressure of squeezing the animal's girth. Onward it galloped, until at last the jeweled sun gave way to the rose-colored mists of dusk and Catherine blinked her eyes at the lush scenery that was beginning to look familiar.

From here, the unicorn announced, slowing to a canter, *you'll be able to find your own way.* Ahead lay the prominent outcropping of blue rock that marked the path of the Goddess' domain.

"Can't you come with me?" Catherine urged, accustomed now to its gentle company.

It is your destiny to go alone, the unicorn replied, kneeling down that she might slide off to the carpet of dew kissed grass. *Mine was simply to delivery you safely.* The blue eyes glistened with life, a bit of sadness and immeasurable warmth. *I shall miss you,* it said.

"Will I see you again?" Catherine asked faintly, propping the sword against her leg so she might stroke the petal-soft nose with her fingers.

It if is the plan of the Goddess, it replied with an innocent nod. *I am only a servant who goes where her wishes send me.*

Above them, an opal-colored moon hung suspended above the treetops. With a pang of sadness Catherine watched the lithe body turn and disappear into a thicket, its hooves hardly making a sound. "Good bye," she called after it, faltering in the eerie silence that now engulfed her.

A light fog rose off the lake's surface as Catherine approached.

A thrill of frightened anticipation touched her spine. "Hello?" she said out loud, chilled by the sound of her own voice in the stillness of the enchanted clearing. "Hello?"

Squinting into the misty darkness, it was impossible now to discern the lake's color or, accordingly, its occupant's mood. Strange and disquieting thoughts began to race through Catherine's mind. What if the Goddess truly had forsaken her? What then?

Anxiety raced through her as she closed her eyes and concentrated as hard as she could. *Please,* her thoughts begged as she nervously bit her lip. *Please hear me. . . .* Hot tears slipped down her cheeks, the last traces of resistance vanishing in her silent prayer for help.

The hand that touched Catherine's shaking shoulder from the back made her jump in alarm. In fright she wheeled around, surprised gratitude exploding on her face as her eyes made contact with the imposing figure whose forehead bore the crescent-shaped scar beneath the blue-black widow's peak.

A flood of words tumbled from Catherine's mouth, her heart skipping a beat with the knowledge that the Goddess *had* heard her and had sent someone to help.

The tall woman's expression remained taut and unaffected as Catherine spilled forth her story. Without speaking, as was their ancient custom, the woman held out both hands.

Reluctantly Catherine looked down at the blood-soaked bundle in her arms. "Can you do something?" she asked tremulously, fearful of relinquishing it. The austere countenance neither smiled nor frowned as strong fingers reached out to take the falcon and pull it to her breast. Unexpectedly her lean hand went out once more in expectation.

Catherine scowled at first, unsure of what the woman wanted. Then she remembered, cautiously opening her fingers to reveal the precious crystal she had held so tightly that it left its mark within her palm. "Please," Catherine whispered, her burning eyes searching for the slightest clue of reassurance as she laid the stone into the outstretched hand. "Please help him."

With a tilt of her head the woman indicated that Catherine could do nothing more than wait. Too weary to argue, Catherine dragged Excalibur along behind her, toward the trees where she might rest, conscious that the woman was watching her.

Moonlight danced off the sword's flat surface as she set it down on the grass, its jeweled hilt sparkling with an intensity that would make the night stars jealous.

A subtle splash across the lake made Catherine turn as she prepared to sit down, her mouth opening in startlement to find herself alone once again. A gentle ripple was slowly dissipating as it reached the shore. It was the black object that trailed along the lake's edge, though, that stunned Catherine into a shocking realization. There, where she had dropped it when she entered the water, lay the cloak of the woman with the crescent-shaped scar. The Goddess herself.

Chapter Twenty-six

RESTLESS THOUGHTS INTERRUPTED Catherine's vain attempts at sleep, her heart chiding itself for taking so long to recognize what now seemed an obvious truth. In retrospect she recalled how the mysterious woman had neither eaten nor slept with the others, assuming instead the role of watchful guardian.

So, too, had she personally watched over Catherine from the beginning, even to the point of dispatching her golden horned emissary to deliver her twice to safety. The unicorn's words slipped back to console her in her lonely midnight vigil by the lake. The Goddess has a reason for this, Catherine silently reminded herself, praying that the reason would justify the soul-tearing pain of the magician's violent death.

The distinctive sound of a wave slapping against the shore brought Catherine instantly alert, her sharp eyes now discerning a slow-moving shadow on the lake's surface. Just below the hovering mist, the dark shape was rhythmically swimming toward land.

In spite of the Goddess' remark that evil knew better than to trespass here, Catherine felt her hand inching its way toward the sword that lay by her side, prepared to defend herself if necessary.

The cadenced strokes stopped as the dark shape neared what must have been the shallow portion of the lake, its silhouette slowly rising as it began to walk in Catherine's direction. The moon softly illuminated its features for the first time.

Her breath caught in her lungs as she leapt to her feet with a cry and plunged toward the water. Its warm waves had swirled the gown up to her slender hips by the time she reached the muscular frame of Kyle Falconer, his body completely naked except for the sparkle of crystal that bobbed at his chest as he quickened his pace to match hers. His voice managed no more than the hoarse whisper of her name as they plummeted into each other's willing arms, the hot caress of his lips on her mouth and along her neck setting her aflame.

His darting tongue sent intimate shivers of desire racing through her as she buried one hand in the thickness of his wet hair and hungrily traced down the outline of his glistening back with the other.

"Catherine," he murmured again with an intensity that reverberated with carnal longing. "My love . . ."

His lips recaptured hers, more demanding this time, as his moist hands slid down to massage her lower back and the roundness pleasingly accentuated by the soaked and clinging material. Urgent and exploratory, he pulled the gown up to her waist, quickly returning to lustfully caress the smooth, bare skin that lay beneath.

Passionately his mouth throbbed with a message that mere words could not have begun to convey. The concave hollow of her spine tingled at his probing touch, her heartbeat skyrocketing as he tenderly stroked the round globes of her bare buttocks. "I've waited so long for you, my darling," he said, his tear-smothered voice echoing her own sweet yearning. As his arm masterfully slid under the back of her knees to lift her from the lake, Catherine knew that the time of waiting was finally was over for both of them.

The damp black curls of his chest ticklishly rubbed against her cheek as he carried her to shore, her inner arm grazing a tender nipple teased to hardness by the burgeoning realization of his long unsated needs.

Lovingly he knelt to lay her down on a thick carpet of verdant moss, his right hand sliding out from under her legs, fluidly trailing up and between them, hesitating just as he reached the core of her womanhood.

"I love you so much," he declared softly, his smoldering eyes intently pleading for the reply that had been in her heart from the first time she saw him . . . the reply *his* heart needed to hear before he could take the step that would change their lives forever.

As if her three words had released him from a prison of his own making, Kyle's warm hand continued on its sensual course, his fingers meeting the moist confirmation that she wanted this as much as he did. A sigh of aching delight hung on Catherine's lips as his right leg slowly swung over hers, his hand massaging her with a steady, circular motion that electrified her with an ecstasy beyond description, an explosive tremor beyond imagination.

As he aroused her to passion his own grew more fierce, the hardness of his chest crushing her beneath him while her lips burned in the pleasure of his total possession. Catherine arched her back as his hands now moved impatiently to disrobe her, drawing the fabric up to her waist, her breasts, stripping it off completely over her head and laying it aside.

In worshipful admiration his eyes roamed over her slim body, sensuously proclaiming without need of words his craving for every part of her. With tantalizing possessiveness he traced a fingertip across her lip, down her chin, and between the soft curves of her upper body, bending his head to fondle with his tongue the dusty pink buds that had swollen to their fullest.

A delicious shudder of excitement heated her entire body as she abandoned herself to the rush of vibrant sensation, raking her fingers through the thick hair that was descending with deliberate lust and purpose down her ribs and taut abdomen.

Seductively he planted a trail of feather-light kisses along the skin of her inner thighs, setting her to breathe in the deep, soul-searching drafts of a lover's ardor, drawing out the dizzying anticipation of his return trip back up to her lips. And then, just as she cried out for him to release her from a sizzling and erotic torture, his hand took hers and placed it on the throbbing muscle between his legs.

"I'm yours, my beloved," he said with a moan as her fingers lovingly curled around its circumference and eagerly reacted to its radiating heat.

Almost in slow motion now, his body closed over hers as her hips raised to accept him, his entry causing both to gasp at the magnitude of hot pleasure that seemed to have no limits. Together they found the harmonious tempo that bound them as one, the pulsating feel of each other's skin exalting them to levels neither had imagined possible.

Over and over, his lips against her ear torridly reaffirmed his love for her, his promise that she alone would possess his heart for all eternity.

Swept up in a raw flood tide of fiery emotions, neither one could harness the sheer outcries of delight that followed, Catherine's insides exploding with the liquid sweetness that united them more completely than anything else on Earth.

In exhaustion his body melted against hers, a groan of contentment sending the last involuntary tremor down the length of his spine. Flesh against flesh, she lay in the protected haven of his arms, savoring the intoxicating feeling of unparalled joy that at long last she had found the one place she belonged . . . always.

The early morning song of silver crickets roused Catherine from sleep, the sky placidly bathed in a mist of dark sapphire that cast the lake world in shadows. A smooth arm lay across her breasts. She turned her head to gaze at the handsome man who still slumbered beside her, a look of total peace softening his face.

It had not been a dream, as at first she had feared. He was hers, as she had longed for him to be, her inner thighs still tingling with remembrance of their escalating passion and searing liberation. Basking in the afterglow of his sweet lovemaking, she could almost bring herself to believe that the Goddess had planned it exactly this way from the very start.

The delicate crystal rose and fell at the end of its gold chain as he breathed, prompting Catherine to notice something she had completely overlooked in the tempestuous fervor of their consummation. His left pectoral and shoulder, which logically should have born evidence of his wound as the falcon, were flawless, a startling condition that further served to enhance her estimation of the Goddess' power.

It was the jeweled sparkle of light, though, that mystified her most. What had the unicorn suspected . . . and yet chose not to share? Her imagination dancing, she wondered why the Goddess had seemed more insistent on the delivery of the crystal to her hand than of the reddish-brown bird to the nurturing cradle of her arms.

With a lazy stretch Kyle stirred beside her, the waning moonlight painting swaying shadows of branches across his hips and down his sturdy thighs. Through half-closed lids his eyes met hers, drinking in the sensuality of her feminine physique. He reached over to trail his fingertips slowly up the line of her jaw and brush back her hair. "I love you," he murmured, raising himself up on one elbow to gaze down at her with tenderness.

His lips touched hers like a whisper yet coaxed her into a drugged euphoria from which she longed never to escape. She drew his virile body close for a renewed embrace, savoring the feeling of satisfaction his nearness generated.

"I want so much for you to be happy," he said into the pulsing hollow at the base of her throat, sealing his wish with a moist kiss.

"I'm happy with *you*," she replied, wanting nothing more at that moment than to remain with him forever in the sheltered cove of enchantment. Her hands feverishly roamed down his back, squeezing the tensed buttocks that now lay exposed to her as he sought to rekindle the evening's scorching flame.

Gusts of desire shook her as she yielded to his impassioned thrust and his hungry search of her body's pleasure points. An overpowering sense of completeness pervaded her entire being as the love flowed between them like a surging current. With groans of uncontrollable delight they surrendered themselves, each to the other, collapsing at last as the first blush of day began to rise over the treetops.

Nearly an hour of blissful rest passed before he stirred again, his dark brows slanting in a frown.

"What is it?" she inquired, sensing his subtle disquiet. The sunlight that hauntingly glanced off Excalibur was an answer in itself. Clearly he was remembering his honor-bound obligation to see it safely to Avalon.

"Last night," he whispered, "and again this morning . . ." His silky voice trailed off. "It all would have been so easy to forget."

The vow weighed heavily upon her, choking her happiness with the painful reality that passion had supplanted so magically. Screams of frustration leapt at the back of her throat as he revealed his intention to continue on to Avalon, as she knew he must.

Her next words barely rose from her pale lips. "When do you have to leave?"

Smiling sadly, he caressed her cheek, his index finger catching the first hint of tears she so desperately was trying to hold in check. "I should leave now," he replied, torn by conflicting emotions and the open sorrow that shadowed her face. His chest heaved with the enormity of the task that confronted him and the void that her departure would carve in his life permanently. "I'll ask the Goddess to send you back."

A resounding splash turned both of their heads toward the lake, its surface slowly turning dark. *If you do,* the disembodied voice announced with brittle clarity, *you'll be wasting your time.*

Kyle's right brow shot up in amazement, more so from the lake's blunt and controversial statement than from her invasion of their intimate privacy. Self-conscious, Catherine scanned for her gown, still unaccustomed to a spirit whose unruffled streak of independence prompted her to intervene without the slightest provocation.

"I'd be sealing her own death sentence if she stayed," he protested as the waters shimmered in swirls of plum and indigo.

Her absence, the lake countered, *would have sealed your own death. Where would that have left you?*

His brown eyes flashed imperiously. "What about Nimue?"

What about her?

His tone was coolly disapproving of the Goddess' casual indifference to his claims of danger. "She knows who Catherine is," he reminded her.

Of course she does, the lake replied. *Why else would she be stalking her so relentlessly if not to kill her all over again?*

"So you agree, then?" he asked probingly. "You'll send her back?"

Nothing of the sort. The waters glittered with the fire of red amber. *The final truth awaits you both at Avalon. Thus both of you must go.*

"What kind of assurance do I have that she'll be safe?" he challenged, his words hardened with cynicism.

As dramatically as it had come, the color began to dissolve back to a tranquil turquoise. *I've been sending you as much assurance as anyone reasonably deserves.* The lake sighed in moderate exasperation, as if weary of wizards and mortals who professed to know more than she did. *If you'd rather be on your own—*

"You win," Kyle bitterly conceded with a sigh, tossing a glance at Catherine, who sat clothed beneath the tree in wait for his decision.

Of course I do, the Goddess concurred, her words fading into the breeze as her last whisper fell on Catherine's ears alone. *There is only one secret that he still keeps to himself. . . .*

"What is it?" Catherine questioned out loud, unaware that Kyle had not heard.

Avalon, the Goddess repeated softly. *You will learn it at Avalon.*

"Is something wrong?" he asked tenderly, disturbed by her vague look of puzzlement.

Elated by the knowledge that she would accompany him, but perplexed by the mystery that still remained, Catherine only shook her head and sat back to wait for him as he donned the tunic and tights the Goddess conveniently had returned while they slept.

High on a rocky and windswept crest above the lake, the underbrush quivered as its imposing visitor lethargically flexed her long talons. Icy contempt flashed in the copper-colored eyes that beheld the loving embrace of the couple below, their bodies now just footsteps away from leaving the lush sanctuary that represented their only protection.

Enough already, the dragon said snorting beneath her foul breath, impatient to reclaim her treasure and put an end to her rival once and for all.

Chapter Twenty-seven

"HOW CAN YOU be so certain?" Catherine asked as they set out past the blue rocks and embarked on the road to the north. Her question about the mention of Nimue's pursuit had touched off his assumption that she and the dragon were one and the same.

"It stands to reason," he said with a shrug. "Dragons were already few and far between back at the time of Arthur. Those that chanced to be slain by knights met their fate because they were either too old or too infirm to get away." He shook his head. "The one you described to me sounds young."

"But why turn herself into anything?" Catherine argued, skirting the issue completely of *how* she had done it. Certainly her tutelage under Merlin had endowed her with the power to do pretty much whatever she wanted.

"Disguise, for one thing," he offered, taking her hand as they forded a cold rivulet, the origins of which sprang from a mountain waterfall. "Betrayal is not soon forgotten here," he explained. "To appear as herself would no doubt invite obstacles to her plan."

After thoughtful reflection he proposed another reason she had chosen to transform herself into so frightening an image. "It's the embodiment of all that is evil, just as your unicorn is a symbol of all that is pure." His eyes combed the landmarks that guided their way. "It wouldn't even surprise me if she's already figured out where we're going."

Niggling doubts still stood in the way of Catherine's acceptance that the monster who had chased her really was the vengeful Nimue. "What about the fire?" she challenged. "You told me she was afraid of it, and yet she was using it herself against me."

"The illusions that one personally controls," he replied, "are never as frightening as the same concept used against you by someone else." His mouth thinned with displeasure, the tensing of his jaw betraying his annoyance. "I suspect that before our quest is through, she will have employed every trick to scare us that I had the poor judgment to teach her."

"But you'll be able to fight her, won't you?" she spoke up, her inflection making it more of a statement than a question. An old conversation jogged her memory. "You said you hadn't taught her *everything,*" she reminded him, hoping that it would encourage him to reveal the one card he had yet to play. "She doesn't know how you got out of the cave."

"I'm afraid the secret of my escape won't do us much good in Avalon," he confessed, declining to elaborate. As they climbed higher and higher into the beckoning hills, a light drizzle of rain had begun to fall.

Time, Catherine had by now decided, could no longer be measured in hours or days, her mind losing track of all but her deepening love for the man who alternately strode ahead and beside her yet was never more than an arm's length away.

Daylight settled into dusk and back again; by the third such cycle she resolved to stop counting. Throughout their journey his care and attentiveness were filling her with even more love. When her legs ached with the strain of climbing, he was the one to suggest that they stop and rest, massaging her feet and calves until the pain had passed. He was also the one who anticipated whenever she might be getting hungry or thirsty, providing for them both with nature's bounty and magic's supplement.

Now and again her concerns would return to the twentieth century, teasing her curiosity about how much time had passed there in her absence. If there was any consolation to be found in her parents being deceased, she rationalized, it was that they had been spared the soul-wrenching distress of worrying about where she had gone and what had become of her. In truth, they were the only ones who really would have mattered. Would they have liked Kyle? she wondered. Her heart longed to believe they would have approved of her choice.

The driving passion that consumed Catherine and Kyle most, however, was the one need that caution dictated he firmly deny. "If I should make myself vulnerable to you," he explained gently, "I would make us both vulnerable at that moment to Nimue's vengeance. Beyond the sacred lake's protection we can't take any chances."

Catherine nodded gravely, dropping her lashes to conceal her disappointment that Nimue continued to cast a dark pall on their relationship. "Do you think she knows where we are?"

"Without question," he affirmed. "If I know Nimue, she's been following us ever since we took leave of the Goddess."

The rain stayed with them as they traveled on, finally culminating in an electrical storm that lit up the sky the evening they reached the dreamscape making the entrance to Avalon.

Twin spires of frosted purple flanked the narrow passageway that began prefacing the road's descent into Britain's Isle of the Dead. Downward it wended, its snaky course reminding Catherine of San Francisco's Lombard Street. At last it spilled out into a misty bayou where fireflies bobbed like marionettes and the trees were so dense with moss that their branches swayed like blue feather boas over the marshy ground.

"Over there," he said pointing. "That's where we're going."

Ahead of them an indefinite shoreline seemed to drop off into a broad channel from which wispy lilac vapors rose and curled like sensuous smoke. Beyond the mist, he told her, lay the invisible island where the souls of Britain's warriors were said to dwell. It was toward this island that they would send Excalibur.

In every moving shadow Catherine began to imagine Nimue's menacing presence; with every rumble of thunder her mind harked back to the heavy sounds of the dragon's arrival. On such a night as this, it would not be difficult for one with wicked cunning and a desperate incentive to use the storm to advantage.

"Do you think maybe we lost her?" Catherine inquired hopefully, telling herself that it would have been impossible for so large an animal to pass through so tight an entry.

"More likely," he contested, "she's changed to a new plan of attack."

Their own plan, he went on, would be for him to start building the barge for Excalibur's transport. "I'll build you a good campfire over there," he continued, indicating an overhanging lip of rock that offered a natural shelter from the elements, "where you can wait for me."

"After all this time I think I can build my own fire," she responded playfully.

Smiling at her twentieth-century independence, he replied, "I have my reasons, Catherine. While I'm working, Excalibur will remain in your possession—until the time comes to lay it out on the pyre."

"But what if Nimue comes?" Catherine queried, fearful for his life on the open exposure of shore.

"It will be safer with you," he reiterated, averse to admit that she was the one in greatest danger from Nimue's wrath. "Just stay close to the fire," he instructed, "and make sure that it doesn't go out."

Restlessly she hugged her knees to her chest trying to stay warm in the clinging dampness of the mystical everglade to which Arthur's paladins had long ago brought him for his final voyage. Beyond the flickering firelight and illumined by the bright jags of lightning, she could see Kyle still at work. The rough-hewn raft was nearly finished. To take her mind off her chill she set it to the task of remembering.

It was now virtually impossible for her to separate what she had read of English legends from what she may have vigorously lived in her own incarnation. To pass the time on the road Kyle had further added to her education with tales of Arthur as a child and himself as a young wizard. And as he spoke, her imagination saw it all, delighting in the adventure, the sorcery, and the glorious color that made her own world drab by comparison.

Which one really *was* her own world, though? Was it the one in which her parents had raised her? Her thoughts floated back to kittens and ice-cream cones, to birthday parties with games and glittered hats, to getting gold stars in school for doing well. Like taking a trip through the pages of a photograph album, she could see herself in cap and gown, waving to her mother as she proudly clutched the diploma that would open doors to the glamorous career of writing. In the blink of an eye she even saw Nat and Larry and her boss, and a host of other faces that had peopled her life, yet still she was left feeling empty and alone.

Then there was *this* world, the one that quite possibly existed only because she believed in it so much. A world in which damsels once waited in ivory towers for knights to find their way through the forest and rescue them. A world where lakes could talk and animals could listen and in which only the foolish dared turn their backs and close their minds against the power of magic.

Most of all, though, it was a world filled with *him*, the soul mate that she had been meant to find. With a wistful smile she looked back over everything that had ever happened to her, recognizing the events now as the pieces of a giant picture puzzle on which she had started to work without any clue of the ordered design.

In its own timing and by its own methods, fate had delivered her to this century and to this place of legend to complete the composition. And as she stepped back in her imagination to admire the finished work, her heart filled in the final touch of a couple entwined on the shallow bank of a misty lake at dawn. This is where she belonged, she told herself. Having tasted his lips and felt his love driven deep inside her, Catherine knew without question that there was no way she could ever live happily anywhere else.

A sputter of flame drew her attention back to the fire. With a start she saw that it had died down during her sensual reverie. She reached for the stick to reawaken the glowing embers. To her satisfaction the gentle prodding coaxed them back to life, their orange glow now casting light on the shadowy white figure that stirred between the trees to her right. With delight she saw that it was none other than the unicorn, no doubt sent by the Goddess to ensure the success of their mission. Yet with a furtive glance toward the shore and the dark-haired man who labored there, it failed to respond to Catherine's enthusiastic greeting.

"It's okay," she said, seeking to reassure it, determining that it probably hadn't recognized who the man was. "It's Merlin."

The sound of the storm, though, was swallowing up her earnest words. Anxious that the unicorn not be too frightened to approach, Catherine rose to her feet and started toward it, her hand outstretched.

As the distance between them shortened, however, her eyes

beheld with alarm that something was terribly wrong. The creature that had previously glowed in the forest with radiant health now looked like a ghostly shell of its former self. A deathly gray pallor had replaced the satin coat of pure white, its diminutive frame nearly skeletal as it trembled behind the curtain of rain-slicked willow branches. Its horn, once polished gold, now protruded like a rusted rod from its sloping forehead, and its mane was dirty and matted. Only when she was finally close enough to see its eyes beneath a bright flash of lightning did Catherine's concern transcend to sheer horror.

As she backed up with a gasp the creature disintegrated like grains of sand through an hourglass, materializing again behind her on the very spot where she had left Excalibur, thwarting her chance to run back and grab it.

With a scream she yelled for Kyle as the dingy creature with eyes that blazed like hot copper set a cracked and yellow hoof arrogantly down on the sword's hilt. Even as the magician ran toward them the illusion was rapidly dissolving into Nimue, her greedy fingers closing around Excalibur's handle as she rose to confront them in a diaphanous gown that left no part of her anatomy to the imagination.

With an angry flick of her wrist a low wall of green flames ripped through the narrow space that separated Kyle from them, its intensity throwing Catherine to the ground. She found herself trapped on the same side as her lover's enemy.

"We meet again, magician!" She laughed wickedly, the earsplitting sound of triumph echoing in the sinister shadows of the storm-tossed night.

"Let her go!" Kyle ordered, his jaw and fists clenched in anger as the wind swept his black hair back like a giant raking comb. "*I'm* the one you *want*, not *her!*"

Nimue licked her full red lips salaciously, appraising the potent strength of the man who dared to oppose her. "All in good time," she purred, strolling toward Catherine, who until now had been too stunned to move.

Teasingly she ran the sword's deadly point along Catherine's throat, inches from grazing her fair skin. "You," she said, snarling, "are becoming an annoyance."

Catherine could hear Kyle shouting above the storm.

"She hasn't *done* anything to you!" he yelled, the fear trembling in his lungs as he watched Nimue enjoy her taunting death game.

Laughter again bubbled from the blond vixen's throat. "And I intend to see that it *stays* that way!" she pronounced, directing her next remark to her victim. "Why couldn't you have stayed dead, where you belonged?"

Across the flickering wall Kyle sought to bargain with the woman whose greed had plunged her to the brink of madness. "Name anything!" he pleaded hotly. "Just tell me what I can give you that will make you let her go!"

Haughtily Nimue tossed back her head and informed him that he lacked the power to order any of her actions, especially now that she possessed all that she could possibly desire.

"Except perhaps *one* thing," she hissed in fiendish delight, her eyes flashing with obvious satisfaction that she had reduced her enemies to quivering children held prisoner and existing entirely at her mercy. The wind and damp bayou plastered the gauzy gown to her voluptuous curves as she slyly proposed her ultimatum to the man she had wantonly seduced for the prize of his power. "Tell me how you escaped."

Chapter Twenty-eight

A WICKED LAUGH underscored Nimue's rejection of the magician's request for her to first release Catherine.

"Why should I?" She sneered childishly. "I have what *you* want, Merlin. *You* only have what I've been content thus far to go without knowing. Perhaps," she said with a shrug, brandishing Excalibur with playful abandon, "I don't even need to know it at all."

Kyle's eyes flashed with a savage inner fire as he appealed to her limitless sense of superiority. "Don't you?" he challenged, his voice cold and exact. "You seem to have lost your desire to be the best."

"I *am* the best!" she spat back, her face a glowering mask of fury and hatred.

"Not as long as I still hold the last secret from you," he taunted, imposing an ironlike control on himself to play her game through until the end.

A bright mockery invaded Nimue's retort. "Are you really that weak to the flesh," she said chidingly, "that life means more to you than magic? Or is it because the final seeds of the prophecy have already been planted?" Impulsively she lunged forward and grabbed Catherine's hair, violently jerking her head back. "*Tell* me!" she yelled at him. "Tell me or she dies!"

Wincing with pain, Catherine could now barely see him through the wicked blaze of green that kept him from reaching her, her senses alone feeling the desperation that had to have been coursing through every muscle of his body and face.

"Swear by the Goddess that you'll let her go!" she heard him command as thunder shook the ground beneath her and the rain fell in blinding sheets.

"I swear by no one!" she proclaimed arrogantly, bringing the sword parallel to Catherine's eyes, her voice hissing like steam. "I sealed your body in the cave forever!" She snarled. "How did you get out?"

Above the wind, Catherine could hardly hear his ominous and calculating reply. "How do you know that I *did*?"

Jags of silver lightning made the sky look as if it were being viciously torn in two and then hastily patched back together, creating a sinister backdrop for the final quest for power that was being waged.

Taut with anger and bristling with indignation at his riddles, Nimue demanded that he explain.

"The oldest magic there is," he shot back, "and the *only* one strong enough to transcend the blackness of your witchcraft."

Catherine could feel even in Nimue's clawlike fingers a definitive tremor of excitement. She *wanted* to know. She *had* to know. Another feeling was coming through, too, a feeling gleaned from the sixth sense that Catherine still awkwardly handled as a novice. Nimue was deathly afraid of something, something that Catherine's intuition couldn't help but perceive was drawing closer while the two voices were locked in battle across the fire.

"You're wasting my time, magician!" Nimue hoarsely barked. "*Tell* me!"

A cold, turbulent wind churned the wet leaves at their feet, setting them to spin recklessly like multicolored tops, chilling Catherine's soul as dramatically as the words that fell next from his lips.

"I escaped through my own dream."

If anger were a color, it would have been a vivid read as Nimue unleashed a hurl of accusations that he was lying. "That's impossible!" she yelled, the wind whipping her hair into a frizzy halo. "I want the *truth*!"

A cataclysmic shiver below the earth sent a broad-limbed tree crashing to its surface, the impact startling Nimue into loosening her grip on Catherine's hair. With a shriek of discovery she let go completely, her eyes frozen on what was now crossing the Channel at the magician's back. In disbelief Catherine saw it, too, and felt her pounding heart leap into her throat.

A contingent of ghostly warriors in silver-and-black armor were riding towards them, their horses caparisoned to match. With a gasp Catherine saw that the horses' hooves neither broke the surface of the water nor sent it splashing to their powerful chests as they galloped forward. And in that moment she realized what the shocked Nimue did not—that the horses and their riders from the Isle of the Dead had been created by illusion.

A terrible scream exploded from Nimue's lungs as she pushed Catherine aside and prepared to meet the attackers who had foolishly chosen to interfere with her time of triumph. In horror Catherine saw Nimue's lips curl back into a recalcitrant grin as she raised Excalibur high above her head with both hands, defying the oncoming warriors to pass within her death sword's range.

In what she would later recall took only a split second to happen, Catherine saw the smile twist into an ugly expression of horror and confusion. For as the riders entered the wall of green flame, there followed explosions like firecrackers, each knight and horse bursting into a pyrotechnic display of hot orange and neon crimson while a disoriented Nimue furiously sought to maintain her wits. With a roar the sky split open. A burning spear of bright lightning came crashing across the vengeful heavens, thrusting itself into the upraised point of Excalibur. Nimue's bloodcurdling screech fused with the north wind as Catherine turned her eyes away from the hideous and lurid sight of electrified death at the unmerciful hands of nature.

Kyle's arms were around her instantly, burying her head against his shoulder as the flames that had held her prisoner slowly died, leaving smoky traces. "It's over," he said, soothing her, his hand anxiously stroking her soaked hair as his quick kisses along her temple brought warmth back to her trembling body. "It's finally over."

The sword was all that remained on the charred ground. Soon the drenching rain subsided to a feather-soft sprinkle and the black clouds parted over a tranquil moon.

The aftermath of the storm's fury and Nimue's destruction had raised more questions that it had resolved. Catherine's lips sought to ask them all at once as Kyle lashed the final strips of wood to the barge.

"Did she know it would happen that way?" Catherine asked, referring to the Goddess, certain that she had been the gathering and inhuman force she had felt, the force that Nimue most feared. "Is that why she sent us to Avalon?"

"She knows *all* that will happen," he thoughtfully replied, his black hair glistening as he bent his head over his work. "As for Avalon, she sent us here because it was the place we were supposed to be." He seemed pensive, neither disturbed nor gratified. "What better setting to put an end to my enemy's evil than the same place where her war with the Goddess began?"

It was impossible for Catherine to shake the sizzling image of Nimue's death. She shuddered with the thought that its memory would haunt her dreams for many years to come. Yet when those nights came, her heart said to console her, she would have Kyle to hold her close in bed and make them go away.

"I was afraid of the horsemen myself," she now confessed freely, replaying in her mind the apparition's unexpected approach and their fiery convergence. "Can you just imagine," she speculated lightly, hoping to lift the somber mood, "if you use them someday in a performance back home?"

Even as she said it, she saw his forearms tighten and heard a sharp intake of breath. A flash of fear stabbed at her as she watched him turn to her with a look of undeniable anguish. Without warning his hands shot out and seized her, pulling her as tightly as he could against the corded muscles of his chest. His clamped lips imprisoned a sob that frightened her, and she floundered in the bewilderment of not knowing what she had said that had upset him so. When at last his words finally came, the effect on her was shattering.

"I can't go back to your time, Catherine . . . any more than you can stay here in mine."

"No!" she blurted out, breaking free of his grasp to confront him with eyes that blinked back hot tears of incredulous shock. "We belong together," she insisted, a flood of arguments bursting forth. "Nimue's dead. We can go on once Excalibur's out to sea—"

"Once Excalibur goes out to sea," he said, interrupting with a firmness that sent icy fingers of terror down her spine, "we each have to return to where we belong."

"But I belong with you!" she cried. "Why can't I stay?"

Immeasurable pain shone on the handsome face she had loved from the beginning. "Because what I told Nimue was the truth," he revealed as his hands squeezed hers with an intensity that otherwise might have hurt. "The moment I return to the cave, I will awaken to be as I was before."

Denial creased Catherine's angry words of protest, for she had feverishly interpreted his disclosure to Nimue as an elaborate ploy to stall for time. "It *can't* be!" she contended with unremitting passion. "You're *real*! You're *here*!" Impatiently she pulled her spinning recollections together. Nothing he had ever said or done validly supported the claim that he was anything less than alive or real. There had to be some other explanation.

With his head bowed in despair he forced himself to summon the courage to unmask what he knew he must.

"For three centuries," he began, "I wallowed in the pity of a man defeated by his own weakness. Because of me, my ward, my king, my very best friend above all others met a death too horrible for words. Because of me, Britain, too, suffered a blow from which it never recovered, a blow that I might have prevented had I possessed the strength to resist mortal temptation."

Catherine began to object to his self-reproach, but he brushed her attempt aside and continued on, his voice laced with bitterness and remorse.

"My dreams became all that comforted me in the darkness, for in dreams alone I could relive the past glory that was Camelot and the power that was once my own." The lines of concentration deepened along his dark brows. "Never in my banishment did the thought come back to me that I had always possessed the key to escape, until the Goddess spoke to me through the crystal that lined my prison and reminded me of the boasts I had made when my skills were at their peak."

It was beginning to return to her, the mystical segment of the second dream for which she had still not found a satisfying answer. The harp . . . the shimmering walls that danced with light . . . the insistent voice of the Goddess that had told him—

Catherine's body suddenly twisted in spasmodic remembrance as the exact words of the maternal spirit played back within her head. *"Nonsense,"* the Goddess had said, teasing him, *"you always said you could do it in your sleep."*

"My will to undo a great wrong," he explained, "broke free of the thick coils of slumber, enabling me to project my spirit to the outside." It was a power, he emphasized, that all men possessed, though few ever put it to use. The power to transcend pain, to recapture the past, to seek solutions in the future and carry them back to the present. As he spoke, Catherine's troubled thoughts returned to their conversation of dreams at Dupont Circle. Dreams were the soul's way of travel, he had told her that day, never revealing until now that they had been his own mode of travel as well.

His hand fingered the crystal at his chest. "Deep in the cave of the Summer Country, its twin lies over the heart of my physical being, awaiting my return. When their images have rejoined as one, the last of my strength as Merlin will be gone."

"But if you can exist outside of it . . ." Catherine cried, at a loss to understand.

"Those were not the terms by which the Goddess offered me my freedom." He shook his head in regret. "The true magic I possessed in my youth is gone, existing only as a shadow of illusion in my present state. Sadly it's a serviceable but still imitative facade of what I once could do." A wry smile curved his lips. "Illusion may have been enough to entertain the twentieth century," he observed, "but not enough to protect you in a land gone black with madness."

"We can protect each other!" she proposed, prepared without doubt or question to accept his world as her own. "We've already proven we can!"

His fingers tenderly glided over her tear-stained cheek. "What's been proven," he whispered, "is that love can exist beyond time and space. Yours is the face that will comfort me now in the darkness, Catherine . . . long after you're gone." The arms that embraced her were shaking as much as hers. "Know that I love you, that you carry a part of me, my darling."

Convulsive sobs racked Catherine's body as she clung to him, begging him to take her with him when he returned to the cave.

"I could never let you see me that way," he said softly. "I am ancient beyond years and ill beyond recovery. In truth, my greatest fear next to losing you is that I should die in my sleep before Excalibur could be reclaimed." His face was warm with love as he searched her eyes for acceptance of his destiny, placing her trembling fingers on the sparkling pendant. "You held my very soul in your hand and kept it safe, Catherine, as you'll hold it always, wherever you are."

Heat rippled under her fair skin as she ached for the sensual assurance of his touch. As involuntary tremors of arousal began, she held fast to the clinging hope that the Goddess would somehow change her mind. Passion pounded the blood through her chest and head as he kissed her with devouring possession, crushing her with a ferocity that made every pore cry out in desire. The turbulence of his love swirled around her, knocking her breath away as the midnight stars spun in reckless orbit.

Suddenly his grasp stiffened as his eyes looked up and over Catherine's shoulder. With a heart that lurched in trepidation she turned to follow his troubled gaze.

As motionless and serene as two statues, she saw the Goddess patiently waiting with the unicorn by her side, a garland of dark flowers draped like reins over its snowy shoulders.

In a panic, Catherine looked to Kyle for an explanation of what they were doing there.

A heaviness centered in his chest as his hesitant voice broke the strained silence. "They've come to take you back."

Chapter Twenty-nine

NOTHING THAT HAD ever come before in her life—including the death of her parents—equaled the quaking sorrow she felt now in the face of their impending separation. "Why does it have to end this way?" she demanded as the grief flowed freely from her heart.

"Because it does," echoed the voice of the Goddess, her countenance stern and immobile across the distance of the peaceable bayou.

"But we haven't had enough time!" Catherine protested.

"You have had more than enough time to learn the lessons for which this journey was meant," she replied, bristling with the impatient desire to return to the serenity of her lake and be done with the both of them.

Pleading fingers clutched at Kyle's tunic, urging him to intercede. In a low, tormented voice he replied that the decision had never been his to make. "Even if I could," he sadly confessed, "I'm not sure that I wouldn't be telling you the same thing she is." The longing and hurt lay naked in his eyes as he took a deep breath and adjusted his smile. "I'm definitely too old for you."

Her arms flew around his neck as she pressed her body against him in fear. "I *can't* go back without you!"

With firm restraint he peeled her away. "You *have* to," he repeated. "And you *must.*"

A gentle tap on Catherine's shoulder prefaced the lilting voice of the unicorn, and she turned to see its golden horn carefully lifting from the spot it had touched. Its approach was so quiet that neither one had heard it until it was there.

It's time to go, it said, its large blue eyes reflecting pained empathy for their star-crossed situation.

Catherine's hurried glance fell on the barge and the sword that had yet to grace its surface. "What about Excalibur?" she contested, reminding him of his personal vow to her that they would sent it on its way together.

"I did make a promise," he awkwardly admitted to the sympathetic beast. With a toss of its head the unicorn looked back at its imposing mistress with a long-lashed blink that implored her to fill this one last request.

Very well, the Lady of the Lake agreed, her sculptured face a mask of flawless marble beneath the moon's incandescence.

With arms wrapped tightly around each other's waists, Catherine and Kyle watched the tide coax the makeshift vessel out toward the center of the channel. Now and then a bright glint of Excalibur's glory shone through the flames that tenderly licked its length and sent spirals of smoke to mingle with the ghostly mist.

"Where will it go?" Catherine whispered, laying her head against his shoulder as the fire began to dance like a host of playful sprites across the splintered wood.

"It will go to Arthur," he replied in a voice choked raw by the significance of this moment. "And there it will remain until the next High King is born and can claim it rightfully."

"And you will be there to help him?" As Excalibur's protector, she remembered from legend the wizard would one day be recalled from death to serve at the new king's side.

"If it's the will of the Goddess." He nodded gravely, his muscles tensing as a sizzle of flame sent part of the barge into the water. Loving hands stroked her back as he set about memorizing this last picture of contentment to take with him in his retreat to the darkness.

"I could never love anyone else," she whispered after a moment, sickened by the thought of the empty future that now awaited her. "I never will."

His hand swept under her chin and tilted back her head. "You mustn't say that, he murmured earnestly, "not when you're a woman with so much precious love to give." His lips sweetly grazed her forehead. " As much as I hate to let you go, my darling, I know the Goddess knows what she's doing." Eyes brimming with tears gazed tenderly into hers. "And I can't believe she'd send you back to spend an entire lifetime alone."

His reference to time made her ask out loud the question that had furrowed her brow on more than one occasion since her arrival. "How long have I been here?" she wondered, conscious of the silky beard that now framed his jaw.

"A little over two months," came his reply, an answer that generated a ludicrous thought on Catherine's part.

"How *can* I go back?" she quipped, half serious. "I probably don't have a job anymore, my rent's way overdue, who knows what the leftovers in the back of my fridge look like."

Amusement flickered in the eyes that met hers. "I promised you long ago," he said, "that I would set right anything that my presence had put asunder." With palm pressed to palm, he interlaced his fingers with hers. "No time will have passed when you return."

A low groan rose from the channel as the barge succumbed to the force and magnitude of the fire, folding into the water in a billow of carmine smoke. With a tinge of pain in his heart Kyle knew that his mission was finally over.

It's time, the unicorn said behind them, kneeling down like an obedient lamb, its hooves neatly tucked in wait below its ivory body.

"But how will I get back?" Catherine quivered as with great reluctance she allowed herself to be put astride her unusual charger.

"Your steed knows where it's going," Kyle reassured her, fresh tears trembling in his eyelids. One last kiss caressed her lips before the unicorn rose to its feet. "I love you, Catherine, as I will love you forever."

Her hand unwillingly slid from his as the unicorn turned to canter toward the solitary figure in the hooded black robe. Wordlessly she and Catherine exchanged a long look as the unicorn paused at the base of the path. It was futile, Catherine realized, to try to appeal once more to the implacable spirit who governed all things. Instead she concentrated on a silent wish for the man she was forced to leave. "Please let him be happy," she prayed, a weak smile of thanks gracing her lips as the Goddess slowly nodded and laid her hand against the unicorn's crest in signal for the journey to begin.

Trusting in the Goddess' wisdom now must be difficult with a love as great as yours, the delicate creature said sympathetically as it plucked its way up the twisting path.

In her tortured mind Catherine was turning over whether it would have been better or worse never to have known him, never to have seen this place to which fate would now forbid her to return.

Time spent on love, the unicorn thoughtfully interjected, *is never time wasted. Think of how much richer you are for giving yourself . . . and how much wiser for knowing who you are.*

Catherine held tight to the rein of larkspurs that circled the unicorn's slender neck. "My mother used to say the same thing," she recalled with wistful longing, relating how tragedy had brought them closer than most mothers and daughters.

Your mother's spirit sounds very wise. The unicorn nodded. *I believe I would strive to be like her if I were human instead of beast.*

Halfway up the hill, Catherine was seized with a compulsion to look back. "Please stop," she urged, wanting to see her love one more time.

I'm not sure the Goddess would approve, the equine servant advised. *She's most particular about these things.*

"Please?"

Moved by compassion, the unicorn eased to a stop and maneuvered its lithesome body so that Catherine might look down through the branches at the two figures who now faced each other. The Goddess was extending her hand, palm upward, toward Kyle.

With a shiver of anxiety Catherine saw a look on his face that she had never seen before. "What's happening?" she asked the unicorn as she watched Kyle slip the chain and crystal off over his head and hand it to the Lady of the Lake.

We should move on, her companion warned her, pawing impatiently at the earth.

"Something's wrong," Catherine blurted out, overcome by the fear that seemed to emanate from Kyle's body, even at a distance. "Something is—"

In one swift motion the Goddess dashed the crystal against the jagged rocks at Kyle's feet, creating an explosion of brilliant reds and white-hot sparks that shot toward the heavens like a geyser.

Catherine's scream split the night as the unicorn broke into speed up the hill, the volume of her cry soon drowned out by the wail of a siren as an ambulance pulled away from the corner of Constitution and 10th Street.

A thousand images swam before Catherine's eyes; a cacophony of sounds assaulted her ears and caused her to moan in excruciating pain. Something was being placed over her nose and mouth, something she sought to rip away with flailing hands. Voices spoke to her, and yet the words came out as amplified gibberish; strong arms that sought to restrain her only set her to writhing even more violently.

Her body felt the sensation of moving, yet she could no longer feel the pulsating muscles of the unicorn beneath her as it surged through the dark forest. She was lying on her back, neither too warm nor too cold, her body gently swaying as the compartment in which she was traveling made sweeping turns as it sailed effortlessly along the ground.

The object again found its way to her face as hands efficiently moved to hold it there. Her nostrils and lungs began to tingle with the sensation of pure air as another set of hands adjusted what felt like a light blanket as it was pulled on top of her.

The crash of discordant sounds began to subside as, above them, a male voice bent close to her ear. "It's okay, ma'am. Take it easy. We're almost there."

Fatigue clogged her senses as she relinquished the desire to fight, clinging desperately instead to an image that was rapidly dissolving behind her closed eyelids.

You can find your way home from here, the unicorn softly told her as she slid from its back, her vision blurred by hot tears. They were at the edge of the forest, an enchanted place where lavender mist rolled from the cracks of hollow logs and the song of nightingales announced the coming of dawn.

A golden tear slipped down the unicorn's muzzle, and Catherine reached her hand up to brush it away.

Perhaps I'll carry you behind my shoulder again someday, the unicorn offered, tossing back the mane that nestled in folds like whipped cream.

Catherine longed to hold tight to its neck, to hold on to every detail of a century and a land that she would never see again.

Hurry, the unicorn urged her, stepping out of her embrace. *They're waiting for you to come back.*

Catherine strained her eyes to watch it go, squinting now into the bright lights of the curtained-off room to which she had been taken.

Hovering above her, the kindly face of an older man was peering at her intently, a stethoscope hanging from his neck.

"Well, that's more like it," he said pleasantly. "How are you feeling, young lady?"

Catherine looked around, disoriented, barely able to get out any words.

"Looks like you had a little fainting spell," he remarked as his fingers comfortingly took hold of the inside of her wrist. "Has this happened to you before?"

Dazed, Catherine shook her head, trying to assimilate what had happened.

"Can you tell us your name?" a female voice on her other side was inquiring.

"Catherine," she murmured drowsily. "It's Catherine. . . ."

"You know, I *thought* you looked familiar," the doctor remarked. "You write for the *Tribune,* don't you?" Pleased with his ability to recognize someone from a newspaper column, he proceeded to tell his nurse who Catherine was. "My daughter Becca's still got your *Cats* review taped to the refrigerator," he told her, holding the stethoscope to her chest.

"Fire," Catherine mumbled.

"What's that?" the nurse inquired as her cool hand brushed the hair back from Catherine's forehead.

"The fire . . ." Catherine repeated. "The fire at the museum."

"Well, I don't know anything about a fire," the doctor replied. "You *did* get a good bump on your head, though, when you fainted."

"Is there someone you want us to call?" the woman asked as she made notes on a clipboard.

"That's okay," the doctor said when he saw that the question was causing her distress. "We'll have plenty of time to take care of that tomorrow."

"Tomorrow?" Catherine repeated, finding it increasingly hard to concentrate.

"Nothing serious to worry about," he said, patting her hand. "It might be a good idea for you to enjoy our hospitality for the night." He reached across to initial what the nurse had written on the chart.

"What's wrong with me?" Catherine muttered as they prepared to have her moved.

"Well, that's what you're in a hospital to find out," he replied with a grandfatherly smile. 'It's up to you, of course, but you might just want to think about having a test in the morning."

"A test?" She blinked in puzzlement.

His concerned reply caught her completely off-guard.

"Is there any possibility you might be pregnant?"

Chapter Thirty

"Dr. Mayes called your office for you this morning," a freckled-faced nurse told her as she delivered Catherine's breakfast tray. "The receptionist said she'd notify your boss as soon as he comes in."

Catherine nodded absently, preoccupied with the test results that had been delivered to her just ten minutes before. Her hand still rested lightly on her stomach as she sat on the edge of the bed, a bittersweet peace pervading her thoughts.

Outside on the streets below, the Monday morning commuter traffic was in full flow. Beyond the door to her hospital room, a new day was teeming with energy. Within her heart, though, Catherine was aching with the memory of another century and the loss of the man whose child she now carried.

With irony she saw how the words of the prophecy had come to pass. She herself had been the daughter of the lake for whom Merlin's love had been intended. "She will bear my only son," his words came back to her, "and even though my own powers will be gone by then, his will be the magic to keep the world safe."

Had he known at the time they parted? She wondered, hoping that somehow he had, that the knowledge would bring him contentment as he closed his eyes and lay back against the shadows of the crystal cave.

Their night and morning together along the banks of the lake floated back to assuage the tears that had started gathering in her eyes. Never in her life would another memory of happiness surpass this one. Her fingertips still felt the warmth of his body, her lips still tingled with the hardness of his kiss. Even in reflection the searing ecstasy of their union sent quivers of flame along her inner thighs, reminding her of how exquisite their love had been.

Her thoughts also turned, to the ever-present attendance of the Goddess on their lives. Certainly it was her loving spirit that had granted them that magical night and whose blessing lay with the child their love had conceived. Maybe she did know, after all, what was best for everyone concerned.

"Dial six first for an outside line," the aide at the nurses' station told her. Larry himself pounced on the call after only two rings.

"Hey, I *thought* it might be you," he prophesied. "Did you know you're not at your desk?"

In the background Catherine could hear the sounds of clattering typewriters and insistent phones, sounds that sounded almost foreign to her after her two-month hiatus from reality.

"Thanks for telling me."

"So where *are* you, anyway?" he asked. It wasn't like Catherine to call in late to the office. "Still got the bug or what?"

"On the mend," she replied. "Am I missing anything?"

"Nah. Johnson took another day for his mouth job. You think we oughta get flowers or something?"

"That would be nice," she agreed.

"Not if he's got allergies." Larry chuckled in malicious mischief. "We're kinda hoping he'll sneeze really hard and lose his brains on his peach strudel. Pretty gross, huh?"

"You're definitely weird, Larry."

"So what's all that noise I hear? Sounds like you're in a bus station or something."

"Actually I'm at Mount Clarion."

"What?" Larry gasped. "You mean Mount Clarion, as in 'hospital'? My God, what's wrong?"

"Nothing a ride back to my apartment won't cure," she said, trying to calm him down. "Since they won't release me unless someone picks me up—"

"I'm on my way," he volunteered instantly. "Wait, do I need to get you anything first? Aspirin? Blankets? Back issues of the *National Enquirer*?"

"I'm fine, "Catherine insisted. "I guess I just let myself get a little run-down, that's all."

"I know you're fine, but do you need anything? I mean, there's this hot story in last month's copy that Elvis is working at a Burger World in Parma, Ohio. You'll kill me if I throw it out."

"Whatever."

"So when do you want me there?"

Catherine casually glanced up as she started to reply, her eyes locking on the black-haired man who was getting directions from a Candy Striper at the end of the corridor.

"Cath? You still there?"

The man's gaze followed the young woman's hand that swept in Catherine's direction. With a smile of loving recognition he was starting to come toward her.

"Never mind," Catherine quickly blurted into the phone to Larry, hastily explaining that someone else would take care of her getting home.

"Yeah, but—"

"I'll call you later." She hung up and broke into an anxious run as Kyle quickened his own speed and opened his arms to embrace her.

Her gasping questions and tearful cries of disbelief were smothered in a hail of kisses. "There'll be time enough for talking," he reassured her huskily, delighting in the glow of her surprised joy to see him.

"How long?" she asked nervously, trembling with the worry that their reunion was only temporary.

"How about a lifetime?" he recommended, oblivious to the impromptu audience that enviously witnessed his lush kiss of promise.

The Washington Monument towered like a protective sentinel behind them as they sat on the cool grass in its shadow.

"It was her plan all along for it to happen exactly this way," he explained, "difficult as it may be for us to look back on her methods and accept them, the Goddess really *did* know what she was doing."

"Then that would mean," Catherine theorized, "that even as far back as Nimue taking Excalibur in the first place . . .

Kyle nodded. "And even farther back than that. All that is governed by her has a place in a tapestry of her own design. Even the times she allowed injustice, it was to pave the way for its subsequent retribution."

Catherine's mind fluttered back to the scene she had witnessed between Kyle and the Goddess, reliving the color and the sound and the heart-tearing agony that he was lost to her forever.

"She told me something that I didn't understand," he explained, his statement accounting for the look Catherine had seen on his face. "She told me that I was no longer needed . . . that my soul had been set free by my own death in the cave."

Catherine's mouth dropped open in astonishment as he related something she never had expected to hear. "I died in my sleep at the very moment Excalibur sank beneath the mists of the channel."

Her hands gripped his in feverish expectation of the story's balance.

"My soul had to go *somewhere*," he said with a shrug. "The Goddess seemed to think that the twentieth century was as good a place as any."

Joy bubbled up in Catherine's laugh and shone in her green eyes as she threw her arms around his neck and sent them both back into the cushion of grass.

"I take it that you don't object," he said, teasing her, losing his hands in her hair.

"I could hardly object," she said, "to spending my life with the man whose child I'm going to have."

Love and elation swept over his face as his gaze traveled downward to her waist and his hand tentatively touched it in unspoken awe.

"A son," Catherine whispered. "I think I already know that."

Fragments of another dream, another memory, came back to her, and she at last recognized its message for what it was. The Goddess had spoken of sending them both assurance that they had nothing to fear. In dreams, too, she had spoken to them, sharing a vision of the future that neither had known until now was the truth.

"We're going to have to move to a bigger place," Catherine proposed, already having an inkling of what the master bedroom would look like.

"I guess that means I'll have to get a job." He sighed ruefully.

"What job?" she laughingly teased. "You're a world-famous magician."

"Unfortunately," he pointed out, "I'm now a world-famous magician without any magic." In response to her puzzled look he explained that the price of his journey had been the cost of all his power. "I don't think I could even do a basic card trick," he confessed.

"We'll think of something." Catherine shrugged. "Seems to me you'd make a pretty good writer." The night of the performance seemed so far away to her now, the memory of the review filling her with warmth as she recalled his desire to make amends.

"Are you sure you don't mind loving someone who doesn't have any magic?" he inquired.

Catherine interlaced her fingers behind his neck. "What you had wasn't magic," she informed him, tilting her head for a kiss. "*This* is."

Epilogue

"Where did you get those big brown eyes?" the little old lady on the park bench sweetly asked of the precocious youngster whose gray-and-white ball had sailed into her crochet basket.

"From my daddy," he said matter-of-factly, pointing to a handsome couple who sat in the shade. At that moment the young woman looked over. "Arthur!" she called out with loving firmness. "Tell the lady you're sorry for bothering her."

"Oh, it's all right." She waved back. "I'm used to little ones." With a smile she settled back to resume her project as the child cheerfully scampered back to his parents. Such a nice sight to see these days, she thought to herself, admiring the young mother's pretty face and the handsome father who clearly adored them both.

With pink tongue peeking out the corner of his mouth, his eyes squinting in fierce determination, Arthur plopped down on the grass to tie his shoe.

"Want Mommy to do that?" Catherine offered, but Arthur resolutely shook his head. "Were you that stubborn when you were little?" she teased Kyle.

"I don't remember." He sighed, leaning in to kiss her. "It was so long ago." With a laugh they turned their conversation back to the latest book Kyle was working on, a book about a place called Camelot.

By far, Arthur decided, he had the world's best parents. His daddy wrote books about castles and things, books that Arthur was excited to read someday when he was old enough to learn how. In the meantime his mommy could tell him stories like she always did before bedtime. Arthur always wondered if his mommy hadn't been a princess or something before she became a mommy. Someday he'd ask.

"Wanna see what I can do, Daddy?"

"Just a second, Arthur."

A second to Arthur, though, may as well have been an eternity, especially when his daddy got to talking about books. Oh, well. He'd use the time to practice what he discovered just the other day that he could do.

With a squeal of delight he tossed the ball as high as he could into the air and clapped his chubby hands twice as it started its descent.

Across the grass, the little old lady's smile of enjoyment turned into a perplexed scowl. "I just can't take the sun like I used to." She sighed, annoyed that her vision had tricked her into seeing the ball turn into a silver dove and fly toward the trees.

Pleased with what he had done, Arthur shaded his eyes and watched until the dove was only a streak of silver against the Washington sky, its wings hovering only a moment above the treetops before it sailed softly away and out of sight.